WINESBURG, OHIO

Winesburg, Ohio

A GROUP OF TALES
OF OHIO
SMALL-TOWN LIFE

by Sherwood Anderson

INTRODUCTION BY
ERNEST BOYD

THE
MODERN LIBRARY
NEW YORK

Random House IS THE PUBLISHER OF

THE MODERN LIBRARY

BENNETT A. CERF · DONALD S. KLOPFER · ROBERT K. HAAS

Manufactured in the United States of America

By H. Wolff

SOME OF THE EPISODES IN THIS BOOK WERE PRINTED IN THE SEVEN ARTS, THE MASSES AND THE LITTLE REVIEW TO WIIICII MAGAZINES THE AUTHOR MAKES DUE ACKNOWLEDGMENT.

INTRODUCTION

By Ernest Boyd

Sherwood Anderson was born at Clyde, Ohio, in 1876, and it was not until his fortieth year that his first book, *Windy McPherson's Son*, was published. When that novel appeared its author was scarcely known beyond the small circle of readers who had seen his powerful stories in the little reviews which can afford out of their poverty to have the courage of their convictions. He was a contributor from the outset to *The Little Review*, whose files contain so many of the names which now give contemporary American literature a quality and a significance that are truly national. It is noteworthy that many of the chapters in *Winesburg, Ohio*, the book which made his name, are reprinted from that and other periodicals of his experimental years. The legend is that Sherwood Anderson had " a trunkful " of fiction when he made his bid for fame with *Windy McPherson's Son* in 1916, and the following year he issued *Marching Men*, followed in 1918 by a volume of poems, excellently entitled *Mid-American Chants*. That was the sum of Sherwood Anderson's work when he published the book which now receives the consecration of being included in a library of the world's modern classics.

Just as the growth and development of America are rapid, so literary history moves quickly in this country, and in the space of five years the writer who was an innovator, an isolated figure, is now counted as one of a school of what is called the new American fiction. When Sherwood Anderson began there was only one novelist who could be seriously regarded as an original figure in modern American realistic fiction, and that was Theodore Dreiser. The latter was still the subject of vituperation and dispute, the single hope of those who believed that the purveyors of cheerful sentimentalities and of red-blooded adventures, were not the beginning and end of the national impulse towards a native American literature Then there were but a few places in which such writers could obtain a hearing; now the weekly and monthly reviews of the adult type in New York can easily stand comparison with those of London. These years of destruction in Europe, by some law of compensation, have been years of creation and development in this country. The rise of a serious periodical literature, whose virtue is neither the eternal negation of conservatism nor the mere success of immense circulation, is part of what seems to be a genuine literary renascence in America.

Sherwood Anderson's work is typical of this renascence, this expression of America to-day in a literature which is no longer provincial but has its roots in the soil. In fiction this movement of independence has taken the form of realism, a resolute insistence upon the fundamentals of life,

upon the facts so strenuously denied, or ignored,
by the conventional imitators of British ortho-
doxy. It is essentially a literature of revolt against
the great illusion of American civilization, the
illusion of optimism, with all its childish evasion
of harsh facts, its puerile cheerfulness, whose inevitable culmination is the school of " glad " books,
which have reduced American literature to the
lowest terms of sentimentality. A generation of
poets, novelists and critics has arisen to repudiate
these old idols of the literary market-place. The
tentative and lonely efforts of such pioneers as
Ambrose Bierce, Frank Norris and Theodore Dreiser
have opened up the way for a new literature. The
speed at which American history moves, whether
it be literary, political or social history, does not,
of course, deprive history of the traditional privilege of repeating itself. Thus America to-day is
witnessing such a conflict as was fought out in
France during the last quarter of the nineteenth
century, when Flaubert and Maupassant, the Gon-
court brothers and Zola, threw off the yoke of
Romanticism. They were accused, as the younger
Americans of to-day are accused, of various crimes,
literary and intellectual. Their books were suppressed for moral reasons; they were denounced
for their constant preoccupation with the ugly, the
drab and the uninspiring; in many cases they were
dismissed by the critical mandarins because of
their lack of style, their indifference to form. If
they more frequently resisted their opponents successfully, as when Flaubert defeated the moral

censors of *Madame Bovary*, it must be remembered
that their fight was more specifically restricted to
the domain of literature. In other words, the
Romanticism which they had to conquer was a
literary doctrine, not a national philosophy. The
American realists have to contend with both, since
this is the country in which life itself is viewed in
terms of romantic fiction.

Indeed, so long as American realism did not seem
to embody any profound challenge to the national
philosophy of romantic optimism, it was allowed
to proceed unhindered. Hence the early regional-
ism of such writers as Sara Orne Jewett, whose
notations of real life were in a minor key, barely
audible in the student din of the popular fictioneers,
each with a message of hope and gladness, and a
considerable mechanical skill in translating the
platitudes of the mob soothsayers into terms of
machine-made romance. When the author of *Sister
Carrie* and *Jennie Gerhardt* came forward with his
dispassionate querying of all the assumptions of
his contemporaries, it was easy to cloak moral in-
dignation in aesthetic criticism, to perform the same
ritual of excommunication as was attempted in
France in the case of Zola, and even of Balzac, to
some extent. But, in time, the influence of Dreiser
triumphed over defects of form which are incredible
only to those who have not submitted, as the true
critic and sensitive reader must submit, to the com-
pelling power of the creative genius. Chaotic,
formless, at times banal, Theodore Dreiser has
nevertheless, imposed a tradition of freedom, of

sincerity, of objective documentation, which has given a new impulse to American fiction. His influence may be compared to the displacement effected by the pressure of the sheer weight of some elemental natural force.

In his first two novels, *Windy McPherson's Son* and *Marching Men*, as in his last, *Poor White*, Sherwood Anderson shows himself no mere imitator of Dreiser. Sam McPherson's boyhood and youth in Canton, Iowa, where he is moulded by the influence of that shiftless, braggart Windy McPherson, provides the occasion for a remarkable study of that mid-American life of which the author has become the interpreter. It is a projection of reality into the pages of a novel which immediately revealed the power and the potentialities of Sherwood Anderson After his struggle for success in Chicago Sam McPherson sets off upon a vague pilgrimage, abandoning his wife, and seeking some tangible answer to the riddle of an existence which cannot be satisfied, as every right-thinking citizen was taught to be, by mere success as defined by the prospectuses of the correspondence schools. The last portion of the book lacks the continuity of interest which gives its power to the earlier narrative portion, but what is a literary weakness serves only to emphasise the difference which separates such literature from the commonplace waves of the old school.

It seems perverse to extend the story, not only beyond the point where the national philosophy receives its glow of warm satisfaction, but beyond the point where craftsmanship is capable of its literary task. When one has nothing to say, but knows how to say it, no such dilemma can present itself. But that is just what makes these writers of the younger generation: they have so much to say that content is often unrestrained by mere form, much to the supercilious delight of the mandarins and the slick business-men of letters. What are they to think, for example, of a novel like *Marching Men*, whose title raises expectations of conventional military glories? It is the curious story of Beaut McGregor, the miner's son, whose groping adventure through life leads him to the idea of physical union in disciplined ranks as the means of creative solidarity amongst the laboring masses. Obviously Sherwood Anderson is as independent of the shibboleths of class-conscious radical fiction as of the no more unreal conventions of the circulationist novel.

In *Poor White*, which followed *Winesburg, Ohio*, there are evident signs of the author's increasing technical skill as a novelist. It is a fine study of the invasion of the pioneer American civilization by modern machinery and industrialism, as well as a superb analysis of the evolution of a human being from the decadent, rather than the primitive, barbarism of a poor white group. The book was slightly overshadowed at the moment of its appearance, by the more sensational eruption of the newcomers into this no longer fallow field of American literature, but it has qualities of a more profound character than its rivals of a season. Yet, in the last analysis, it is the stories of Sherwood Anderson

which are his best achievement hitherto, and to
that *genre* he has returned in his new book, *The
Triumph of the Egg*. The present collection of
Winesburg stories gives the measure of his genius.
In their unpremeditated narrative art they have a
power of suggestion and revelation which we are ac-
customed to find in the great Russians, in Chekhov
more than in Dostoyevsky, for there one admires the
same economy of means, the same rich synthesis
of life.

Winesburg, Ohio is like that wheel of many colors,
of which Anatole France writes, which had only
to revolve to give a harmony of all the parts, which
becomes the truth. These separate fragments of
mid-American society combine to make a picture
of American life which carries the inescapable conviction of reality. The stories are written out of
the depths of imagination and intuition, out of a
prolonged brooding over the fascinating spectacle
of existence, but they combine that quality with
a marvelous faculty of precise observation. Thus,
the impression of surface realism is reinforced by
that deeper realism which sees beyond and beneath
the exterior world to the hidden reality which is the
essence of things. Did not Schopenhauer, inter-
preting Goethe's own confessions, point out that
this is precisely the quality of the artist: that it is
given to him alone to perceive the metaphysically
Real—*das Ding an sich?*

THE TALES AND THE PERSONS

PAGE
1 THE BOOK OF THE GROTESQUE.
7 HANDS—*concerning* WING BIDDLEBAUM.
18 PAPER PILLS—*concerning* DOCTOR REEFY.
24 MOTHER—*concerning* ELIZABETH WILLARD.
38 THE PHILOSOPHER—*concerning* DOCTOR PARCIVAL.
49 NOBODY KNOWS—*concerning* LOUISE TRUNNION.
55 GODLINESS (PARTS I AND II)—*concerning* JESSE BENTLEY.
88 SURRENDER (PART III)—*concerning* LOUISE BENTLEY.
102 TERROR (PART IV)—*concerning* DAVID HARDY.
110 A MAN OF IDEAS—*concerning* JOE WELLING.
123 ADVENTURE—*concerning* ALICE HINDMAN.
135 RESPECTABILITY—*concerning* WASH WILLIAMS.
145 THE THINKER—*concerning* SETH RICHMOND.
166 TANDY—*concerning* TANDY HARD.
171 THE STRENGTH OF GOD—*concerning* THE REVEREND CURTIS HARTMAN.
184 THE TEACHER—*concerning* KATE SWIFT.
197 LONELINESS—*concerning* ENOCH ROBINSON.
213 AN AWAKENING—*concerning* BELLE CARPENTER.
228 "QUEER"—*concerning* ELMER COWLEY.
244 THE UNTOLD LIE—*concerning* RAY PEARSON.
254 DRINK—*concerning* TOM FOSTER.
268 DEATH—*concerning* DOCTOR REEFY *and* ELIZABETH WILLARD.
285 SOPHISTICATION—*concerning* HELEN WHITE.
299 DEPARTURE—*concerning* GEORGE WILLARD.

THE BOOK OF THE GROTESQUE

THE writer, an old man with a white mustache, had some difficulty in getting into
bed. The windows of the house in which
he lived were high and he wanted to look at the
trees when he awoke in the morning. A carpenter came to fix the bed so that it would be on a
level with the window.

Quite a fuss was made about the matter. The
carpenter, who had been a soldier in the Civil
War, came into the writer's room and sat down
to talk of building a platform for the purpose of
raising the bed. The writer had cigars lying
about and the carpenter smoked.

For a time the two men talked of the raising
of the bed and then they talked of other things.
The soldier got on the subject of the war. The
writer, in fact, led him to that subject. The carpenter had once been a prisoner in Andersonville
prison and had lost a brother. The brother had
died of starvation, and whenever the carpenter
got upon that subject he cried. He, like the old
writer, had a white mustache, and when he cried
he puckered up his lips and the mustache bobbed

1

up and down. The weeping old man with the cigar in his mouth was ludicrous. The plan the writer had for the raising of his bed was forgotten and later the carpenter did it in his own way and the writer, who was past sixty, had to help himself with a chair when he went to bed at night.

In his bed the writer rolled over on his side and lay quite still. For years he had been beset with notions concerning his heart. He was a hard smoker and his heart fluttered. The idea had got into his mind that he would some time die unexpectedly and always when he got into bed he thought of that. It did not alarm him. The effect in fact was quite a special thing and not easily explained. It made him more alive, there in bed, than at any other time. Perfectly still he lay and his body was old and not of much use any more, but something inside him was altogether young. He was like a pregnant woman, only that the thing inside him was not a baby but a youth. No, it wasn't a youth, it was a woman, young, and wearing a coat of mail like a knight. It is absurd, you see, to try to tell what was inside the old writer as he lay on his high bed and listened to the fluttering of his heart. The thing to get at is what the writer, or the young thing within the writer, was thinking about.

The old writer, like all of the people in the

world, had got, during his long life, a great many notions in his head. He had once been quite handsome and a number of women had been in love with him. And then, of course, he had known people, many people, known them in a peculiarly intimate way that was different from the way in which you and I know people. At least that is what the writer thought and the thought pleased him. Why quarrel with an old man concerning his thoughts?

In the bed the writer had a dream that was not a dream. As he grew somewhat sleepy but was still conscious, figures began to appear before his eyes. He imagined the young indescribable thing within himself was driving a long procession of figures before his eyes.

You see the interest in all this lies in the figures that went before the eyes of the writer. They were all grotesques. All of the men and women the writer had ever known had become grotesques.

The grotesques were not all horrible. Some were amusing, some almost beautiful, and one, a woman all drawn out of shape, hurt the old man by her grotesqueness. When she passed he made a noise like a small dog whimpering. Had you come into the room you might have supposed the old man had unpleasant dreams or perhaps indigestion.

For an hour the procession of grotesques passed

before the eyes of the old man, and then, although it was a painful thing to do, he crept out of bed and began to write. Some one of the grotesques had made a deep impression on his mind and he wanted to describe it.

At his desk the writer worked for an hour. In the end he wrote a book which he called "The Book of the Grotesque." It was never published, but I saw it once and it made an indelible impression on my mind. The book had one central thought that is very strange and has always remained with me. By remembering it I have been able to understand many people and things that I was never able to understand before. The thought was involved but a simple statement of it would be something like this:

That in the beginning when the world was young there were a great many thoughts but no such thing as a truth. Man made the truths himself and each truth was a composite of a great many vague thoughts. All about in the world were the truths and they were all beautiful.

The old man had listed hundreds of the truths in his book. I will not try to tell you of all of them. There was the truth of virginity and the truth of passion, the truth of wealth and of poverty, of thrift and of profligacy, of carelessness and abandon. Hundreds and hundreds were the truths and they were all beautiful.

And then the people came along. Each as he appeared snatched up one of the truths and some who were quite strong snatched up a dozen of them.

It was the truths that made the people grotesques. The old man had quite an elaborate theory concerning the matter. It was his notion that the moment one of the people took one of the truths to himself, called it his truth, and tried to live his life by it, he became a grotesque and the truth he embraced became a falsehood.

You can see for yourself how the old man, who had spent all of his life writing and was filled with words, would write hundreds of pages concerning this matter. The subject would become so big in his mind that he himself would be in danger of becoming a grotesque. He didn't, I suppose, for the same reason that he never published the book. It was the young thing inside him that saved the old man.

Concerning the old carpenter who fixed the bed for the writer, I only mentioned him because he, like many of what are called very common people, became the nearest thing to what is understandable and lovable of all the grotesques in the writer's book.

Winesburg, Ohio

HANDS

UPON the half decayed veranda of a small frame house that stood near the edge of a ravine near the town of Winesburg, Ohio, a fat little old man walked nervously up and down. Across a long field that has been seeded for clover but that had produced only a dense crop of yellow mustard weeds, he could see the public highway along which went a wagon filled with berry pickers returning from the fields. The berry pickers, youths and maidens, laughed and shouted boisterously. A boy clad in a blue shirt leaped from the wagon and attempted to drag after him one of the maidens who screamed and protested shrilly. The feet of the boy in the road kicked up a cloud of dust that floated across the face of the departing sun. Over the long field came a thin girlish voice. "Oh, you Wing Biddlebaum, comb your hair, it's falling into your eyes," commanded the voice to the man, who was bald and whose nervous little hands fiddled about the bare white forehead as though arranging a mass of tangled locks.

Wing Biddlebaum, forever frightened and be-set by a ghostly band of doubts, did not think of himself as in any way a part of the life of the town where he had lived for twenty years. Among all the people of Winesburg but one had come close to him. With George Willard, son of Tom Willard, the proprietor of the new Wil-lard House, he had formed something like a friendship. George Willard was the reporter on the *Winesburg Eagle* and sometimes in the eve-nings he walked out along the highway to Wing Biddlebaum's house. Now as the old man walked up and down on the veranda, his hands moving nervously about, he was hoping that George Willard would come and spend the evening with him. After the wagon containing the berry pickers had passed, he went across the field through the tall mustard weeds and climbing a rail fence peered anxiously along the road to the town. For a moment he stood thus, rubbing his hands together and looking up and down the road, and then, fear overcoming him, ran back to walk again upon the porch on his own house.

In the presence of George Willard, Wing Biddlebaum, who for twenty years had been the town mystery, lost something of his timidity, and his shadowy personality, submerged in a sea of doubts, came forth to look at the world. With the young reporter at his side, he ventured in the light of day into Main Street or strode up and down on the rickety front porch of his own house, talking excitedly. The voice that had been low and trembling became shrill and loud. The bent figure straightened. With a kind of wriggle, like a fish returned to the brook by the fisherman, Biddlebaum the silent began to talk, striving to put into words the ideas that had been accumulated by his mind during long years of silence.

Wing Biddlebaum talked much with his hands. The slender expressive fingers, forever active, forever striving to conceal themselves in his pockets or behind his back, came forth and became the piston rods of his machinery of expression.

The story of Wing Biddlebaum is a story of hands. Their restless activity, like unto the beating of the wings of an imprisoned bird, had given him his name. Some obscure poet of the town had thought of it. The hands alarmed their owner. He wanted to keep them hidden away and looked with amazement at the quiet inexpressive hands of other men who worked beside him in the fields, or passed, driving sleepy teams on country roads.

When he talked to George Willard, Wing Biddlebaum closed his fists and beat with them upon a table or on the walls of his house. The action made him more comfortable. If the desire to talk came to him when the two were walking in the fields, he sought out a stump or the top board of a fence and with his hands pounding busily talked with renewed ease.

The story of Wing Biddlebaum's hands is worth a book in itself. Sympathetically set forth it would tap many strange, beautiful qualities in obscure men. It is a job for a poet. In Winesburg the hands had attracted attention merely because of their activity. With them Wing Biddlebaum had picked as high as a hundred and forty quarts of strawberries in a day. They became his distinguishing feature, the source of his fame. Also they made more grotesque an already grotesque and elusive individuality. Winesburg was proud of the hands of Wing Biddlebaum in the same spirit in which it was proud of Banker White's new stone house and Wesley Moyer's bay stallion, Tony Tip, that had won the two-fifteen trot at the fall races in Cleveland.

As for George Willard, he had many times wanted to ask about the hands. At times an almost overwhelming curiosity had taken hold of him. He felt that there must be a reason for their strange activity and their inclination to keep hidden away and only a growing respect for

Wing Biddlebaum kept him from blurting out
the questions that were often in his mind.

Once he had been on the point of asking. The
two were walking in the fields on a summer afternoon and had stopped to sit upon a grassy bank.
All afternoon Wing Biddlebaum had talked as
one inspired. By a fence he had stopped and
beating like a giant woodpecker upon the top
board had shouted at George Willard, condemn-
ing his tendency to be too much influenced by the
people about him. "You are destroying yourself," he cried. "You have the inclination to be
alone and to dream and you are afraid of dreams.
You want to be like others in town here. You
hear them talk and you try to imitate them."

On the grassy bank Wing Biddlebaum had tried
again to drive his point home. His voice became
soft and reminiscent, and with a sigh of content-
ment he launched into a long rambling talk, speaking as one lost in a dream.

Out of the dream Wing Biddlebaum made a
picture for George Willard. In the picture men
lived again in a kind of pastoral golden age.
Across a green open country came clean-limbed
young men, some afoot, some mounted upon
horses. In crowds the young men came to gather
about the feet of an old man who sat beneath
a tree in a tiny garden and who talked to them.

Wing Biddlebaum became wholly inspired.

For once he forgot the hands. Slowly they stole forth and lay upon George Willard's shoulders. Something new and bold came into the voice that talked. "You must try to forget all you have learned," said the old man. "You must begin to dream. From this time on you must shut your ears to the roaring of the voices."

Pausing in his speech, Wing Biddlebaum looked long and earnestly at George Willard. His eyes glowed. Again he raised the hands to caress the boy and then a look of horror swept over his face.

With a convulsive movement of his body, Wing Biddlebaum sprang to his feet and thrust his hands deep into his trousers pockets. Tears came to his eyes. "I must be getting along home. I can talk no more with you," he said nervously.

Without looking back, the old man had hurried down the hillside and across a meadow, leaving George Willard perplexed and frightened upon the grassy slope. With a shiver of dread the boy arose and went along the road toward town. "I'll not ask him about his hands," he thought, touched by the memory of the terror he had seen in the man's eyes. "There's something wrong, but I don't want to know what it is. His hands have something to do with his fear of me and of everyone."

And George Willard was right. Let us look

briefly into the story of the hands. Perhaps our talking of them will arouse the poet who will tell the hidden wonder story of the influence for which the hands were but fluttering pennants of promise.

In his youth Wing Biddlebaum had been a school teacher in a town in Pennsylvania. He was not then known as Wing Biddlebaum, but went by the less euphonic name of Adolph Myers. As Adolph Myers he was much loved by the boys of his school.

Adolph Myers was meant by nature to be a teacher of youth. He was one of those rare, little-understood men who rule by a power so gentle that it passes as a lovable weakness. In their feeling for the boys under their charge such men are not unlike the finer sort of women in their love of men.

And yet that is but crudely stated. It needs the poet there. With the boys of his school, Adolph Myers had walked in the evening or had sat talking until dusk upon the schoolhouse steps lost in a kind of dream. Here and there went his hands, caressing the shoulders of the boys, playing about the tousled heads. As he talked his voice became soft and musical. There was a caress in that also. In a way the voice and the hands, the stroking of the shoulders and the touching of the hair was a part of the school-master's effort to carry a dream into the young minds. By the caress that was in his fingers he expressed himself. He was one of those men in whom the force that creates life is diffused, not centralized. Under the caress of his hands doubt and disbelief went out of the minds of the boys and they began also to dream.

And then the tragedy. A half-witted boy of the school became enamored of the young master. In his bed at night he imagined unspeakable things and in the morning went forth to tell his dreams as facts. Strange, hideous accusations fell from his loose-hung lips. Through the Pennsylvania town went a shiver. Hidden, shadowy doubts that had been in men's minds concerning Adolph Myers were galvanized into beliefs.

The tragedy did not linger. Trembling lads were jerked out of bed and questioned. "He put his arms about me," said one. "His fingers were always playing in my hair," said another.

One afternoon a man of the town, Henry Bradford, who kept a saloon, came to the schoolhouse door. Calling Adolph Myers into the school yard he began to beat him with his fists. As his hard knuckles beat down into the frightened face of the schoolmaster, his wrath became more and more terrible. Screaming with dismay, the children ran here and there like disturbed insects. "I'll teach you to put your hands on my boy, you beast," roared the saloon keeper, who, tired of beating the master, had begun to kick him about the yard.

Adolph Myers was driven from the Pennsylvania town in the night. With lanterns in their hands a dozen men came to the door of the house where he lived alone and commanded that he dress and come forth. It was raining and one of the men had a rope in his hands. They had intended to hang the schoolmaster, but something in his figure, so small, white, and pitiful, touched their hearts and they let him escape. As he ran away into the darkness they repented of their weakness and ran after him, swearing and throwing sticks and great balls of soft mud at the figure that screamed and ran faster and faster into the darkness.

For twenty years Adolph Myers had lived alone in Winesburg. He was but forty but looked sixty-five. The name of Biddlebaum he got from a box of goods seen at a freight station as he hurried through an eastern Ohio town. He had an aunt in Winesburg, a black-toothed old woman who raised chickens, and with her he lived until she died. He had been ill for a year after the experience in Pennsylvania, and after his recovery worked as a day laborer in the fields, going timidly about and striving to conceal his hands. Although he did not understand what had happened he felt that the hands must be to blame

Again and again the fathers of the boys had talked of the hands. "Keep your hands to yourself," the saloon keeper had roared, dancing with fury in the schoolhouse yard.

Upon the veranda of his house by the ravine, Wing Biddlebaum continued to walk up and down until the sun had disappeared and the road beyond the field was lost in the grey shadows. Going into his house he cut slices of bread and spread honey upon them. When the rumble of the evening train that took away the express cars loaded with the day's harvest of berries had passed and restored the silence of the summer night, he went again to walk upon the veranda. In the darkness he could not see the hands and they became quiet. Although he still hungered for the presence of the boy, who was the medium through which he expressed his love of man, the hunger became again a part of his loneliness and his waiting. Lighting a lamp, Wing Biddlebaum washed the few dishes soiled by his simple meal and, setting up a folding cot by the screen door that led to the porch, prepared to undress for the night. A few stray white bread crumbs lay on the cleanly washed floor by the table; putting the lamp upon a low stool he began to pick up the crumbs, carrying them to his mouth one by one with unbelievable rapidity. In the dense blotch of light beneath the table, the kneeling figure looked like a priest engaged in some service of his church. The nervous expressive fingers, flashing in and out of the light, might well have been mistaken for the fingers of the devotee going swiftly through decade after decade of his rosary.

PAPER PILLS

HE was an old man with a white beard and huge nose and hands. Long before the time during which we will know him, he was a doctor and drove a jaded white horse from house to house through the streets of Winesburg. Later he married a girl who had money. She had been left a large fertile farm when her father died. The girl was quiet, tall, and dark, and to many people she seemed very beautiful. Everyone in Winesburg wondered why she married the doctor. Within a year after the marriage she died.

The knuckles of the doctor's hand were extraordinarily large. When the hands were closed they looked like clusters of unpainted wooden balls as large as walnuts fastened together by steel rods. He smoked a cob pipe and after his wife's death sat all day in his empty office close by a window that was covered with cobwebs. He never opened the window. Once on a hot day in August he tried but found it stuck fast and after that he forgot all about it.

Winesburg had forgotten the old man, but in Doctor Reefy there were the seeds of something very fine. Alone in his musty office in the Heffner Block above the Paris Dry Goods Company's Store, he worked ceaselessly, building up something that he himself destroyed. Little pyramids of truth he erected and after erecting knocked them down again that he might have the truths to erect other pyramids.

Doctor Reefy was a tall man who had worn one suit of clothes for ten years. It was frayed at the sleeves and little holes had appeared at the knees and elbows. In the office he wore also a linen duster with huge pockets into which he continually stuffed scraps of paper. After some weeks the scraps of paper became little hard round balls, and when the pockets were filled he dumped them out upon the floor. For ten years he had but one friend, another old man named John Spaniard who owned a tree nursery. Sometimes, in a playful mood, old Doctor Reefy took from his pockets a handful of the paper balls and threw them at the nursery man. "That is to confound you, you blithering old sentimentalist," he cried, shaking with laughter.

The story of Doctor Reefy and his courtship of the tall dark girl who became his wife and left her money to him is a very curious story. It is delicious, like the twisted little apples that grow in the orchards of Winesburg. In the fall one walks in the orchards and the ground is hard with frost underfoot. The apples have been taken from the trees by the pickers. They have been put in barrels and shipped to the cities where they will be eaten in apartments that are filled with books, magazines, furniture, and people. On the trees are only a few gnarled apples that the pickers have rejected. They look like the knuckles of Doctor Reefy's hands. One nibbles at them and they are delicious. Into a little round place at the side of the apple has been gathered all of its sweetness. One runs from tree to tree over the frosted ground picking the gnarled, twisted apples and filling his pockets with them. Only the few know the sweetness of the twisted apples.

The girl and Doctor Reefy began their courtship on a summer afternoon. He was forty-five then and already he had begun the practice of filling his pockets with the scraps of paper that became hard balls and were thrown away. The habit had been formed as he sat in his buggy behind the jaded grey horse and went slowly along country roads. On the papers were written thoughts, ends of thoughts, beginnings of thoughts.

One by one the mind of Doctor Reefy had made the thoughts. Out of many of them he formed a truth that arose gigantic in his mind. The truth clouded the world. It became terrible and then faded away and the little thoughts began again.

The tall dark girl came to see Doctor Reefy because she was in the family way and had become frightened. She was in that condition because of a series of circumstances also curious.

The death of her father and mother and the rich acres of land that had come down to her had set a train of suitors on her heels. For two years she saw suitors almost every evening. Except two they were all alike. They talked to her of passion and there was a strained eager quality in their voices and in their eyes when they looked at her. The two who were different were much unlike each other. One of them, a slender young man with white hands, the son of a jeweler in Winesburg, talked continually of virginity. When he was with her he was never off the subject. The other, a black-haired boy with large ears, said nothing at all but always managed to get her into the darkness where he began to kiss her.

For a time the tall dark girl thought she would marry the jeweler's son. For hours she sat in silence listening as he talked to her and then she began to be afraid of something. Beneath his talk of virginity she began to think there was a lust greater than in all the others. At times it seemed to her that as he talked he was holding her body in his hands. She imagined him turning it slowly about in the white hands and staring at it. At night she dreamed that he had bitten into her body and that his jaws were dripping. She had the dream three times then she became in the family way to the one who said nothing at all but who in the moment of his passion actually did bite her shoulder so that for days the marks of his teeth showed.

After the tall dark girl came to know Doctor Reefy it seemed to her that she never wanted to leave him again. She went into his office one morning and without her saying anything he seemed to know what had happened to her.

In the office of the doctor there was a woman, the wife of the man who kept the bookstore in Winesburg. Like all old-fashioned country practitioners, Doctor Reefy pulled teeth, and the woman who waited held a handkerchief to her teeth and groaned. Her husband was with her and when the tooth was taken out they both screamed and blood ran down on the woman's white dress. The tall dark girl did not pay any attention. When the woman and the man had gone the doctor smiled. "I will take you driving into the country with me," he said.

For several weeks the tall dark girl and the doctor were together almost every day. The condition that had brought her to him passed in an illness, but she was like one who has discovered the sweetness of the twisted apples, she could not get her mind fixed again upon the round perfect fruit that is eaten in the city apartments.   In the fall after the beginning of her acquaintanceship with him she married Doctor Reefy and in the following spring she died.   During the winter he read to her all of the odds and ends of thoughts he had scribbled on the bits of paper.   After he had read them he laughed and stuffed them away in his pockets to become round hard balls.

MOTHER

ELIZABETH WILLARD, the mother of George Willard, was tall and gaunt and her face was marked with smallpox scars. Although she was but forty-five, some obscure disease had taken the fire out of her figure. Listlessly she went about the disorderly old hotel looking at the faded wall-paper and the ragged carpets and, when she was able to be about, doing the work of a chambermaid among beds soiled by the slumbers of fat traveling men. Her husband, Tom Willard, a slender, graceful man with square shoulders, a quick military step, and a black mustache, trained to turn sharply up at the ends, tried to put the wife out of his mind. The presence of the tall ghostly figure, moving slowly through the halls, he took as a reproach to himself. When he thought of her he grew angry and swore. The hotel was unprofitable and forever on the edge of failure and he wished himself out of it. He thought of the old house and the woman who lived there with him as things defeated and done for. The hotel in which he had begun life so hopefully was now a mere ghost of

24

what a hotel should be. As he went spruce and
businesslike through the streets of Winesburg, he
sometimes stopped and turned quickly about as
though fearing that the spirit of the hotel and
of the woman would follow him even into the
streets. "Damn such a life, damn it!" he sputtered aimlessly.

Tom Willard had a passion for village politics
and for years had been the leading Democrat in
a strongly Republican community. Some day, he
told himself, the tide of things political will turn
in my favor and the years of ineffectual service
count big in the bestowal of rewards. He
dreamed of going to Congress and even of becoming governor. Once when a younger member
of the party arose at a political conference and
began to boast of his faithful service, Tom Willard grew white with fury. "Shut up, you," he
roared, glaring about. "What do you know of
service? What are you but a boy? Look at
what I've done here! I was a Democrat here in
Winesburg when it was a crime to be a Democrat. In the old days they fairly hunted us with
guns."

Between Elizabeth and her one son George
there was a deep unexpressed bond of sympathy,
based on a girlhood dream that had long ago
died. In the son's presence she was timid and
reserved, but sometimes while he hurried about

town intent upon his duties as a reporter, she
went into his room and closing the door knelt by
a little desk, made of a kitchen table, that sat near
a window. In the room by the desk she went
through a ceremony that was half a prayer, half
a demand, addressed to the skies. In the boyish
figure she yearned to see something half forgotten that had once been a part of herself re-
created. The prayer concerned that. "Even
though I die, I will in some way keep defeat
from you," she cried, and so deep was her determination that her whole body shook. Her
eyes glowed and she clenched her fists. "If I am
dead and see him becoming a meaningless drab
figure like myself, I will come back," she declared.
"I ask God now to give me that privilege. I demand it. I will pay for it. God may beat me
with his fists. I will take any blow that may be-
fall if but this my boy be allowed to express something for us both." Pausing uncertainly, the
woman stared about the boy's room. "And do
not let him become smart and successful either,"
she added vaguely.

The communion between George Willard and
his mother was outwardly a formal thing without
meaning. When she was ill and sat by the window in her room he sometimes went in the evening
to make her a visit. They sat by a window that
looked over the roof of a small frame building

into Main Street.   By turning their heads they
could see, through another window, along an alleyway that ran behind the Main Street stores and
into the back door of Abner Groff's bakery.
Sometimes as they sat thus a picture of village
life presented itself to them.   At the back door of
his shop appeared Abner Groff with a stick or an
empty milk bottle in his hand.   For a long time
there was a feud between the baker and a grey cat
that belonged to Sylvester West, the druggist.
The boy and his mother saw the cat creep into the
door of the bakery and presently emerge followed
by the baker who swore and waved his arms about.
The baker's eyes were small and red and his black
hair and beard were filled with flour dust.
Sometimes he was so angry that, although the cat
had disappeared, he hurled sticks, bits of broken
glass, and even some of the tools of his trade
about.   Once he broke a window at the back of
Sinning's Hardware Store.   In the alley the grey
cat crouched behind barrels filled with torn paper
and broken bottles above which flew a black
swarm of flies.   Once when she was alone, and
after watching a prolonged and ineffectual outburst on the part of the baker, Elizabeth Willard
put her head down on her long white hands and
wept.   After that she did not look along the alleyway any more, but tried to forget the contest between the bearded man and the cat.   It seemed

like a rehearsal of her own life, terrible in its vividness.

In the evening when the son sat in the room with his mother, the silence made them both feel awkward. Darkness came on and the evening train came in at the station. In the street below feet tramped up and down upon a board sidewalk. In the station yard, after the evening train had gone, there was a heavy silence. Perhaps Skinner Leason, the express agent, moved a truck the length of the station platform. Over on Main Street sounded a man's voice, laughing. The door of the express office banged. George Willard arose and crossing the room fumbled for the doorknob. Sometimes he knocked against a chair, making it scrape along the floor. By the window sat the sick woman, perfectly still, listless. Her long hands, white and bloodless, could be seen drooping over the ends of the arms of the chair. "I think you had better be out among the boys. You are too much indoors," she said, striving to relieve the embarrassment of the departure. "I thought I would take a walk." replied George Willard, who felt awkward and confused.

One evening in July, when the transient guests who made the New Willard House their temporary homes had become scarce, and the hallways, lighted only by kerosene lamps turned low, were plunged in gloom, Elizabeth Willard had an adventure. She had been ill in bed for several days and her son had not come to visit her. She was alarmed. The feeble blaze of life that remained in her body was blown into a flame by her anxiety and she crept out of bed, dressed and hurried along the hallway toward her son's room, shaking with exaggerated fears. As she went along she steadied herself with her hand, slipped along the papered walls of the hall and breathed with difficulty. The air whistled through her teeth. As she hurried forward she thought how foolish she was. "He is concerned with boyish affairs," she told herself. "Perhaps he has now begun to walk about in the evening with girls."

Elizabeth Willard had a dread of being seen by guests in the hotel that had once belonged to her father and the ownership of which still stood recorded in her name in the county courthouse. The hotel was continually losing patronage because of its shabbiness and she thought of herself as also shabby. Her own room was in an obscure corner and when she felt able to work she voluntarily worked among the beds, preferring the labor that could be done when the guests were abroad seeking trade among the merchants of Winesburg.

By the door of her son's room the mother knelt upon the floor and listened for some sound from within. When she heard the boy moving about and talking in low tones a smile came to her lips. George Willard had a habit of talking aloud to himself and to hear him doing so had always given his mother a peculiar pleasure. The habit in him, she felt, strengthened the secret bond that existed between them. A thousand times she had whispered to herself of the matter. "He is groping about, trying to find himself," she thought. "He is not a dull clod, all words and smartness. Within him there is a secret something that is striving to grow. It is the thing I let be killed in myself."

In the darkness in the hallway by the door the sick woman arose and started again toward her own room. She was afraid that the door would open and the boy come upon her. When she had reached a safe distance and was about to turn a corner into a second hallway she stopped and bracing herself with her hands waited, thinking to shake off a trembling fit of weakness that had come upon her. The presence of the boy in the room had made her happy. In her bed, during the long hours alone, the little fears that had visited her had become giants. Now they were all gone. "When I get back to my room I shall sleep," she murmured gratefully.

But Elizabeth Willard was not to return to her bed and to sleep. As she stood trembling in the

darkness the door of her son's room opened and
the boy's father, Tom Willard, stepped out. In
the light that streamed out at the door he stood
with the knob in his hand and talked. What he
said infuriated the woman.

Tom Willard was ambitious for his son. He
had always thought of himself as a successful
man, although nothing he had ever done had
turned out successfully. However, when he was
out of sight of the New Willard House and had
no fear of coming upon his wife, he swaggered
and began to dramatize himself as one of the
chief men of the town. He wanted his son to succeed. He it was who had secured for the boy
the position on the *Winesburg Eagle*. Now, with
a ring of earnestness in his voice, he was advis-
ing concerning some course of conduct. "I tell
you what, George, you've got to wake up," he said
sharply. "Will Henderson has spoken to me
three times concerning the matter. He says you
go along for hours not hearing when you are
spoken to and acting like a gawky girl. What
ails you?" Tom Willard laughed good-natur-
edly. "Well, I guess you'll get over it," he said.
"I told Will that. You're not a fool and you're
not a woman. You're Tom Willard's son
and you'll wake up. I'm not afraid. What you
say clears things up. If being a newspaper man
had put the notion of becoming a writer into your

mind that's all right.   Only I guess you'll have
to wake up to do that too, eh?"

Tom Willard went briskly along the hallway
and down a flight of stairs to the office.   The
woman in the darkness could hear him laughing
and talking with a guest who was striving to wear
away a dull evening by dozing in a chair by the
office door.   She returned to the door of her
son's room.   The weakness had passed from her
body as by a miracle and she stepped boldly along.
A thousand ideas raced through her head.   When
she heard the scraping of a chair and the sound
of a pen scratching upon paper, she again turned
and went back along the hallway to her own room.

A definite determination had come into the
mind of the defeated wife of the Winesburg Hotel
keeper.   The determination was the result of long
years of quiet and rather ineffectual thinking.
"Now," she told herself, "I will act.   There is
something threatening my boy and I will ward it
off."   The fact that the conversation between
Tom Willard and his son had been rather quiet
and natural, as though an understanding existed
between them, maddened her.   Although for
years she had hated her husband, her hatred had
always before been a quite impersonal thing.   He
had been merely a part of something else that she
hated.   Now, and by the few words at the door,
he had become the thing personified.   In the dark-

ness of her own room she clenched her fists and glared about. Going to a cloth bag that hung on a nail by the wall she took out a long pair of sewing scissors and held them in her hand like a dagger. "I will stab him," she said aloud. "He has chosen to be the voice of evil and I will kill him. When I have killed him something will snap within myself and I will die also. It will be a release for all of us."

In her girlhood and before her marriage with Tom Willard, Elizabeth had borne a somewhat shaky reputation in Winesburg. For years she had been what is called "stage-struck" and had paraded through the streets with traveling men guests at her father's hotel, wearing loud clothes and urging them to tell her of life in the cities out of which they had come. Once she startled the town by putting on men's clothes and riding a bicycle down Main Street.

In her own mind the tall dark girl had been in those days much confused. A great restlessness was in her and it expressed itself in two ways. First there was an uneasy desire for change, for some big definite movement to her life. It was this feeling that had turned her mind to the stage. She dreamed of joining some company and wandering over the world, seeing always new faces and giving something out of herself to all people. Sometimes at night she was quite beside herself with the thought, but when she tried to talk of the matter to the members of the theatrical companies that came to Winesburg and stopped at her father's hotel, she got nowhere. They did not seem to know what she meant, or if she did get something of her passion expressed, they only laughed. "It's not like that," they said. "It's as dull and uninteresting as this here. Nothing comes of it."

With the traveling men when she walked about with them, and later with Tom Willard, it was quite different. Always they seemed to understand and sympathize with her. On the side streets of the village, in the darkness under the trees, they took hold of her hand and she thought that something unexpressed in herself came forth and became a part of an unexpressed something in them.

And then there was the second expression of her restlessness. When that came she felt for a time released and happy. She did not blame the men who walked with her and later she did not blame Tom Willard. It was always the same, beginning with kisses and ending, after strange wild emotions, with peace and then sobbing repentance. When she sobbed she put her hand upon the face of the man and had always the same thought. Even though he were large and bearded she thought he had become suddenly a little boy. She wondered why he did not sob also.

In her room, tucked away in a corner of the old Willard House, Elizabeth Willard lighted a lamp and put it on a dressing table that stood by the door. A thought had come into her mind and she went to a closet and brought out a small square box and set it on the table. The box contained material for make-up and had been left with other things by a theatrical company that had once been stranded in Winesburg. Elizabeth Willard had decided that she would be beautiful. Her hair was still black and there was a great mass of it braided and coiled about her head. The scene that was to take place in the office below began to grow in her mind. No ghostly worn-out figure should confront Tom Willard, but something quite unexpected and startling. Tall and with dusky cheeks and hair that fell in a mass from her shoulders, a figure should come striding down the stairway before the startled loungers in the hotel office. The figure would be silent—it would be swift and terrible. As a tigress whose cub had been threatened would she appear, coming out of the shadows, stealing noiselessly along and holding the long wicked scissors in her hand.

With a little broken sob in her throat, Elizabeth Willard blew out the light that stood upon the table and stood weak and trembling in the darkness. The strength that had been as a miracle in her body left and she half reeled across the floor, clutching at the back of the chair in which she had spent so many long days staring out over the tin roofs into the main street of Winesburg. In the hallway there was the sound of footsteps and George Willard came in at the door. Sitting in a chair beside his mother he began to talk. "I'm going to get out of here," he said. "I don't know where I shall go or what I shall do but I am going away."

The woman in the chair waited and trembled. An impulse came to her. "I suppose you had better wake up," she said. "You think that? You will go to the city and make money, eh? It will be better for you, you think, to be a business man, to be brisk and smart and alive?" She waited and trembled.

The son shook his head. "I suppose I can't make you understand, but oh, I wish I could," he said earnestly. "I can't even talk to father about it. I don't try. There isn't any use. I don't know what I shall do. I just want to go away and look at people and think."

Silence fell upon the room where the boy and woman sat together. Again, as on the other evenings, they were embarrassed. After a time the boy tried again to talk. "I suppose it won't be for a year or two but I've been thinking about it."

he said, rising and going toward the door.
"Something father said makes it sure that I shall
have to go away." He fumbled with the door
knob. In the room the silence became unbearable to the woman. She wanted to cry out with
joy because of the words that had come from the
lips of her son, but the expression of joy had
become impossible to her. "I think you had better go out among the boys. You are too much
indoors," she said. "I thought I would go for
a little walk," replied the son stepping awkwardly out of the room and closing the door.

THE PHILOSOPHER

DOCTOR PARCIVAL was a large man with a drooping mouth covered by a yellow mustache. He always wore a dirty white waistcoat out of the pockets of which protruded a number of the kind of black cigars known as stogies. His teeth were black and irregular and there was something strange about his eyes. The lid of the left eye twitched; it fell down and snapped up; it was exactly as though the lid of the eye were a window shade and someone stood inside the doctor's head playing with the cord.

Doctor Parcival had a liking for the boy, George Willard. It began when George had been working for a year on the *Winesburg Eagle* and the acquaintanceship was entirely a matter of the doctor's own making.

In the late afternoon Will Henderson, owner and editor of the *Eagle*, went over to Tom Willy's saloon. Along an alleyway he went and slipping in at the back door of the saloon began drinking a drink made of a combination of sloe gin and soda water. Will Henderson was a sensualist and had reached the age of forty-five.

He imagined the gin renewed the youth in him. Like most sensualists he enjoyed talking of women, and for an hour he lingered about gossiping with Tom Willy. The saloon keeper was a short, broad-shouldered man with peculiarly marked hands. That flaming kind of birthmark that sometimes paints with red the faces of men and women had touched with red Tom Willy's fingers and the backs of his hands. As he stood by the bar talking to Will Henderson he rubbed the hands together. As he grew more and more excited the red of his fingers deepened. It was as though the hands had been dipped in blood that had dried and faded.

As Will Henderson stood at the bar looking at the red hands and talking of women, his assistant, George Willard, sat in the office of the *Winesburg Eagle* and listened to the talk of Doctor Parcival.

Doctor Parcival appeared immediately after Will Henderson had disappeared. One might have supposed that the doctor had been watching from his office window and had seen the editor going along the alleyway. Coming in at the front door and finding himself a chair, he lighted one of the stogies and crossing his legs began to talk. He seemed intent upon convincing the boy of the advisability of adopting a line of conduct that he was himself unable to define.

"If you have your eyes open you will see that although I call myself a doctor I have mighty few patients," he began. "There is a reason for that. It is not an accident and it is not because I do not know as much of medicine as anyone here. I do not want patients. The reason, you see, does not appear on the surface. It lies in fact in my character, which has, if you think about it, many strange turns. Why I want to talk to you of the matter I don't know. I might keep still and get more credit in your eyes. I have a desire to make you admire me, that's a fact. I don't know why. That's why I talk. It's very amusing, eh?"

Sometimes the doctor launched into long tales concerning himself. To the boy the tales were very real and full of meaning. He began to admire the fat unclean-looking man and, in the afternoon when Will Henderson had gone, looked forward with keen interest to the doctor's coming.

Doctor Parcival had been in Winesburg about five years. He came from Chicago and when he arrived was drunk and got into a fight with Albert Longworth, the baggageman. The fight concerned a trunk and ended by the doctor's being escorted to the village lockup. When he was released he rented a room above a shoe-repairing shop at the lower end of Main Street and put out the sign that announced himself as a doctor. Although he had but few patients and these of the poorer sort who were unable to pay, he seemed to have plenty of money for his needs. He slept in the office that was unspeakably dirty and dined at Biff Carter's lunch room in a small frame building opposite the railroad station. In the summer the lunch room was filled with flies and Biff Carter's white apron was more dirty than his floor. Doctor Parcival did not mind. Into the lunch room he stalked and deposited twenty cents upon the counter. "Feed me what you wish for that," he said laughing. "Use up food that you wouldn't otherwise sell. It makes no difference to me. I am a man of distinction, you see. Why should I concern myself with what I eat."

The tales that Doctor Parcival told George Willard began nowhere and ended nowhere. Sometimes the boy thought they must all be inventions, a pack of lies. And then again he was convinced that they contained the very essence of truth.

"I was a reporter like you here," Doctor Parcival began. "It was in a town in Iowa—or was it in Illinois? I don't remember and anyway it makes no difference. Perhaps I am trying to conceal my identity and don't want to be very definite. Have you ever thought it strange that I have money for my needs although I do nothing? I may have stolen a great sum of money or been

involved in a murder before I came here. There
is food for thought in that, eh? If you were a
really smart newspaper reporter you would look
me up. In Chicago there was a Doctor Cronin
who was murdered. Have you heard of that?
Some men murdered him and put him in a trunk.
In the early morning they hauled the trunk across
the city. It sat on the back of an express wagon
and they were on the seat as unconcerned as anything. Along they went through quiet streets
where everyone was asleep. The sun was just
coming up over the lake. Funny, eh—just to
think of them smoking pipes and chattering as
they drove along as unconcerned as I am now.
Perhaps I was one of those men. That would be
a strange turn of things, now wouldn't it, eh?"
Again Doctor Parcival began his tale: "Well,
anyway there I was, a reporter on a paper just
as you are here, running about and getting little
items to print. My mother was poor. She took
in washing. Her dream was to make me a Presbyterian minister and I was studying with that end
in view.

"My father had been insane for a number of
years. He was in an asylum over at Dayton,
Ohio. There you see I have let it slip out! All
of this took place in Ohio, right here in Ohio.
There is a clew if you ever get the notion of looking me up.

"I was going to tell you of my brother. That's the object of all this. That's what I'm getting at. My brother was a railroad painter and had a job on the Big Four. You know that road runs through Ohio here. With other men he lived in a box car and away they went from town to town painting the railroad property—switches, crossing gates, bridges, and stations.

"The Big Four paints its stations a nasty orange color. How I hated that color! My brother was always covered with it. On pay days he used to get drunk and come home wearing his paint-covered clothes and bringing his money with him. He did not give it to mother but laid it in a pile on our kitchen table.

"About the house he went in the clothes covered with the nasty orange colored paint. I can see the picture. My mother, who was small and had red, sad-looking eyes, would come into the house from a little shed at the back. That's where she spent her time over the washtub scrubbing people's dirty clothes. In she would come and stand by the table, rubbing her eyes with her apron that was covered with soap-suds.

" 'Don't touch it! Don't you dare touch that money,' my brother roared, and then he himself took five or ten dollars and went tramping off to the saloons. When he had spent what he had taken he came back for more. He never gave my mother any money at all but stayed about until he had spent it all, a little at a time. Then he went back to his job with the painting crew on the railroad. After he had gone things began to arrive at our house, groceries and such things. Sometimes there would be a dress for mother or a pair of shoes for me.

"Strange, eh? My mother loved my brother much more than she did me, although he never said a kind word to either of us and always raved up and down threatening us if we dared so much as touch the money that sometimes lay on the table three days.

"We got along pretty well. I studied to be a minister and prayed. I was a regular ass about saying prayers. You should have heard me. When my father died I prayed all night, just as I did sometimes when my brother was in town drinking and going about buying the things for us. In the evening after supper I knelt by the table where the money lay and prayed for hours. When no one was looking I stole a dollar or two and put it in my pocket. That makes me laugh now but then it was terrible. It was on my mind all the time. I got six dollars a week from my job on the paper and always took it straight home to mother. The few dollars I stole from my brother's pile I spent on myself, you know, for trifles, candy and cigarettes and such things.

"When my father died at the asylum over at Dayton, I went over there. I borrowed some money from the man for whom I worked and went on the train at night. It was raining. In the asylum they treated me as though I were a king.

"The men who had jobs in the asylum had found out I was a newspaper reporter. That made them afraid. There had been some negligence, some carelessness, you see, when father was ill. They thought perhaps I would write it up in the paper and make a fuss. I never intended to do anything of the kind.

"Anyway, in I went to the room where my father lay dead and blessed the dead body. I wonder what put that notion into my head. Wouldn't my brother, the painter, have laughed, though. There I stood over the dead body and spread out my hands. The superintendent of the asylum and some of his helpers came in and stood about looking sheepish. It was very amusing. I spread out my hands and said, 'Let peace brood over this carcass.' That's what I said."

Jumping to his feet and breaking off the tale, Doctor Parcival began to walk up and down in the office of the *Winesburg Eagle* where George Willard sat listening. He was awkward and, as the office was small, continually knocked against things. "What a fool I am to be talking," he said. "That is not my object in coming here and forcing my acquaintanceship upon you. I have something else in mind. You are a reporter just as I was once and you have attracted my attention. You may end by becoming just such another fool. I want to warn you and keep on warning you. That's why I seek you out."

Doctor Parcival began talking of George Willard's attitude toward men. It seemed to the boy that the man had but one object in view, to make everyone seem despicable. "I want to fill you with hatred and contempt so that you will be a superior being," he declared. "Look at my brother. There was a fellow, eh? He despised everyone, you see. You have no idea with what contempt he looked upon mother and me. And was he not our superior? You know he was. You have not seen him and yet I have made you feel that. I have given you a sense of it. He is dead. Once when he was drunk he lay down on the tracks and the car in which he lived with the other painters ran over him."

.   .   .   .

One day in August Doctor Parcival had an adventure in Winesburg. For a month George Willard had been going each morning to spend an hour in the doctor's office. The visits came about through a desire on the part of the doctor to read to the boy from the pages of a book he was in the process of writing. To write the book Doctor Parcival declared was the object of his coming to Winesburg to live.

On the morning in August before the coming of the boy, an incident had happened in the doctor's office. There had been an accident on Main Street. A team of horses had been frightened by a train and had run away. A little girl, the daughter of a farmer, had been thrown from a buggy and killed.

On Main Street everyone had become excited and a cry for doctors had gone up. All three of the active practitioners of the town had come quickly but had found the child dead. From the crowd someone had run to the office of Doctor Parcival who had bluntly refused to go down out of his office to the dead child. The useless cruelty of his refusal had passed unnoticed. Indeed, the man who had come up the stairway to summon him had hurried away without hearing the refusal.

All of this, Doctor Parcival did not know and when George Willard came to his office he found the man shaking with terror. "What I have done will arouse the people of this town," he declared excitedly. "Do I not know human nature? Do I not know what will happen? Word of my refusal will be whispered about. Presently men will get together in groups and talk of it. They will come here. We will quarrel and there will be talk of hanging. Then they will come again bearing a rope in their hands."

Doctor Parcival shook with fright. "I have a presentiment," he declared emphatically. "It may be that what I am talking about will not occur this morning. It may be put off until to-night but I will be hanged. Everyone will get excited. I will be hanged to a lamp-post on Main Street."

Going to the door of his dirty little office, Doctor Parcival looked timidly down the stairway leading to the street. When he returned the fright that had been in his eyes was beginning to be replaced by doubt. Coming on tip-toe across the room he tapped George Willard on the shoulder. "If not now, sometime," he whispered, shaking his head. "In the end I will be crucified, uselessly crucified."

Doctor Parcival began to plead with George Willard. "You must pay attention to me," he urged. "If something happens perhaps you will be able to write the book that I may never get written. The idea is very simple, so simple that if you are not careful you will forget it. It is this—that everyone in the world is Christ and they are all crucified. That's what I want to say. Don't you forget that. Whatever happens, don't you dare let yourself forget."

NOBODY KNOWS

LOOKING cautiously about, George Willard arose from his desk in the office of the *Winesburg Eagle* and went hurriedly out at the back door. The night was warm and cloudy and although it was not yet eight o'clock, the alleyway back of the *Eagle* office was pitch dark. A team of horses tied to a post somewhere in the darkness stamped on the hard-baked ground. A cat sprang from under George Willard's feet and ran away into the night. The young man was nervous. All day he had gone about his work like one dazed by a blow. In the alleyway he trembled as though with fright.

In the darkness George Willard walked along the alleyway, going carefully and cautiously. The back doors of the Winesburg stores were open and he could see men sitting about under the store lamps. In Myerbaum's Notion Store Mrs. Willy the saloon keeper's wife stood by the counter with a basket on her arm. Sid Green the clerk was waiting on her. He leaned over the counter and talked earnestly.

George Willard crouched and then jumped

through the path of light that came out at the door. He began to run forward in the darkness. Behind Ed Griffith's saloon old Jerry Bird the town drunkard lay asleep on the ground. The runner stumbled over the sprawling legs. He laughed brokenly.

George Willard had set forth upon an adventure. All day he had been trying to make up his mind to go through with the adventure and now he was acting. In the office of the *Winesburg Eagle* he had been sitting since six o'clock trying to think.

There had been no decision. He had just jumped to his feet, hurried past Will Henderson who was reading proof in the print shop and started to run along the alleyway.

Through street after street went George Willard, avoiding the people who passed. He crossed and recrossed the road. When he passed a street lamp he pulled his hat down over his face. He did not dare think. In his mind there was a fear but it was a new kind of fear. He was afraid the adventure on which he had set out would be spoiled, that he would lose courage and turn back.

George Willard found Louise Trunnion in the kitchen of her father's house. She was washing dishes by the light of a kerosene lamp. There she stood behind the screen door in the little shed-like kitchen at the back of the house. George Willard stopped by a picket fence and tried to control the shaking of his body. Only a narrow potato patch separated him from the adventure. Five minutes passed before he felt sure enough of himself to call to her. "Louise! Oh Louise!" he called. The cry stuck in his throat. His voice became a hoarse whisper.

Louise Trunnion came out across the potato patch holding the dish cloth in her hand. "How do you know I want to go out with you," she said sulkily. "What makes you so sure?"

George Willard did not answer. In silence the two stood in the darkness with the fence between them. "You go on along," she said. "Pa's in there. I'll come along. You wait by William's barn."

The young newspaper reporter had received a letter from Louise Trunnion. It had come that morning to the office of the *Winesburg Eagle*. The letter was brief. "I'm yours if you want me," it said. He thought it annoying that in the darkness by the fence she had pretended there was nothing between them. "She has a nerve! Well, gracious sakes, she has a nerve," he muttered as he went along the street and passed a row of vacant lots where corn grew. The corn was shoulder high and had been planted right down to the sidewalk.

When Louise Trunnion came out of the front door of her house she still wore the gingham dress in which she had been washing dishes.   There was no hat on her head.   The boy could see her standing with the doorknob in her hand talking to someone within, no doubt to old Jake Trunnion, her father.   Old Jake was half deaf and she shouted.   The door closed and everything was dark and silent in the little side street.   George Willard trembled more violently than ever.

In the shadows by William's barn George and Louise stood, not daring to talk.   She was not particularly comely and there was a black smudge on the side of her nose.   George thought she must have rubbed her nose with her finger after she had been handling some of the kitchen pots.

The young man began to laugh nervously. "It's warm," he said.   He wanted to touch her with his hand.   "I'm not very bold," he thought. Just to touch the folds of the soiled gingham dress would, he decided, be an exquisite pleasure.   She began to quibble.   "You think you're better than I am.   Don't tell me, I guess I know," she said drawing closer to him.

A flood of words burst from George Willard. He remembered the look that had lurked in the girl's eyes when they had met on the streets and thought of the note she had written.   Doubt left him.   The whispered tales concerning her that had gone about town gave him confidence. He became wholly the male, bold and aggressive. In his heart there was no sympathy for her. "Ah, come on, it'll be all right. There won't be anyone know anything. How can they know?" he urged.

They began to walk along a narrow brick sidewalk between the cracks of which tall weeds grew. Some of the bricks were missing and the sidewalk was rough and irregular. He took hold of her hand that was also rough and thought it delightfully small. "I can't go far," she said and her voice was quiet, unperturbed.

They crossed a bridge that ran over a tiny stream and passed another vacant lot in which corn grew. The street ended. In the path at the side of the road they were compelled to walk one behind the other. Will Overton's berry field lay beside the road and there was a pile of boards. "Will is going to build a shed to store berry crates here," said George and they sat down upon the boards.

.   .   .   .

When George Willard got back into Main Street it was past ten o'clock and had begun to rain. Three times he walked up and down the length of Main Street. Sylvester West's Drug Store was still open and he went in and bought a cigar. When Shorty Crandall the clerk came out at the door with him he was pleased. For five minutes the two stood in the shelter of the store awning and talked. George Willard felt satisfied. He had wanted more than anything else to talk to some man. Around a corner toward the New Willard House he went whistling softly.

On the sidewalk at the side of Winny's Dry Goods Store where there was a high board fence covered with circus pictures, he stopped whistling and stood perfectly still in the darkness, attentive, listening as though for a voice calling his name. Then again he laughed nervously. "She hasn't got anything on me. Nobody knows," he muttered doggedly and went on his way.

GODLINESS

A TALE IN FOUR PARTS

PART ONE

THERE were always three or four old people sitting on the front porch of the house or puttering about the garden of the Bentley farm. Three of the old people were women and sisters to Jesse. They were a colorless, soft-voiced lot. Then there was a silent old man with thin white hair who was Jesse's uncle.

The farmhouse was built of wood, a board outer-covering over a framework of logs. It was in reality not one house but a cluster of houses joined together in a rather haphazard manner. Inside, the place was full of surprises. One went up steps from the living room into the dining room and there were always steps to be ascended or descended in passing from one room to another. At meal times the place was like a beehive. At one moment all was quiet, then doors began to open, feet clattered on stairs, a murmur of soft voices arose and people appeared from a dozen obscure corners.

Beside the old people, already mentioned, many others lived in the Bentley house. There were four hired men, a woman named Aunt Callie Beebe, who was in charge of the housekeeping, a dull-witted girl named Eliza Stoughton, who made beds and helped with the milking, a boy who worked in the stables, and Jesse Bentley himself, the owner and overlord of it all.

By the time the American Civil War had been over for twenty years, that part of Northern Ohio where the Bentley farms lay had begun to emerge from pioneer life. Jesse then owned machinery for harvesting grain. He had built modern barns and most of his land was drained with carefully laid tile drain, but in order to understand the man we will have to go back to an earlier day.

The Bentley family had been in Northern Ohio for several generations before Jesse's time. They came from New York State and took up land when the country was new and land could be had at a low price. For a long time they, in common with all the other Middle Western people, were very poor. The land they had settled upon was heavily wooded and covered with fallen logs and underbrush. After the long hard labor of clearing these away and cutting the timber, there were still the stumps to be reckoned with. Plows run through the fields caught on hidden roots, stones lay all about, on the low places water gathered, and the young corn turned yellow, sickened and died.

When Jesse Bentley's father and brothers had come into their ownership of the place, much of the harder part of the work of clearing had been done, but they clung to old traditions and worked like driven animals. They lived as practically all of the farming people of the time lived. In the spring and through most of the winter the highways leading into the town of Winesburg were a sea of mud. The four young men of the family worked hard all day in the fields, they ate heavily of coarse, greasy food, and at night slept like tired beasts on beds of straw. Into their lives came little that was not coarse and brutal and out-wardly they were themselves coarse and brutal. On Saturday afternoons they hitched a team of horses to a three-seated wagon and went off to town. In town they stood about the stoves in the stores talking to other farmers or to the store keepers. They were dressed in overalls and in the winter wore heavy coats that were flecked with mud. Their hands as they stretched them out to the heat of the stoves were cracked and red. It was difficult for them to talk and so they for the most part kept silent. When they had bought meat, flour, sugar, and salt, they went into one of the Winesburg saloons and drank beer. Under

the influence of drink the naturally strong lusts of
their natures, kept suppressed by the heroic labor
of breaking up new ground, were released.   A
kind of crude and animal-like poetic fervor took
possession of them.   On the road home they stood
up on the wagon seats and shouted at the stars.
Sometimes they fought long and bitterly and at
other times they broke forth into songs.   Once
Enoch Bentley, the older one of the boys, struck
his father, old Tom Bentley, with the butt of a
teamster's whip, and the old man seemed likely to
die.   For days Enoch lay hid in the straw in the
loft of the stable ready to flee if the result of his
momentary passion turned out to be murder.
He was kept alive with food brought by his
mother who also kept him informed of the in-
jured man's condition.   When all turned out well
he emerged from his hiding place and went back
to the work of clearing land as though nothing
had happened.

.   .   .   .

The Civil War brought a sharp turn to the
fortunes of the Bentleys and was responsible for
the rise of the youngest son, Jesse.   Enoch, Edward, Harry, and Will Bentley all enlisted and
before the long war ended they were all killed.
For a time after they went away to the South,
old Tom tried to run the place, but he was not

successful. When the last of the four had been killed he sent word to Jesse that he would have to come home.

Then the mother, who had not been well for a year, died suddenly, and the father became altogether discouraged. He talked of selling the farm and moving into town. All day he went about shaking his head and muttering. The work in the fields was neglected and weeds grew high in the corn. Old Tom hired men but he did not use them intelligently. When they had gone away to the fields in the morning he wandered into the woods and sat down on a log. Sometimes he forgot to come home at night and one of the daughters had to go in search of him.

When Jesse Bentley came home to the farm and began to take charge of things he was a slight, sensitive-looking man of twenty-two. At eighteen he had left home to go to school to become a scholar and eventually to become a minister of the Presbyterian Church. All through his boyhood he had been what in our country was called an "odd sheep" and had not got on with his brothers. Of all the family only his mother had understood him and she was now dead. When he came home to take charge of the farm, that had at that time grown to more than six hundred acres, everyone on the farms about and in the nearby town of Winesburg smiled at the idea of his trying to handle the work that had been done by his four strong brothers.

There was indeed good cause to smile. By the standards of his day Jesse did not look like a man at all. He was small and very slender and womanish of body and, true to the traditions of young ministers, wore a long black coat and a narrow black string tie. The neighbors were amused when they saw him, after the years away, and they were even more amused when they saw the woman he had married in the city.

As a matter of fact, Jesse's wife did soon go under. That was perhaps Jesse's fault. A farm in Northern Ohio in the hard years after the Civil War was no place for a delicate woman, and Katherine Bentley was delicate. Jesse was hard with her as he was with everybody about him in those days. She tried to do such work as all the neighbor women about her did and he let her go on without interference. She helped to do the milking and did part of the housework; she made the beds for the men and prepared their food. For a year she worked every day from sunrise until late at night and then after giving birth to a child she died.

As for Jesse Bentley—although he was a delicately built man there was something within him that could not easily be killed. He had brown curly hair and grey eyes that were at times hard

and direct, at times wavering and uncertain. Not
only was he slender but he was also short of stature. His mouth was like the mouth of a sensitive
and very determined child. Jesse Bentley was a
fanatic. He was a man born out of his time and
place and for this he suffered and made others
suffer. Never did he succeed in getting what he
wanted out of life and he did not know what he
wanted. Within a very short time after he came
home to the Bentley farm he made everyone there
a little afraid of him, and his wife, who should
have been close to him as his mother had been,
was afraid also. At the end of two weeks after
his coming, old Tom Bentley made over to him
the entire ownership of the place and retired into
the background. Everyone retired into the background. In spite of his youth and inexperience,
Jesse had the trick of mastering the souls of his
people. He was so in earnest in everything he
did and said that no one understood him. He
made everyone on the farm work as they had never
worked before and yet there was no joy in the
work. If things went well they went well for
Jesse and never for the people who were his de-
pendents. Like a thousand other strong men who
have come into the world here in America in
these later times, Jesse was but half strong. He
could master others but he could not master himself. The running of the farm as it had never

been run before was easy for him.　When he came
home from Cleveland where he had been in
school, he shut himself off from all of his people
and began to make plans.　He thought about the
farm night and day and that made him successful.
Other men on the farms about him worked too
hard and were too tired to think, but to think of
the farm and to be everlastingly making plans for
its success was a relief to Jesse.　It partially satisfied something in his passionate nature.　Immediately after he came home he had a wing built on
to the old house and in a large room facing the
west he had windows that looked into the barnyard and other windows that looked off across the
fields.　By the window he sat down to think.
Hour after hour and day after day he sat and
looked over the land and thought out his new place
in life.　The passionate burning thing in his
nature flamed up and his eyes became hard.　He
wanted to make the farm produce as no farm in
his state had ever produced before and then he
wanted something else.　It was the indefinable
hunger within that made his eyes waver and that
kept him always more and more silent before
people.　He would have given much to achieve
peace and in him was a fear that peace was the
thing he could not achieve.

All over his body Jesse Bentley was alive.　In
his small frame was gathered the force of a long

'line of strong men. He had always been extraordinarily alive when he was a small boy on the farm and later when he was a young man in school. In the school he had studied and thought of God and the Bible with his whole mind and heart. As time passed and he grew to know people better, he began to think of himself as an extraordinary man, one set apart from his fellows. He wanted terribly to make his life a thing of great importance, and as he looked about at his fellow men and saw how like clods they lived it seemed to him that he could not bear to become also such a clod. Although in his absorption in himself and in his own destiny he was blind to the fact that his young wife was doing a strong woman's work even after she had become large with child and that she was killing herself in his service, he did not intend to be unkind to her. When his father, who was old and twisted with toil, made over to him the ownership of the farm and seemed content to creep away to a corner and wait for death, he shrugged his shoulders and dismissed the old man from his mind.

In the room by the window overlooking the land that had come down to him sat Jesse thinking of his own affairs. In the stables he could hear the tramping of his horses and the restless movement of his cattle. Away in the fields he could see other cattle wandering over green hills.

The voices of men, his men who worked for him, came in to him through the window. From the milkhouse there was the steady thump, thump of a churn being manipulated by the half-witted girl, Eliza Stoughton. Jesse's mind went back to the men of Old Testament days who had also owned lands and herds. He remembered how God had come down out of the skies and talked to these men and he wanted God to notice and to talk to him also. A kind of feverish boyish eagerness to in some way achieve in his own life the flavor of significance that had hung over these men took possession of him. Being a prayerful man he spoke of the matter aloud to God and the sound of his own words strengthened and fed his eagerness.

"I am a new kind of man come into possession of these fields," he declared. "Look upon me, O God, and look Thou also upon my neighbors and all the men who have gone before me here! O God, create in me another Jesse, like that one of old, to rule over men and to be the father of sons who shall be rulers!" Jesse grew excited as he talked aloud and jumping to his feet walked up and down in the room. In fancy he saw himself living in old times and among old peoples. The land that lay stretched out before him became of vast significance, a place peopled by his fancy with a new race of men sprung from himself. It seemed to him that in his day as in those other and older days, kingdoms might be created and new impulses given to the lives of men by the power of God speaking through a chosen servant. He longed to be such a servant. "It is God's work I have come to the land to do," he declared in a loud voice and his short figure straightened and he thought that something like a halo of Godly approval hung over him.

. . . .

It will perhaps be somewhat difficult for the men and women of a later day to understand Jesse Bentley. In the last fifty years a vast change has taken place in the lives of our people. A revolution has in fact taken place. The coming of industrialism, attended by all the roar and rattle of affairs, the shrill cries of millions of new voices that have come among us from over seas, the going and coming of trains, the growth of cities, the building of the interurban car lines that weave in and out of towns and past farmhouses, and now in these later days the coming of the automobiles has worked a tremendous change in the lives and in the habits of thought of our people of Mid-America. Books, badly imagined and written though they may be in the hurry of our times, are in every household, magazines circulate by the millions of copies, newspapers are everywhere. In our day a farmer standing by the stove in the store in his village has his mind filled to overflowing with the words of other men. The newspapers and the magazines have pumped him full. Much of the old brutal ignorance that had in it also a kind of beautiful childlike innocence is gone forever. The farmer by the stove is brother to the men of the cities, and if you listen you will find him talking as glibly and as senselessly as the best city man of us all.

In Jesse Bentley's time and in the country districts of the whole Middle West in the years after the Civil War it was not so. Men labored too hard and were too tired to read. In them was no desire for words printed upon paper. As they worked in the fields, vague, half-formed thoughts took possession of them. They believed in God and in God's power to control their lives. In the little Protestant churches they gathered on Sunday to hear of God and his works. The churches were the center of the social and intellectual life of the times. The figure of God was big in the hearts of men.

And so, having been born an imaginative child and having within him a great intellectual eagerness, Jesse Bentley had turned wholeheartedly toward God. When the war took his brothers away, he saw the hand of God in that. When his father became ill and could no longer attend to the running of the farm, he took that also as a sign from God. In the city, when the word came to him, he walked about at night through the streets thinking of the matter and when he had come home and had got the work on the farm well under way, he went again at night to walk through the forests and over the low hills and to think of God.

As he walked the importance of his own figure in some divine plan grew in his mind. He grew avaricious and was impatient that the farm contained only six hundred acres. Kneeling in a fence corner at the edge of some meadow, he sent his voice abroad into the silence and looking up he saw the stars shining down at him.

One evening, some months after his father's death, and when his wife Katherine was expecting at any moment to be laid abed of childbirth, Jesse left his house and went for a long walk. The Bentley farm was situated in a tiny valley watered by Wine Creek, and Jesse walked along the banks of the stream to the end of his own land and on through the fields of his neighbors. As he walked the valley broadened and then narrowed again. Great open stretches of field and wood lay before him. The moon came out from behind clouds, and, climbing a low hill, he sat down to think.

Jesse thought that as the true servant of God
the entire stretch of country through which he had
walked should have come into his possession. He
thought of his dead brothers and blamed them
that they had not worked harder and achieved
more. Before him in the moonlight the tiny
stream ran down over stones, and he began to
think of the men of old times who like himself had
owned flocks and lands.

A fantastic impulse, half fear, half greediness
took possession of Jesse Bentley. He remembered how in the old Bible story the Lord had
appeared to that other Jesse and told him to send
his son David to where Saul and the men of Israel
were fighting the Philistines in the Valley of Elah.
Into Jesse's mind came the conviction that all of
the Ohio farmers who owned land in the valley
of Wine Creek were Philistines and enemies of
God. "Suppose," he whispered to himself, "there
should come from among them one who, like
Goliath the Philistine of Gath, could defeat me
and take from me my possessions." In fancy he
felt the sickening dread that he thought must have
lain heavy on the heart of Saul before the coming
of David. Jumping to his feet, he began to run
through the night. As he ran he called to God.
His voice carried far over the low hills. "Jeho-
vah of Hosts," he cried, "send to me this night
out of the womb of Katherine, a son. Let thy

grace alight upon me. Send me a son to be called David who shall help me to pluck at last all of these lands out of the hands of the Philistines and turn them to Thy service and to the building of Thy kingdom on earth."

GODLINESS

PART TWO

DAVID HARDY of Winesburg, Ohio was the grandson of Jesse Bentley, the owner of Bentley farms. When he was twelve years old he went to the old Bentley place to live. His mother, Louise Bentley, the girl who came into the world on that night when Jesse ran through the fields crying to God that he be given a son, had grown to womanhood on the farm and had married young John Hardy of Winesburg who became a banker. Louise and her husband did not live happily together and everyone agreed that she was to blame. She was a small woman with sharp grey eyes and black hair. From childhood she had been inclined to fits of temper and when not angry she was often morose and silent. In Winesburg it was said that she drank. Her husband, the banker, who was a careful, shrewd man, tried hard to make her happy. When he began to make money he bought for her a large brick house on Elm Street in Winesburg and he was the first man in that town to keep a manservant to drive his wife's carriage.

But Louise could not be made happy. She flew into half insane fits of temper during which she was sometimes silent, sometimes noisy and quarrelsome. She swore and cried out in her anger. She got a knife from the kitchen and threatened her husband's life. Once she deliberately set fire to the house, and often she hid herself away for days in her own room and would see no one. Her life, lived as a half recluse, gave rise to all sorts of stories concerning her. It was said that she took drugs and that she hid herself away from people because she was often so under the influence of drink that her condition could not be concealed. Sometimes on summer afternoons she came out of the house and got into her carriage. Dismissing the driver she took the reins in her own hands and drove off at top speed through the streets. If a pedestrian got in her way she drove straight ahead and the frightened citizen had to escape as best he could. To the people of the town it seemed as though she wanted to run them down. When she had driven through several streets, tearing around corners and beating the horses with the whip, she drove off into the country. On the country roads after she had gotten out of sight of the houses she let the horses slow down to a walk and her wild, reckless mood passed. She became thoughtful and muttered words. Sometimes tears came into her eyes. And then when she came back into town she again drove furiously through the quiet streets. But for the influence of her husband and the respect he inspired in people's minds she would have been arrested more than once by the town marshal.

Young David Hardy grew up in the house with this woman and as can well be imagined there was not much joy in his childhood. He was too young then to have opinions of his own about people, but at times it was difficult for him not to have very definite opinions about the woman who was his mother. David was always a quiet orderly boy and for a long time was thought by the people of Winesburg to be something of a dullard. His eyes were brown and as a child he had a habit of looking at things and people a long time without appearing to see what he was looking at. When he heard his mother spoken of harshly or when he overheard her berating his father, he was frightened and ran away to hide. Sometimes he could not find a hiding place and that confused him. Turning his face toward a tree or if he were indoors toward the wall, he closed his eyes and tried not to think of anything. He had a habit of talking aloud to himself, and early in life a spirit of quiet sadness often took possession of him.

On the occasions when David went to visit his

grandfather on the Bentley farm, he was altogether contented and happy. Often he wished that he would never have to go back to town and once when he had come home from the farm after a long visit, something happened that had a lasting effect on his mind.

David had come back into town with one of the hired men. The man was in a hurry to go about his own affairs and left the boy at the head of the street in which the Hardy house stood. It was early dusk of a fall evening and the sky was overcast with clouds. Something happened to David. He could not bear to go into the house where his mother and father lived, and on an impulse he decided to run away from home. He intended to go back to the farm and to his grandfather, but lost his way and for hours he wandered weeping and frightened on country roads. It started to rain and lightning flashed in the sky. The boy's imagination was excited and he fancied that he could see and hear strange things in the darkness. Into his mind came the conviction that he was walking and running in some terrible void where no one had ever been before. The darkness about him seemed limitless. The sound of the wind blowing in trees was terrifying. When a team of horses approached along the road in which he walked he was frightened and climbed a fence. Through a field he ran until he came

into another road and getting upon his knees felt
of the soft ground with his fingers. But for the
figure of his grandfather, whom he was afraid he
would never find in the darkness, he thought the
world must be altogether empty. When his cries
were heard by a farmer who was walking home
from town and he was brought back to his father's house, he was so tired and excited that he did
not know what was happening to him.

By chance David's father knew that he had disappeared. On the street he had met the farm
hand from the Bentley place and knew of his son's
return to town. When the boy did not come
home an alarm was set up and John Hardy with
several men of the town went to search the country. The report that David had been kidnapped
ran about through the streets of Winesburg.
When he came home there were no lights in the
house, but his mother appeared and clutched him
eagerly in her arms. David thought she had suddenly become another woman. He could not believe that so delightful a thing had happened.
With her own hands Louise Hardy bathed his
tired young body and cooked him food. She
would not let him go to bed but, when he had put
on his nightgown, blew out the lights and sat down
in a chair to hold him in her arms. For an hour
the woman sat in the darkness and held her boy.
All the time she kept talking in a low voice.

David could not understand what had so changed her. Her habitually dissatisfied face had become, he thought, the most peaceful and lovely thing he had ever seen. When he began to weep she held him more and more tightly. On and on went her voice. It was not harsh or shrill as when she talked to her husband, but was like rain falling on trees. Presently men began coming to the door to report that he had not been found, but she made him hide and be silent until she had sent them away. He thought it must be a game his mother and the men of the town were playing with him and laughed joyously. Into his mind came the thought that his having been lost and frightened in the darkness was an altogether unimportant matter. He thought that he would have been willing to go through the frightful experience a thousand times to be sure of finding at the end of the long black road a thing so lovely as his mother had suddenly become.

. . . .

During the last years of young David's boyhood he saw his mother but seldom and she became for him just a woman with whom he had once lived. Still he could not get her figure out of his mind and as he grew older it became more definite. When he was twelve years old he went to the Bentley farm to live. Old Jesse came into town and fairly demanded that he be given charge of the boy. The old man was excited and determined on having his own way. He talked to John Hardy in the office of the Winesburg Savings Bank and then the two men went to the house on Elm Street to talk with Louise. They both expected her to make trouble but were mistaken. She was very quiet and when Jesse had explained his mission and had gone on at some length about the advantages to come through having the boy out of doors and in the quiet atmosphere of the old farmhouse, she nodded her head in approval. "It is an atmosphere not corrupted by my presence," she said sharply. Her shoulders shook and she seemed about to fly into a fit of temper. "It is a place for a man child, although it was never a place for me," she went on. "You never wanted me there and of course the air of your house did me no good. It was like poison in my blood but it will be different with him."

Louise turned and went out of the room, leaving the two men to sit in embarrassed silence. As very often happened she later stayed in her room for days. Even when the boy's clothes were packed and he was taken away she did not appear. The loss of her son made a sharp break in her life and she seemed less inclined to quarrel with her husband. John Hardy thought it had all turned out very well indeed.

And so young David went to live in the Bentley

farmhouse with Jesse. Two of the old farmer's sisters were alive and still lived in the house. They were afraid of Jesse and rarely spoke when he was about. One of the women who had been noted for her flaming red hair when she was younger was a born mother and became the boy's caretaker. Every night when he had gone to bed she went into his room and sat on the floor until he fell asleep. When he became drowsy she became bold and whispered things that he later thought he must have dreamed.

Her soft low voice called him endearing names and he dreamed that his mother had come to him and that she had changed so that she was always as she had been that time after he ran away. He also grew bold and reaching out his hand stroked the face of the woman on the floor so that she was ecstatically happy. Everyone in the old house became happy after the boy went there. The hard insistent thing in Jesse Bentley that had kept the people in the house silent and timid and that had never been dispelled by the presence of the girl Louise was apparently swept away by the coming of the boy. It was as though God had relented and sent a son to the man.

The man who had proclaimed himself the only true servant of God in all the valley of Wine Creek, and who had wanted God to send him a sign of approval by way of a son out of the womb of Katherine, began to think that at last his prayers had been answered.   Although he was at that time only fifty-five years old he looked seventy and was worn out with much thinking and scheming.   The effort he had made to extend his land holdings had been successful and there were few farms in the valley that did not belong to him, but until David came he was a bitterly disappointed man.

There were two influences at work in Jesse Bentley and all his life his mind had been a battleground for these influences.   First there was the old thing in him.   He wanted to be a man of God and a leader among men of God.   His walking in the fields and through the forests at night had brought him close to nature and there were forces in the passionately religious man that ran out to the forces in nature.   The disappointment that had come to him when a daughter and not a son had been born to Katherine had fallen upon him like a blow struck by some unseen hand and the blow had somewhat softened his egotism.   He still believed that God might at any moment make himself manifest out of the winds or the clouds, but he no longer demanded such recognition.   Instead he prayed for it.   Sometimes he was altogether doubtful and thought God had deserted the world.   He regretted the fate that had not let him live in a simpler and sweeter time when at the beckoning of some strange cloud in the sky men left their lands and houses and went forth into the wilderness to create new races. While he worked night and day to make his farms more productive and to extend his holdings of land, he regretted that he could not use his own restless energy in the building of temples, the slaying of unbelievers and in general in the work of glorifying God's name on earth.

That is what Jesse hungered for and then also he hungered for something else. He had grown into maturity in America in the years after the Civil War and he, like all men of his time, had been touched by the deep influences that were at work in the country during those years when modern industrialism was being born. He began to buy machines that would permit him to do the work of the farms while employing fewer men and he sometimes thought that if he were a younger man he would give up farming altogether and start a factory in Winesburg for the making of machinery. Jesse formed the habit of reading newspapers and magazines. He invented a machine for the making of fence out of wire. Faintly he realized that the atmosphere of old times and places that he had always cultivated in his own mind was strange and foreign to the thing that was growing up in the minds of others. The beginning of the most materialistic age in the

history of the world, when wars would be fought
without patriotism, when men would forget God
and only pay attention to moral standards, when
the will to power would replace the will to serve
and beauty would be well-nigh forgotten in the
terrible headlong rush of mankind toward the
acquiring of possessions, was telling its story to
Jesse the man of God as it was to the men about
him.   The greedy thing in him wanted to make
money faster than it could be made by tilling the
land.   More than once he went into Winesburg
to talk with his son-in-law John Hardy about it.
"You are a banker and you will have chances I
never had," he said and his eyes shone.   "I am
thinking about it all the time.   Big things are going to be done in the country and there will be
more money to be made than I ever dreamed of.
You get into it.   I wish I were younger and had
your chance."   Jesse Bentley walked up and down
in the bank office and grew more and more excited as he talked.   At one time in his life he had
been threatened with paralysis and his left side
remained somewhat weakened.   As he talked his
left eyelid twitched.   Later when he drove back
home and when night came on and the stars came
out it was harder to get back the old feeling of
a close and personal God who lived in the sky
overhead and who might at any moment reach out
his hand, touch him on the shoulder, and appoint

for him some heroic task to be done. Jesse's mind was fixed upon the things read in newspapers and magazines, on fortunes to be made almost without effort by shrewd men who bought and sold. For him the coming of the boy David did much to bring back with renewed force the old faith and it seemed to him that God had at last looked with favor upon him.

As for the boy on the farm, life began to reveal itself to him in a thousand new and delightful ways. The kindly attitude of all about him expanded his quiet nature and he lost the half timid, hesitating manner he had always had with his people. At night when he went to bed after a long day of adventures in the stables, in the fields, or driving about from farm to farm with his grandfather he wanted to embrace everyone in the house. If Sherley Bentley, the woman who came each night to sit on the floor by his bedside, did not appear at once, he went to the head of the stairs and shouted, his young voice ringing through the narrow halls where for so long there had been a tradition of silence. In the morning when he awoke and lay still in bed, the sounds that came in to him through the windows filled him with delight. He thought with a shudder of the life in the house in Winesburg and of his mother's angry voice that had always made him tremble. There in the country all sounds were pleasant

sounds. When he awoke at dawn the barnyard
back of the house also awoke. In the house people stirred about. Eliza Stoughton the half-
witted girl was poked in the ribs by a farm hand
and giggled noisily, in some distant field a cow
bawled and was answered by the cattle in the
stables, and one of the farm hands spoke sharply
to the horse he was grooming by the stable door.
David leaped out of bed and ran to a window.
All of the people stirring about excited his mind,
and he wondered what his mother was doing in
the house in town.

From the windows of his own room he could
not see directly into the barnyard where the farm
hands had now all assembled to do the morning
chores, but he could hear the voices of the men
and the neighing of the horses. When one of the
men laughed, he laughed also. Leaning out at
the open window, he looked into an orchard where
a fat sow wandered about with a litter of tiny pigs
at her heels. Every morning he counted the pigs.
"Four, five, six, seven," he said slowly, wetting
his finger and making straight up and down marks
on the window ledge. David ran to put on his
trousers and shirt. A feverish desire to get out
of doors took possession of him. Every morning he made such a noise coming down stairs that
Aunt Sallie, the housekeeper, declared he was trying to tear the house down. When he had run

through the long old house, shutting doors behind him with a bang, he came into the barnyard and looked about with an amazed air of expectancy. It seemed to him that in such a place tremendous things might have happened during the night. The farm hands looked at him and laughed. Henry Strader, an old man who had been on the farm since Jesse came into possession and who before David's time had never been known to make a joke, made the same joke every morning. It amused David so that he laughed and clapped his hands. "See, come here and look," cried the old man, "Grandfather Jesse's white mare has torn the black stocking she wears on her foot."

Day after day through the long summer, Jesse Bentley drove from farm to farm up and down the valley of Wine Creek, and his grandson went with him. They rode in a comfortable old phaeton drawn by the white horse. The old man scratched his thin white beard and talked to himself of his plans for increasing the productiveness of the fields they visited and of God's part in the plans all men made. Sometimes he looked at David and smiled happily and then for a long time he appeared to forget the boy's existence. More and more every day now his mind turned back again to the dreams that had filled his mind when he had first come out of the city to live on the land. One afternoon he startled David by letting

his dreams take entire possession of him.   With
the boy as a witness, he went through a ceremony
and brought about an accident that nearly destroyed the companionship that was growing up
between them.

Jesse and his grandson were driving in a distant
part of the valley some miles from home.   A
forest came down to the road and through the
forest Wine Creek wriggled its way over stones
toward a distant river.   All the afternoon Jesse
had been in a meditative mood and now he began
to talk.   His mind went back to the night when
he had been frightened by thoughts of a giant that
might come to rob and plunder him of his possessions, and again as on that night when he had
run through the fields crying for a son, he became
excited to the edge of insanity.   Stopping the
horse he got out of the buggy and asked David
to get out also.   The two climbed over a fence
and walked along the bank of the stream.   The
boy paid no attention to the muttering of his
grandfather, but ran along beside him and wondered what was going to happen.   When a rab-
bit jumped up and ran away through the woods, he
clapped his hands and danced with delight.   He
looked at the tall trees and was sorry that he was
not a little animal to climb high in the air without
being frightened.   Stooping, he picked up a small
stone and threw it over the head of his grand-

father into a clump of bushes. "Wake up, little animal. Go and climb to the top of the trees," he shouted in a shrill voice.

Jesse Bentley went along under the trees with his head bowed and with his mind in a ferment. His earnestness affected the boy who presently became silent and a little alarmed. Into the old man's mind had come the notion that now he could bring from God a word or a sign out of the sky, that the presence of the boy and man on their knees in some lonely spot in the forest would make the miracle he had been waiting for almost inevitable. "It was in just such a place as this that other David tended the sheep when his father came and told him to go down unto Saul," he muttered.

Taking the boy rather roughly by the shoulder, he climbed over a fallen log and when he had come to an open place among the trees, he dropped upon his knees and began to pray in a loud voice.

A kind of terror he had never known before took possession of David. Crouching beneath a tree he watched the man on the ground before him and his own knees began to tremble. It seemed to him that he was in the presence, not only of his grandfather but of someone else, someone who might hurt him, someone who was not kindly but dangerous and brutal. He began to cry and reaching down picked up a small stick which he held tightly gripped in his fingers. When Jesse Bentley, absorbed in his own idea, suddenly arose and advanced toward him, his terror grew until his whole body shook. In the woods an intense silence seemed to lie over everything and suddenly out of the silence came the old man's harsh and insistent voice. Gripping the boy's shoulders, Jesse turned his face to the sky and shouted. The whole left side of his face twitched and his hand on the boy's shoulder twitched also. "Make a sign to me, God," he cried, "here I stand with the boy David. Come down to me out of the sky and make Thy presence known to me."

With a cry of fear, David turned and shaking himself loose from the hands that held him, ran away through the forest. He did not believe that the man who turned up his face and in a harsh voice shouted at the sky, was his grandfather at all. The man did not look like his grandfather. The conviction that something strange and terrible had happened, that by some miracle a new and dangerous person had come into the body of the kindly old man took possession of him. On and on he ran down the hillside sobbing as he ran. When he fell over the roots of a tree and in falling struck his head, he arose and tried to run on again. His head hurt so that presently he fell down and lay still, but it was only after

Jesse had carried him to the buggy and he awoke to find the old man's hand stroking his head tenderly, that the terror left him. "Take me away. There is a terrible man back there in the woods," he declared firmly, while Jesse looked away over the tops of the trees and again his lips cried out to God. "What have I done that Thou doest not approve of me," he whispered softly, saying the words over and over as he drove rapidly along the road with the boy's cut and bleeding head held tenderly against his shoulder.

GODLINESS

PART THREE

SURRENDER

THE story of Louise Bentley, who became
Mrs. John Hardy and lived with her hus-
band in a brick house on Elm Street in
Winesburg, is a story of misunderstanding.

Before such women as Louise can be understood and their lives made livable, much will have
to be done. Thoughtful books will have to be
written and thoughtful lives lived by people
about them.

Born of a delicate and overworked mother, and
an impulsive, hard, imaginative father, who did
not look with favor upon her coming into the
world, Louise was from childhood a neurotic, one
of the race of over-sensitive women that in later
days industrialism was to bring in such great num-
bers into the world.

During her early years she lived on the Bentley
farm, a silent, moody child, wanting love more
than anything else in the world and not getting it.
When she was fifteen she went to live in Winesburg with the family of Albert Hardy who had

a store for the sale of buggies and wagons, and
who was a member of the town board of education.

Louise went into town to be a student in the
Winesburg High School and she went to live at
the Hardy's because Albert Hardy and her father
were friends.

Hardy, the vehicle merchant of Winesburg,
like thousands of other men of his times, was an
enthusiast on the subject of education. He had
made his own way in the world without learning
got from books, but he was convinced that had
he but known books things would have gone better with him. To everyone who came into his
shop he talked of the matter, and in his own
household he drove his family distracted by his
constant harping on the subject.

He had two daughters and one son, John
Hardy, and more than once the daughters threatened to leave school altogether. As a matter of
principle they did just enough work in their classes
to avoid punishment. "I hate books and I hate
anyone who likes books," Harriet, the younger of
the two girls, declared passionately.

In Winesburg as on the farm Louise was not
happy. For years she had dreamed of the time
when she could go forth into the world, and she
looked upon the move into the Hardy household
as a great step in the direction of freedom. Al-

ways when she had thought of the matter, it had seemed to her that in town all must be gaiety and life, that there men and women must live happily and freely, giving and taking friendship and affection as one takes the feel of a wind on the cheek. After the silence and the cheerlessness of life in the Bentley house, she dreamed of stepping forth into an atmosphere that was warm and pulsating with life and reality. And in the Hardy household Louise might have got something of the thing for which she so hungered but for a mistake she made when she had just come to town.

Louise won the disfavor of the two Hardy girls, Mary and Harriet, by her application to her studies in school. She did not come to the house until the day when school was to begin and knew nothing of the feeling they had in the matter. She was timid and during the first month made no acquaintances. Every Friday afternoon one of the hired men from the farm drove into Winesburg and took her home for the week-end, so that she did not spend the Saturday holiday with the town people. Because she was embarrassed and lonely she worked constantly at her studies. To Mary and Harriet, it seemed as though she tried to make trouble for them by her proficiency. In her eagerness to appear well Louise wanted to answer every question put to the class by the

teacher. She jumped up and down and her eyes
flashed. Then when she had answered some
question the others in the class had been unable to
answer, she smiled happily. "See, I have done
it for you," her eyes seemed to say. "You need
not bother about the matter. I will answer all
questions. For the whole class it will be easy
while I am here."

In the evening after supper in the Hardy house,
Albert Hardy began to praise Louise. One of
the teachers had spoken highly of her and he was
delighted. "Well, again I have heard of it," he
began, looking hard at his daughters and then
turning to smile at Louise. "Another of the
teachers has told me of the good work Louise is
doing. Everyone in Winesburg is telling me how
smart she is. I am ashamed that they do not
speak so of my own girls." Arising, the merchant marched about the room and lighted his
evening cigar.

The two girls looked at each other and shook
their heads wearily. Seeing their indifference the
father became angry. "I tell you it is something
for you two to be thinking about," he cried, glaring at them. "There is a big change coming here
in America and in learning is the only hope of the
coming generations. Louise is the daughter of a
rich man but she is not ashamed to study. It

should make you ashamed to see what she does."

The merchant took his hat from a rack by the door and prepared to depart for the evening. At the door he stopped and glared back. So fierce was his manner that Louise was frightened and ran upstairs to her own room. The daughters began to speak of their own affairs. "Pay attention to me," roared the merchant. "Your minds are lazy. Your indifference to education is affecting your characters. You will amount to nothing. Now mark what I say—Louise will be so far ahead of you that you will never catch up."

The distracted man went out of the house and into the street shaking with wrath. He went along muttering words and swearing, but when he got into Main Street his anger passed. He stopped to talk of the weather or the crops with some other merchant or with a farmer who had come into town and forgot his daughters altogether or, if he thought of them, only shrugged his shoulders. "Oh, well, girls will be girls," he muttered philosophically.

In the house when Louise came down into the room where the two girls sat, they would have nothing to do with her. One evening after she had been there for more than six weeks and was heartbroken because of the continued air of coldness with which she was always greeted, she burst into tears. "Shut up your crying and go back to

your own room and to your books," Mary Hardy
said sharply.

.   .   .   .

The room occupied by Louise was on the second
floor of the Hardy house, and her window looked
out upon an orchard.   There was a stove in the
room and every evening young John Hardy carried up an armful of wood and put it in a box that
stood by the wall.   During the second month
after she came to the house, Louise gave up all
hope of getting on a friendly footing with the
Hardy girls and went to her own room as soon
as the evening meal was at an end.

Her mind began to play with thoughts of making friends with John Hardy.   When he came
into the room with the wood in his arms, she pretended to be busy with her studies but watched
him eagerly.   When he had put the wood in the
box and turned to go out, she put down her head
and blushed.   She tried to make talk but could
say nothing, and after he had gone she was angry
at herself for her stupidity.

The mind of the country girl became filled with
the idea of drawing close to the young man.   She
thought that in him might be found the quality she
had all her life been seeking in people.   It seemed
to her that between herself and all the other people in the world, a wall had been built up and that
she was living just on the edge of some warm

inner circle of life that must be quite open and
understandable to others. She became obsessed
with the thought that it wanted but a courageous
act on her part to make all of her association with
people something quite different, and that it was
possible by such an act to pass into a new life as
one opens a door and goes into a room. Day
and night she thought of the matter, but although
the thing she wanted so earnestly was something
very warm and close it had as yet no conscious
connection with sex. It had not become that
definite, and her mind had only alighted upon the
person of John Hardy because he was at hand
and unlike his sisters had not been unfriendly to
her.

The Hardy sisters, Mary and Harriet, were
both older than Louise. In a certain kind of
knowledge of the world they were years older.
They lived as all of the young women of Middle
Western towns lived. In those days young women
did not go out of our towns to eastern colleges
and ideas in regard to social classes had hardly
begun to exist. A daughter of a laborer was in
much the same social position as a daughter of a
farmer or a merchant, and there were no leisure
classes. A girl was "nice" or she was "not nice."
If a nice girl, she had a young man who came to
her house to see her on Sunday and on Wednesday evenings. Sometimes she went with her

young man to a dance or a church social. At
other times she received him at the house and was
given the use of the parlor for that purpose. No
one intruded upon her. For hours the two sat
behind closed doors. Sometimes the lights were
turned low and the young man and woman embraced. Cheeks became hot and hair disarranged.
After a year or two, if the impulse within them
became strong and insistent enough, they married.

One evening during her first winter in Winesburg, Louise had an adventure that gave a new
impulse to her desire to break down the wall that
she thought stood between her and John Hardy.
It was Wednesday and immediately after the evening meal Albert Hardy put on his hat and went
away. Young John brought the wood and put it
in the box in Louise's room. "You do work hard,
don't you?" he said awkwardly, and then before
she could answer he also went away.

Louise heard him go out of the house and had
a mad desire to run after him. Opening her window she leaned out and called softly. "John,
dear John, come back, don't go away." The
night was cloudy and she could not see far into
the darkness, but as she waited she fancied she
could hear a soft little noise as of someone going
on tiptoes through the trees in the orchard. She
was frightened and closed the window quickly.
For an hour she moved about the room trembling

with excitement and when she could not longer bear the waiting, she crept into the hall and down the stairs into a closet-like room that opened off the parlor.

Louise had decided that she would perform the courageous act that had for weeks been in her mind. She was convinced that John Hardy had concealed himself in the orchard beneath her window and she was determined to find him and tell him that she wanted him to come close to her, to hold her in his arms, to tell her of his thoughts and dreams and to listen while she told him her thoughts and dreams. "In the darkness it will be easier to say things," she whispered to herself, as she stood in the little room groping for the door.

And then suddenly Louise realized that she was not alone in the house. In the parlor on the other side of the door a man's voice spoke softly and the door opened. Louise just had time to conceal herself in a little opening beneath the stairway when Mary Hardy, accompanied by her young man, came into the little dark room.

For an hour Louise sat on the floor in the darkness and listened. Without words Mary Hardy, with the aid of the man who had come to spend the evening with her, brought to the country girl a knowledge of men and women. Putting her head down until she was curled into a little ball she lay perfectly still. It seemed to her that by

some strange impulse of the gods, a great gift
had been brought to Mary Hardy and she could
not understand the older woman's determined
protest.

The young man took Mary Hardy into his arms
and kissed her. When she struggled and laughed,
he but held her the more tightly. For an hour
the contest between them went on and then they
went back into the parlor and Louise escaped up
the stairs. "I hope you were quiet out there.
You must not disturb the little mouse at her
studies," she heard Harriet saying to her sister
as she stood by her own door in the hallway above.

Louise wrote a note to John Hardy and late
that night when all in the house were asleep, she
crept downstairs and slipped it under his door.
She was afraid that if she did not do the thing
at once her courage would fail. In the note she
tried to be quite definite about what she wanted.
"I want someone to love me and I want to love
someone," she wrote. "If you are the one for
me I want you to come into the orchard at night
and make a noise under my window. It will be
easy for me to crawl down over the shed and come
to you. I am thinking about it all the time, so
if you are to come at all you must come soon."

For a long time Louise did not know what
would be the outcome of her bold attempt to
secure for herself a lover. In a way she still did

not know whether or not she wanted him to come. Sometimes it seemed to her that to be held tightly and kissed was the whole secret of life, and then a new impulse came and she was terribly afraid. The age-old woman's desire to be possessed had taken possession of her, but so vague was her notion of life that it seemed to her just the touch of John Hardy's hand upon her own hand would satisfy. She wondered if he would understand that. At the table next day while Albert Hardy talked and the two girls whispered and laughed, she did not look at John but at the table and as soon as possible escaped. In the evening she went out of the house until she was sure he had taken the wood to her room and gone away. When after several evenings of intense listening she heard no call from the darkness in the orchard, she was half beside herself with grief and decided that for her there was no way to break through the wall that had shut her off from the joy of life.

And then on a Monday evening two or three weeks after the writing of the note, John Hardy came for her. Louise had so entirely given up the thought of his coming that for a long time she did not hear the call that came up from the orchard. On the Friday evening before, as she was being driven back to the farm for the week-end by one of the hired men, she had on an impulse done a thing that had startled her, and as John Hardy stood in the darkness below and called her name softly and insistently, she walked about in her room and wondered what new impulse had led her to commit so ridiculous an act.

The farm hand, a young fellow with black curly hair, had come for her somewhat late on that Friday evening and they drove home in the darkness. Louise, whose mind was filled with thoughts of John Hardy, tried to make talk but the country boy was embarrassed and would say nothing. Her mind began to review the loneliness of her childhood and she remembered with a pang the sharp new loneliness that had just come to her. "I hate everyone," she cried suddenly, and then broke forth into a tirade that frightened her escort. "I hate father and old man Hardy, too," she declared vehemently. "I get my lessons there in the school in town but I hate that also."

Louise frightened the farm hand still more by turning and putting her cheek down upon his shoulder. Vaguely she hoped that he like that young man who had stood in the darkness with Mary would put his arms about her and kiss her, but the country boy was only alarmed. He struck the horse with the whip and began to whistle. "The road is rough, eh?" he said loudly. Louise was so angry that reaching up she snatched his hat from his head and threw it into the road. When he jumped out of the buggy and went to get it, she drove off and left him to walk the rest of the way back to the farm.

Louise Bentley took John Hardy to be her lover. That was not what she wanted but it was so the young man had interpreted her approach to him, and so anxious was she to achieve something else that she made no resistance. When after a few months they were both afraid that she was about to become a mother, they went one evening to the county seat and were married. For a few months they lived in the Hardy house and then took a house of their own. All during the first year Louise tried to make her husband understand the vague and intangible hunger that had led to the writing of the note and that was still unsatisfied. Again and again she crept into his arms and tried to talk of it, but always without success. Filled with his own notions of love between men and women, he did not listen but began to kiss her upon the lips. That confused her so that in the end she did not want to be kissed. She did not know what she wanted.

When the alarm that had tricked them into marriage proved to be groundless, she was angry and said bitter, hurtful things. Later when her son David was born, she could not nurse him and did not know whether she wanted him or not. Sometimes she stayed in the room with him all day.

walking about and occasionally creeping close to touch him tenderly with her hands, and then other days came when she did not want to see or be near the tiny bit of humanity that had come into the house. When John Hardy reproached her for her cruelty, she laughed. "It is a man child and will get what it wants anyway," she said sharply. "Had it been a woman child there is nothing in the world I would not have done for it."

GODLINESS

PART FOUR

TERROR

WHEN David Hardy was a tall boy of fifteen, he, like his mother, had an adventure that changed the whole current of his life and sent him out of his quiet corner into the world. The shell of the circumstances of his life was broken and he was compelled to start forth. He left Winesburg and no one there ever saw him again. After his disappearance, his mother and grandfather both died and his father became very rich. He spent much money in trying to locate his son, but that is no part of this story.

It was in the late fall of an unusual year on the Bentley farms. Everywhere the crops had been heavy. That spring, Jesse had bought part of a long strip of black swamp land that lay in the valley of Wine Creek. He got the land at a low price but had spent a large sum of money to improve it. Great ditches had to be dug and thousands of tile laid. Neighboring farmers shook their heads over the expense. Some of them

laughed and hoped that Jesse would lose heavily
by the venture, but the old man went silently on
with the work and said nothing.

When the land was drained he planted it to
cabbages and onions, and again the neighbors
laughed. The crop was, however, enormous and
brought high prices. In the one year Jesse made
enough money to pay for all the cost of preparing
the land and had a surplus that enabled him to buy
two more farms. He was exultant and could
not conceal his delight. For the first time in all
the history of his ownership of the farms, he went
among his men with a smiling face.

Jesse bought a great many new machines for
cutting down the cost of labor and all of the re-
maining acres in the strip of black fertile swamp
land. One day he went into Winesburg and
bought a bicycle and a new suit of clothes for
David and he gave his two sisters money with
which to go to a religious convention at Cleveland,
Ohio.

In the fall of that year when the frost came
and the trees in the forests along Wine Creek were
golden brown, David spent every moment when
he did not have to attend school, out in the open.
Alone or with other boys he went every afternoon into the woods to gather nuts. The other
boys of the countryside, most of them sons of
laborers on the Bentley farms, had guns with

which they went hunting rabbits and squirrels, but
David did not go with them.   He made himself
a sling with rubber bands and a forked stick and
went off by himself to gather nuts.   As he went
about thoughts came to him.   He realized that
he was almost a man and wondered what he would
do in life, but before they came to anything, the
thoughts passed and he was a boy again.   One
day he killed a squirrel that sat on one of the
lower branches of a tree and chattered at him.
Home he ran with the squirrel in his hand.   One
of the Bentley sisters cooked the little animal and
he ate it with great gusto.   The skin he tacked on
a board and suspended the board by a string from
his bedroom window.

That gave his mind a new turn.   After that
he never went into the woods without carrying
the sling in his pocket and he spent hours shooting at imaginary animals concealed among the
brown leaves in the trees.   Thoughts of his coming manhood passed and he was content to be a
boy with a boy's impulses.

One Saturday morning when he was about to
set off for the woods with the sling in his pocket
and a bag for nuts on his shoulder, his grandfather stopped him.   In the eyes of the old man
was the strained serious look that always a little
frightened David.   At such times Jesse Bentley's
eyes did not look straight ahead but wavered and

seemed to be looking at nothing. Something like an invisible curtain appeared to have come between the man and all the rest of the world. "I want you to come with me," he said briefly, and his eyes looked over the boy's head into the sky. "We have something important to do to-day. You may bring the bag for nuts if you wish. It does not matter and anyway we will be going into the woods."

Jesse and David set out from the Bentley farmhouse in the old phaeton that was drawn by the white horse. When they had gone along in silence for a long way they stopped at the edge of a field where a flock of sheep were grazing. Among the sheep was a lamb that had been born out of season, and this David and his grandfather caught and tied so tightly that it looked like a little white ball. When they drove on again Jesse let David hold the lamb in his arms. "I saw it yesterday and it put me in mind of what I have long wanted to do," he said, and again he looked away over the head of the boy with the wavering, uncertain stare in his eyes.

After the feeling of exaltation that had come to the farmer as a result of his successful year, another mood had taken possession of him. For a long time he had been going about feeling very humble and prayerful. Again he walked alone at night thinking of God and as he walked he again connected his own figure with the figures of old days. Under the stars he knelt on the wet grass and raised up his voice in prayer. Now he had decided that like the men whose stories filled the pages of the Bible, he would make a sacrifice to God. "I have been given these abundant crops and God has also sent me a boy who is called David," he whispered to himself. "Perhaps I should have done this thing long ago." He was sorry the idea had not come into his mind in the days before his daughter Louise had been born and thought that surely now when he had erected a pile of burning sticks in some lonely place in the woods and had offered the body of a lamb as a burnt offering, God would appear to him and give him a message.

More and more as he thought of the matter, he thought also of David and his passionate self love was partially forgotten. "It is time for the boy to begin thinking of going out into the world and the message will be one concerning him," he decided. "God will make a pathway for him. He will tell me what place David is to take in life and when he shall set out on his journey. It is right that the boy should be there. If I am fortunate and an angel of God should appear, David will see the beauty and glory of God made manifest to man. It will make a true man of God of him also."

In silence Jesse and David drove along the
road until they came to that place where Jesse
had once before appealed to God and had frightened his grandson.   The morning had been bright
and cheerful, but a cold wind now began to blow
and clouds hid the sun. When David saw the place
to which they had come he began to tremble with
fright, and when they stopped by the bridge where
the creek came down from among the trees, he
wanted to spring out of the phaeton and run away.

A dozen plans for escape ran through David's
head, but when Jesse stopped the horse and
climbed over the fence into the wood, he followed.
"It is foolish to be afraid. Nothing will happen," he told himself as he went along with the
lamb in his arms. There was something in the
helplessness of the little animal, held so tightly
in his arms that gave him courage. He could
feel the rapid beating of the beast's heart and
that made his own heart beat less rapidly. As
he walked swiftly along behind his grandfather,
he untied the string with which the four legs of
the lamb were fastened together. "If anything
happens we will run away together," he thought.

In the woods, after they had gone a long way
from the road, Jesse stopped in an opening among
the trees where a clearing, overgrown with small
bushes, ran up from the creek. He was still
silent but began at once to erect a heap of dry

sticks which he presently set afire. The boy sat
on the ground with the lamb in his arms. His
imagination began to invest every movement of
the old man with significance and he became every
moment more afraid. "I must put the blood of
the lamb on the head of the boy," Jesse muttered
when the sticks had begun to blaze greedily, and
taking a long knife from his pocket he turned and
walked rapidly across the clearing toward David.

Terror seized upon the soul of the boy. He
was sick with it. For a moment he sat perfectly
still and then his body stiffened and he sprang to
his feet. His face became as white as the fleece
of the lamb, that now finding itself suddenly released, ran down the hill. David ran also. Fear
made his feet fly. Over the low bushes and logs
he leaped frantically. As he ran he put his hand
into his pocket and took out the branched stick
from which the sling for shooting squirrels was
suspended. When he came to the creek that was
shallow and splashed down over the stones, he
dashed into the water and turned to look back,
and when he saw his grandfather still running
toward him with the long knife held tightly in his
hand he did not hesitate but reaching down,
selected a stone and put it in the sling. With all
his strength he drew back the heavy rubber bands
and the stone whistled through the air. It hit
Jesse, who had entirely forgotten the boy and was

pursuing the lamb, squarely in the head. With a groan he pitched forward and fell almost at the boy's feet. When David saw that he lay still and that he was apparently dead, his fright increased immeasurably. It became an insane panic.

With a cry he turned and ran off through the woods weeping convulsively. "I don't care—I killed him, but I don't care," he sobbed. As he ran on and on he decided suddenly that he would never go back again to the Bentley farms or to the town of Winesburg. "I have killed the man of God and now I will myself be a man and go into the world," he said stoutly as he stopped running and walked rapidly down a road that followed the windings of Wine Creek as it ran through fields and forests into the west.

On the ground by the creek Jesse Bentley moved uneasily about. He groaned and opened his eyes. For a long time he lay perfectly still and looked at the sky. When at last he got to his feet, his mind was confused and he was not surprised by the boy's disappearance. By the roadside he sat down on a log and began to talk about God. That is all they ever got out of him. Whenever David's name was mentioned he looked vaguely at the sky and said that a messenger from God had taken the boy. "It happened because I was too greedy for glory," he declared, and would have no more to say in the matter.

A MAN OF IDEAS

HE lived with his mother, a grey, silent woman with a peculiar ashy complexion. The house in which they lived stood in a little grove of trees beyond where the main street of Winesburg crossed Wine Creek. His name was Joe Welling, and his father had been a man of some dignity in the community, a lawyer and a member of the state legislature at Columbus. Joe himself was small of body and in his character unlike anyone else in town. He was like a tiny little volcano that lies silent for days and then suddenly spouts fire. No, he wasn't like that——he was like a man who is subject to fits, one who walks among his fellow men inspiring fear because a fit may come upon him suddenly and blow him away into a strange uncanny physical state in which his eyes roll and his legs and arms jerk. He was like that, only that the visitation that descended upon Joe Welling was a mental and not a physical thing. He was beset by ideas and in the throes of one of his ideas was uncontrollable. Words rolled and tumbled from his mouth. A peculiar smile came upon his lips..

110

The edges of his teeth that were tipped with gold glistened in the light. Pouncing upon a bystander he began to talk. For the bystander there was no escape. The excited man breathed into his face, peered into his eyes, pounded upon his chest with a shaking forefinger, demanded, compelled attention.

In those days the Standard Oil Company did not deliver oil to the consumer in big wagons and motor trucks as it does now, but delivered instead to retail grocers, hardware stores and the like. Joe was the Standard Oil agent in Winesburg and in several towns up and down the railroad that went through Winesburg. He collected bills, booked orders, and did other things. His father, the legislator, had secured the job for him.

In and out of the stores of Winesburg went Joe Welling—silent, excessively polite, intent upon his business. Men watched him with eyes in which lurked amusement tempered by alarm. They were waiting for him to break forth, preparing to flee. Although the seizures that came upon him were harmless enough, they could not be laughed away. They were overwhelming. Astride an idea, Joe was overmastering. His personality became gigantic. It overrode the man to whom he talked, swept him away, swept all away, all who stood within sound of his voice.

In Sylvester West's Drug Store stood four men

who were talking of horse racing.   Wesley Moyer's stallion, Tony Tip, was to race at the June meeting at Tiffin, Ohio, and there was a rumor that he would meet the stiffest competition of his career.   It was said that Pop Geers, the great racing driver, would himself be there.   A doubt of the success of Tony Tip hung heavy in the air of Winesburg.

Into the drug store came Joe Welling, brushing the screen door violently aside.   With a strange absorbed light in his eyes he pounced upon Ed Thomas, he who knew Pop Geers and whose opinion of Tony Tip's chances was worth considering.

"The water is up in Wine Creek," cried Joe Welling with the air of Pheidippides bringing news of the victory of the Greeks in the struggle at Marathon.   His finger beat a tattoo upon Ed Thomas' broad chest.   "By Trunion bridge it is within eleven and a half inches of the flooring," he went on, the words coming quickly and with a little whistling noise from between his teeth.   An expression of helpless annoyance crept over the faces of the four.

"I have my facts correct.   Depend upon that. I went to Sinning's Hardware Store and got a rule. Then I went back and measured.   I could hardly believe my own eyes.   It hasn't rained you see for ten days.   At first I didn't know what to think.

Thoughts rushed through my head.   I thought of subterranean passages and springs.   Down under the ground went my mind, delving about.   I sat on the floor of the bridge and rubbed my head. There wasn't a cloud in the sky, not one.   Come out into the street and you'll see.   There wasn't a cloud.   There isn't a cloud now.   Yes, there was a cloud.   I don't want to keep back any facts. There was a cloud in the west down near the horizon, a cloud no bigger than a man's hand.

"Not that I think that has anything to do with it.   There it is you see.   You understand how puzzled I was.

"Then an idea came to me.   I laughed.   You'll laugh, too.   Of course it rained over in Medina County.   That's interesting, eh?   If we had no trains, no mails, no telegraph, we would know that it rained over in Medina County.   That's where Wine Creek comes from.   Everyone knows that. Little old Wine Creek brought us the news. That's interesting.   I laughed.   I thought I'd tell you—it's interesting, eh?"

Joe Welling turned and went out at the door. Taking a book from his pocket, he stopped and ran a finger down one of the pages.   Again he was absorbed in his duties as agent of the Standard Oil Company.   "Hern's Grocery will be getting low on coal oil.   I'll see them," he muttered, hurrying along the street, and bowing politely to the right and left at the people walking past.

When George Willard went to work for the *Winesburg Eagle* he was besieged by Joe Welling. Joe envied the boy. It seemed to him that he was meant by Nature to be a reporter on a newspaper. "It is what I should be doing, there is no doubt of that," he declared, stopping George Willard on the sidewalk before Daugherty's Feed Store. His eyes began to glisten and his forefinger to tremble. "Of course I make more money with the Standard Oil Company and I'm only telling you," he added. "I've got nothing against you, but I should have your place. I could do the work at odd moments. Here and there I would run finding out things you'll never see."

Becoming more excited Joe Welling crowded the young reporter against the front of the feed store. He appeared to be lost in thought, rolling his eyes about and running a thin nervous hand through his hair. A smile spread over his face and his gold teeth glittered. "You get out your note book," he commanded. "You carry a little pad of paper in your pocket, don't you? I knew you did. Well, you set this down. I thought of it the other day. Let's take decay. Now what is decay? It's fire. It burns up wood and other things. You never thought of that? Of course not. This sidewalk here and this feed store, the trees down the street there—they're all on fire.

They're burning up. Decay you see is always going on. It don't stop. Water and paint can't stop it. If a thing is iron, then what? It rusts, you see. That's fire, too. The world is on fire. Start your pieces in the paper that way. Just say in big letters 'The World Is On Fire.' That will make 'em look up. They'll say you're a smart one. I don't care. I don't envy you. I just snatched that idea out of the air. I would make a newspaper hum. You got to admit that."

Turning quickly, Joe Welling walked rapidly away. When he had taken several steps he stopped and looked back. "I'm going to stick to you," he said. "I'm going to make you a regular hummer. I should start a newspaper myself, that's what I should do. I'd be a marvel. Everybody knows that."

When George Willard had been for a year on the *Winesburg Eagle,* four things happened to Joe Welling. His mother died, he came to live at the New Willard House, he became involved in a love affair, and he organized the Winesburg Baseball Club.

Joe organized the baseball club because he wanted to be a coach and in that position he began to win the respect of his townsmen. "He is a wonder," they declared after Joe's team had whipped the team from Medina County. "He gets everybody working together. You just watch him."

Upon the baseball field Joe Welling stood by first base, his whole body quivering with excitement. In spite of themselves all of the players watched him closely. The opposing pitcher became confused.

"Now! Now! Now! Now!" shouted the excited man. "Watch me! Watch me! Watch my fingers! Watch my hands! Watch my feet! Watch my eyes! Let's work together here! Watch me! In me you see all the movements of the game! Work with me! Work with me! Watch me! Watch me! Watch me!"

With runners of the Winesburg team on bases, Joe Welling became as one inspired. Before they knew what had come over them, the base runners were watching the man, edging off the bases, advancing, retreating, held as by an invisible cord. The players of the opposing team also watched Joe. They were fascinated. For a moment they watched and then as though to break a spell that hung over them, they began hurling the ball wildly about, and amid a series of fierce animal-like cries from the coach, the runners of the Winesburg team scampered home.

Joe Welling's love affair set the town of Winesburg on edge. When it began everyone whispered and shook his head. When people tried to

laugh, the laughter was forced and unnatural.
Joe fell in love with Sarah King, a lean, sad-looking woman who lived with her father and brother
in a brick house that stood opposite the gate leading to the Winesburg Cemetery.

The two Kings, Edward the father, and Tom
the son, were not popular in Winesburg. They
were called proud and dangerous. They had
come to Winesburg from some place in the South
and ran a cider mill on the Trunion Pike. Tom
King was reported to have killed a man before
he came to Winesburg. He was twenty-seven
years old and rode about town on a grey pony.
Also he had a long yellow mustache that dropped
down over his teeth, and always carried a heavy,
wicked-looking walking stick in his hand. Once
he killed a dog with the stick. The dog belonged
to Win Pawsey, the shoe merchant, and stood on
the sidewalk wagging its tail. Tom King killed
it with one blow. He was arrested and paid a
fine of ten dollars.

Old Edward King was small of stature and
when he passed people in the street laughed a
queer unmirthful laugh. When he laughed he
scratched his left elbow with his right hand. The
sleeve of his coat was almost worn through from
the habit. As he walked along the street, looking
nervously about and laughing, he seemed more
dangerous than his silent, fierce looking son.

When Sarah King began walking out in the evening with Joe Welling, people shook their heads in alarm. She was tall and pale and had dark rings under her eyes. The couple looked ridiculous together. Under the trees they walked and Joe talked. His passionate eager protestations of love, heard coming out of the darkness by the cemetery wall, or from the deep shadows of the trees on the hill that ran up to the Fair Grounds from Waterworks Pond, were repeated in the stores. Men stood by the bar in the New Willard House laughing and talking of Joe's courtship. After the laughter came silence. The Winesburg baseball team, under his management, was winning game after game, and the town had begun to respect him. Sensing a tragedy, they waited, laughing nervously.

Late on a Saturday afternoon the meeting between Joe Welling and the two Kings, the anticipation of which had set the town on edge, took place in Joe Welling's room in the New Willard House. George Willard was a witness to the meeting. It came about in this way:

When the young reporter went to his room after the evening meal he saw Tom King and his father sitting in the half darkness in Joe's room. The son had the heavy walking stick in his hand and sat near the door. Old Edward King walked nervously about, scratching his left elbow with his right hand.   The hallways were empty and silent.

George Willard went to his own room and sat down at his desk.   He tried to write but his hand trembled so that he could not hold the pen.   He also walked nervously up and down.   Like the rest of the town of Winesburg he was perplexed and knew not what to do.

It was seven-thirty and fast growing dark when Joe Welling came along the station platform toward the New Willard House.   In his arms he held a bundle of weeds and grasses.   In spite of the terror that made his body shake, George Willard was amused at the sight of the small spry figure holding the grasses and half running along the platform.

Shaking with fright and anxiety, the young reporter lurked in the hallway outside the door of the room in which Joe Welling talked to the two Kings.   There had been an oath, the nervous giggle of old Edward King, and then silence.   Now the voice of Joe Welling, sharp and clear, broke forth.   George Willard began to laugh.   He understood.   As he had swept all men before him, so now Joe Welling was carrying the two men in the room off their feet with a tidal wave of words.   The listener in the hall walked up and down, lost in amazement.

Inside the room Joe Welling had paid no attention to the grumbled threat of Tom King.   Absorbed in an idea he closed the door and lighting a lamp, spread the handful of weeds and grasses upon the floor. "I've got something here," he announced solemnly. "I was going to tell George Willard about it, let him make a piece out of it for the paper. I'm glad you're here. I wish Sarah were here also. I've been going to come to your house and tell you of some of my ideas. They're interesting. Sarah wouldn't let me. She said we'd quarrel. That's foolish."

Running up and down before the two perplexed men, Joe Welling began to explain. "Don't you make a mistake now," he cried. "This is something big." His voice was shrill with excitement. "You just follow me, you'll be interested. I know you will. Suppose this—suppose all of the wheat, the corn, the oats, the peas, the potatoes, were all by some miracle swept away. Now here we are, you see, in this county. There is a high fence built all around us. We'll suppose that. No one can get over the fence and all the fruits of the earth are destroyed, nothing left but these wild things, these grasses. Would we be done for? I ask you that. Would we be done for?" Again Tom King growled and for a moment there was silence in the room. Then again Joe plunged into the exposition of his idea. "Things would go hard for a time. I admit that. I've got to admit that. No getting around it. We'd be hard put to it. More than one fat stomach would cave in. But they couldn't down us. I should say not."

Tom King laughed good naturedly and the shivery, nervous laugh of Edward King rang through the house. Joe Welling hurried on. "We'd begin, you see, to breed up new vegetables and fruits. Soon we'd regain all we had lost. Mind, I don't say the new things would be the same as the old. They wouldn't. Maybe they'd be better, maybe not so good. That's interesting, eh? You can think about that. It starts your mind working, now don't it?"

In the room there was silence and then again old Edward King laughed nervously. "Say, I wish Sarah was here," cried Joe Welling. "Let's go up to your house. I want to tell her of this."

There was a scraping of chairs in the room. It was then that George Willard retreated to his own room. Leaning out at the window he saw Joe Welling going along the street with the two Kings. Tom King was forced to take extraordinary long strides to keep pace with the little man. As he strode along, he leaned over, listening—absorbed, fascinated. Joe Welling again talked excitedly. "Take milkweed now," he cried. "A lot might be done with milkweed, eh? It's almost unbelievable. I want you to think about it. I want you two to think about it. There would be a new vegetable kingdom you see. It's interesting, eh? It's an idea. Wait till you see Sarah, she'll get the idea. She'll be interested. Sarah is always interested in ideas. You can't be too smart for Sarah, now can you? Of course you can't. You know that."

ADVENTURE

ALICE HINDMAN, a woman of twenty-seven when George Willard was a mere boy, had lived in Winesburg all her life. She clerked in Winney's Dry Goods Store and lived with her mother who had married a second husband.

Alice's step-father was a carriage painter, and given to drink. His story is an odd one. It will be worth telling some day.

At twenty-seven Alice was tall and somewhat slight. Her head was large and overshadowed her body. Her shoulders were a little stooped and her hair and eyes brown. She was very quiet but beneath a placid exterior a continual ferment went on.

When she was a girl of sixteen and before she began to work in the store, Alice had an affair with a young man. The young man, named Ned Currie, was older than Alice. He, like George Willard, was employed on the *Winesburg Eagle* and for a long time he went to see Alice almost every evening. Together the two walked under the trees through the streets of the town and talked of what they would do with their lives. Alice was then a very pretty girl and Ned Currie took her into his arms and kissed her. He became excited and said things he did not intend to say and Alice, betrayed by her desire to have something beautiful come into her rather narrow life, also grew excited. She also talked. The outer crust of her life, all of her natural diffidence and reserve, was torn away and she gave herself over to the emotions of love. When, late in the fall of her sixteenth year, Ned Currie went away to Cleveland where he hoped to get a place on a city newspaper and rise in the world, she wanted to go with him. With a trembling voice she told him what was in her mind. "I will work and you can work," she said. "I do not want to harness you to a needless expense that will prevent your making progress. Don't marry me now. We will get along without that and we can be together. Even though we live in the same house no one will say anything. In the city we will be unknown and people will pay no attention to us."

Ned Currie was puzzled by the determination and abandon of his sweetheart and was also deeply touched. He had wanted the girl to become his mistress but changed his mind. He wanted to protect and care for her. "You don't know what you're talking about," he said sharply; "you may be sure I'll let you do no such thing. As soon as I get a good job I'll come back. For the present you'll have to stay here. It's the only thing we can do."

On the evening before he left Winesburg to take up his new life in the city, Ned Currie went to call on Alice. They walked about through the streets for an hour and then got a rig from Wesley Moyer's livery and went for a drive in the country. The moon came up and they found themselves unable to talk. In his sadness the young man forgot the resolutions he had made regarding his conduct with the girl.

They got out of the buggy at a place where a long meadow ran down to the bank of Wine Creek and there in the dim light became lovers. When at midnight they returned to town they were both glad. It did not seem to them that anything that could happen in the future could blot out the wonder and beauty of the thing that had happened. "Now we will have to stick to each other, whatever happens we will have to do that," Ned Currie said as he left the girl at her father's door.

The young newspaper man did not succeed in getting a place on a Cleveland paper and went west to Chicago. For a time he was lonely and wrote to Alice almost every day. Then he was caught up by the life of the city; he began to make friends and found new interests in life. In Chicago he boarded at a house where there were several women.   One of them attracted his attention and he forgot Alice in Winesburg.   At the end of a year he had stopped writing letters, and only once in a long time, when he was lonely or when he went into one of the city parks and saw the moon shining on the grass as it had shone that night on the meadow by Wine Creek, did he think of her at all.

In Winesburg the girl who had been loved grew to be a woman.   When she was twenty-two years old her father, who owned a harness repair shop, died suddenly.   The harness maker was an old soldier, and after a few months his wife received a widow's pension.   She used the first money she got to buy a loom and became a weaver of carpets, and Alice got a place in Winney's store.   For a number of years nothing could have induced her to believe that Ned Currie would not in the end return to her.

She was glad to be employed because the daily round of toil in the store made the time of waiting seem less long and uninteresting.   She began to save money, thinking that when she had saved two or three hundred dollars she would follow her lover to the city and try if her presence would not win back his affections.

Alice did not blame Ned Currie for what had happened in the moonlight in the field, but felt that she could never marry another man.   To her the thought of giving to another what she still felt could belong only to Ned seemed monstrous. When other young men tried to attract her attention she would have nothing to do with them. "I am his wife and shall remain his wife whether he comes back or not," she whispered to herself, and for all of her willingness to support herself could not have understood the growing modern idea of a woman's owning herself and giving and taking for her own ends in life.

Alice worked in the dry goods store from eight in the morning until six at night and on three evenings a week went back to the store to stay from seven until nine. As time passed and she became more and more lonely she began to practice the devices common to lonely people. When at night she went upstairs into her own room she knelt on the floor to pray and in her prayers whispered things she wanted to say to her lover. She became attached to inanimate objects, and because it was her own, could not bear to have anyone touch the furniture of her room. The trick of saving money, begun for a purpose, was carried on after the scheme of going to the city to find Ned Currie had been given up. It became a fixed habit, and when she needed new clothes she did not get them   Sometimes on rainy afternoons in the store she got out her bank book and, letting it lie open before her, spent hours dreaming impossible dreams of saving money enough so that the interest would support both herself and her future husband.

"Ned always liked to travel about," she thought. "I'll give him the chance. Some day when we are married and I can save both his money and my own, we will be rich. Then we can travel together all over the world."

In the dry goods store weeks ran into months and months into years as Alice waited and dreamed of her lover's return. Her employer, a grey old man with false teeth and a thin grey mustache that drooped down over his mouth, was not given to conversation, and sometimes, on rainy days and in the winter when a storm raged in Main Street, long hours passed when no customers came in. Alice arranged and rearranged the stock. She stood near the front window where she could look down the deserted street and thought of the evenings when she had walked with Ned Currie and of what he had said. "We will have to stick to each other now." The words echoed and re-echoed through the mind of the maturing woman. Tears came into her eyes. Sometimes when her employer had gone out and she was alone in the store she put her head on the counter and wept. "Oh, Ned, I am waiting," she whispered over and over, and all the time the creeping fear that he would never come back grew stronger within her.

In the spring when the rains have passed and before the long hot days of summer have come, the country about Winesburg is delightful. The town lies in the midst of open fields, but beyond the fields are pleasant patches of woodlands. In the wooded places are many little cloistered nooks, quiet places where lovers go to sit on Sunday afternoons. Through the trees they look out across the fields and see farmers at work about the barns or people driving up and down on the roads. In the town bells ring and occasionally a train passes, looking like a toy thing in the distance.

For several years after Ned Currie went away Alice did not go into the wood with other young people on Sunday, but one day after he had been gone for two or three years and when her loneliness seemed unbearable, she put on her best dress and set out. Finding a little sheltered place from which she could see the town and a long stretch of the fields, she sat down. Fear of age and ineffectuality took possession of her. She could not sit still, and arose. As she stood looking out over the land something, perhaps the thought of never ceasing life as it expresses itself in the flow of the seasons, fixed her mind on the passing years. With a shiver of dread, she realized that for her the beauty and freshness of youth had passed. For the first time she felt that she had been cheated. She did not blame Ned Currie and did not know what to blame. Sadness swept over her. Dropping to her knees, she tried to pray, but instead of prayers words of protest came to her lips. "It is not going to come to me. I will never find happiness. Why do I tell myself lies?" she cried, and an odd sense of relief came with this, her first bold attempt to face the fear that had become a part of her everyday life.

In the year when Alice Hindman became twenty-five two things happened to disturb the dull uneventfulness of her days. Her mother married Bush Milton, the carriage painter of Winesburg, and she herself became a member of the Winesburg Methodist Church. Alice joined the church because she had become frightened by the loneliness of her position in life. Her mother's second marriage had emphasized her isolation. "I am becoming old and queer. If Ned comes he will not want me. In the city where he is living men are perpetually young. There is so much going on that they do not have time to grow old," she told herself with a grim little smile, and went resolutely about the business of becoming acquainted with people. Every Thursday evening when the store had closed she went to a prayer meeting in the basement of the church and on Sunday eve-

ning attended a meeting of an organization called
The Epworth League.

When Will Hurley, a middle-aged man who
clerked in a drug store and who also belonged to
the church, offered to walk home with her she did
not protest. "Of course I will not let him make
a practice of being with me, but if he comes to see
me once in a long time there can be no harm in
that," she told herself, still determined in her loy-
alty to Ned Currie.

Without realizing what was happening, Alice
was trying feebly at first, but with growing determination, to get a new hold upon life. Beside
the drug clerk she walked in silence, but sometimes
in the darkness as they went stolidly along she put
out her hand and touched softly the folds of his
coat. When he left her at the gate before her
mother's house she did not go indoors, but stood
for a moment by the door. She wanted to call to
the drug clerk, to ask him to sit with her in the
darkness on the porch before the house, but was
afraid he would not understand. "It is not him
that I want," she told herself; "I want to avoid
being so much alone. If I am not careful I will
grow unaccustomed to being with people."

. . . .

During the early fall of her twenty-seventh year
a passionate restlessness took possession of Alice.
She could not bear to be in the company of the

drug clerk, and when, in the evening, he came to walk with her she sent him away. Her mind became intensely active and when, weary from the long hours of standing behind the counter in the store, she went home and crawled into bed, she could not sleep. With staring eyes she looked into the darkness. Her imagination, like a child awakened from long sleep, played about the room. Deep within her there was something that would not be cheated by phantasies and that demanded some definite answer from life.

Alice took a pillow into her arms and held it tightly against her breasts. Getting out of bed, she arranged a blanket so that in the darkness it looked like a form lying between the sheets and, kneeling beside the bed, she caressed it, whispering words over and over, like a refrain. "Why doesn't something happen? Why am I left here alone?" she muttered. Although she sometimes thought of Ned Currie, she no longer depended on him. Her desire had grown vague. She did not want Ned Currie or any other man. She wanted to be loved, to have something answer the call that was growing louder and louder within her.

And then one night when it rained Alice had an adventure. It frightened and confused her. She had come home from the store at nine and found the house empty. Bush Milton had gone off to

town and her mother to the house of a neighbor.
Alice went upstairs to her room and undressed in
the darkness.   For a moment she stood by the
window hearing the rain beat against the glass
and then a strange desire took possession of her.
Without stopping to think of what she intended to
do, she ran downstairs through the dark house
and out into the rain.   As she stood on the little
grass plot before the house and felt the cold rain
on her body a mad desire to run naked through
the streets took possession of her.

She thought that the rain would have some creative and wonderful effect on her body.   Not for
years had she felt so full of youth and courage.
She wanted to leap and run, to cry out, to find
some other lonely human and embrace him.   On
the brick sidewalk before the house a man stumbled homeward.   Alice started to run.   A wild,
desperate mood took possession of her.   "What
do I care who it is.   He is alone, and I will go
to him," she thought; and then without stopping
to consider the possible result of her madness,
called softly.   "Wait!" she cried.   "Don't go
away.   Whoever you are, you must wait."

The man on the sidewalk stopped and stood lis-
tening.   He was an old man and somewhat deaf.
Putting his hand to his mouth, he shouted:
"What?   What say?" he called.

Alice dropped to the ground and lay trembling.

She was so frightened at the thought of what she had done that when the man had gone on his way she did not dare get to her feet, but crawled on hands and knees through the grass to the house. When she got to her own room she bolted the door and drew her dressing table across the door-way. Her body shook as with a chill and her hands trembled so that she had difficulty getting into her nightdress. When she got into bed she buried her face in the pillow and wept broken-heartedly. "What is the matter with me? I will do something dreadful if I am not careful," she thought, and turning her face to the wall, be-gan trying to force herself to face bravely the fact that many people must live and die alone, even in Winesburg.

RESPECTABILITY

IF you have lived in cities and have walked in the park on a summer afternoon, you have perhaps seen, blinking in a corner of his iron cage, a huge, grotesque kind of monkey, a creature with ugly, sagging, hairless skin below his eyes and a bright purple underbody. This monkey is a true monster. In the completeness of his ugliness he achieved a kind of perverted beauty. Children stopping before the cage are fascinated, men turn away with an air of disgust, and women linger for a moment, trying perhaps to remember which one of their male acquaintances the thing in some faint way resembles.

Had you been in the earlier years of your life a citizen of the village of Winesburg, Ohio, there would have been for you no mystery in regard to the beast in his cage. "It is like Wash Williams," you would have said. "As he sits in the corner there, the beast is exactly like old Wash sitting on the grass in the station yard on a summer evening after he has closed his office for the night."

Wash Williams, the telegraph operator of Winesburg, was the ugliest thing in town. His girth was immense, his neck thin, his legs feeble. He was dirty. Everything about him was unclean. Even the whites of his eyes looked soiled.

I go too fast. Not everything about Wash was unclean. He took care of his hands. His fingers were fat, but there was something sensitive and shapely in the hand that lay on the table by the instrument in the telegraph office. In his youth Wash Williams had been called the best telegraph operator in the state, and in spite of his degradement to the obscure office at Winesburg, he was still proud of his ability.

Wash Williams did not associate with the men of the town in which he lived. "I'll have nothing to do with them," he said, looking with bleary eyes at the men who walked along the station platform past the telegraph office. Up along Main Street he went in the evening to Ed Griffith's saloon, and after drinking unbelievable quantities of beer staggered off to his room in the New Willard House and to his bed for the night.

Wash Williams was a man of courage. A thing had happened to him that made him hate life, and he hated it whole-heartedly, with the abandon of a poet. First of all, he hated women. "Bitches," he called them. His feeling toward men was somewhat different. He pitied them. "Does not every man let his life be managed for him by some bitch or another?" he asked.

In Winesburg no attention was paid to Wash Williams and his hatred of his fellows. Once Mrs. White, the banker's wife, complained to the telegraph company, saying that the office in Winesburg was dirty and smelled abominably, but nothing came of her complaint- Here and there a man respected the operator. Instinctively the man felt in him a glowing resentment of something he had not the courage to resent. When Wash walked through the streets such a one had an instinct to pay him homage, to raise his hat or to bow before him. The superintendent who had supervision over the telegraph operators on the railroad that went through Winesburg felt that way. He had put Wash into the obscure office at Winesburg to avoid discharging him, and he meant to keep him there. When he received the letter of complaint from the banker's wife, he tore it up and laughed unpleasantly. For some reason he thought of his own wife as he tore up the letter.

Wash Williams once had a wife. When he was still a young man he married a woman at Dayton, Ohio. The woman was tall and slender and had blue eyes and yellow hair. Wash was himself a comely youth. He loved the woman with a love as absorbing as the hatred he later felt for all women.

In all of Winesburg there was but one person

who knew the story of the thing that had made
ugly the person and the character of Wash Williams.   He once told the story to George Willard
and the telling of the tale came about in this
way:

George Willard went one evening to walk with
Belle Carpenter, a trimmer of women's hats who
worked in a millinery shop kept by Mrs. Kate
McHugh.   The young man was not in love with
the woman, who, in fact, had a suitor who worked
as bartender in Ed Griffith's saloon, but as they
walked about under the trees they occasionally embraced.   The night and their own thoughts had
aroused something in them.   As they were returning to Main Street they passed the little lawn
beside the railroad station and saw Wash Williams apparently asleep on the grass beneath a
tree.   On the next evening the operator and
George Willard walked out together.   Down the
railroad they went and sat on a pile of decaying
railroad ties beside the tracks.   It was then that
the operator told the young reporter his story
of hate.

Perhaps a dozen times George Willard and the
strange, shapeless man who lived at his father's
hotel had been on the point of talking.   The
young man looked at the hideous, leering face
staring about the hotel dining room and was con-
sumed with curiosity.   Something he saw lurking

in the staring eyes told him that the man who had nothing to say to others had nevertheless something to say to him. On the pile of railroad ties on the summer evening, he waited expectantly. When the operator remained silent and seemed to have changed his mind about talking, he tried to make conversation. "Were you ever married, Mr. Williams?" he began. "I suppose you were and your wife is dead, is that it?"

Wash Williams spat forth a succession of vile oaths. "Yes, she is dead," he agreed. "She is dead as all women are dead. She is a living-dead thing, walking in the sight of men and making the earth foul by her presence." Staring into the boy's eyes, the man became purple with rage. "Don't have fool notions in your head," he commanded. "My wife, she is dead; yes, surely. I tell you, all women are dead, my mother, your mother, that tall dark woman who works in the millinery store and with whom I saw you walking about yesterday,—all of them, they are all dead. I tell you there is something rotten about them. I was married, sure. My wife was dead before she married me, she was a foul thing come out of a woman more foul. She was a thing sent to make life unbearable to me. I was a fool, do you see, as you are now, and so I married this woman. I would like to see men a little begin to understand women. They are sent to prevent men making the world worth while. It is a trick in Nature. Ugh! They are creeping, crawling, squirming things, they with their soft hands and their blue eyes. The sight of a woman sickens me. Why I don't kill every woman I see I don't know."

Half frightened and yet fascinated by the light burning in the eyes of the hideous old man, George Willard listened, afire with curiosity. Darkness came on and he leaned forward trying to see the face of the man who talked. When, in the gathering darkness, he could no longer see the purple, bloated face and the burning eyes, a curious fancy came to him. Wash Williams talked in low even tones that made his words seem the more terrible. In the darkness the young reporter found himself imagining that he sat on the railroad ties beside a comely young man with black hair and black shining eyes. There was something almost beautiful in the voice of Wash Williams, the hideous, telling his story of hate.

The telegraph operator of Winesburg, sitting in the darkness on the railroad ties, had become a poet. Hatred had raised him to that elevation. "It is because I saw you kissing the lips of that Belle Carpenter that I tell you my story," he said. "What happened to me may next happen to you. I want to put you on your guard. Already you may be having dreams in your head. I want to destroy them."

Wash Williams began telling the story of his married life with the tall blonde girl with blue eyes whom he had met when he was a young operator at Dayton, Ohio. Here and there his story was touched with moments of beauty intermingled with strings of vile curses. The operator had married the daughter of a dentist who was the youngest of three sisters. On his marriage day, because of his ability, he was promoted to a position as dispatcher at an increased salary and sent to an office at Columbus, Ohio. There he settled down with his young wife and began buying a house on the installment plan.

The young telegraph operator was madly in love. With a kind of religious fervor he had managed to go through the pitfalls of his youth and to remain virginal until after his marriage. He made for George Willard a picture of his life in the house at Columbus, Ohio, with the young wife. "In the garden back of our house we planted vegetables," he said, "you know, peas and corn and such things. We went to Columbus in early March and as soon as the days became warm I went to work in the garden. With a spade I turned up the black ground while she ran about laughing and pretending to be afraid of the worms I uncovered. Late in April came the planting.

In the little paths among the seed beds she stood holding a paper bag in her hand. The bag was filled with seeds. A few at a time she handed me the seeds that I might thrust them into the warm, soft ground."

For a moment there was a catch in the voice of the man talking in the darkness. "I loved her," he said. "I don't claim not to be a fool. I love her yet. There in the dusk in the spring evening I crawled along the black ground to her feet and groveled before her. I kissed her shoes and the ankles above her shoes. When the hem of her garment touched my face I trembled. When after two years of that life I found she had managed to acquire three other lovers who came regularly to our house when I was away at work, I didn't want to touch them or her. I just sent her home to her mother and said nothing. There was nothing to say. I had four hundred dollars in the bank and I gave her that. I didn't ask her reasons. I didn't say anything. When she had gone I cried like a silly boy. Pretty soon I had a chance to sell the house and I sent that money to her."

Wash Williams and George Willard arose from the pile of railroad ties and walked along the tracks toward town. The operator finished his tale quickly, breathlessly.

"Her mother sent for me," he said. "She

wrote me a letter and asked me to come to their
house at Dayton. When I got there it was evening about this time."

Wash Williams' voice rose to a half scream.
"I sat in the parlor of that house two hours. Her
mother took me in there and left me. Their
house was stylish. They were what is called respectable people. There were plush chairs and
a couch in the room. I was trembling all over.
I hated the men I thought had wronged her. I
was sick of living alone and wanted her back.
The longer I waited the more raw and tender I
became. I thought that if she came in and just
touched me with her hand I would perhaps faint
away. I ached to forgive and forget."

Wash Williams stopped and stood staring at
George Willard. The boy's body shook as from
a chill. Again the man's voice became soft and
low. "She came into the room naked," he went
on. "Her mother did that. While I sat there
she was taking the girl's clothes off, perhaps coax-
ing her to do it. First I heard voices at the door
that led into a little hallway and then it opened
softly. The girl was ashamed and stood perfectly still staring at the floor. The mother
didn't come into the room. When she had pushed
the girl in through the door she stood in the hallway waiting, hoping we would—well, you see—
waiting."

George Willard and the telegraph operator came into the main street of Winesburg. The lights from the store windows lay bright and shining on the sidewalks. People moved about laughing and talking. The young reporter felt ill and weak. In imagination, he also become old and shapeless. "I didn't get the mother killed," said Wash Williams, staring up and down the street. "I struck her once with a chair and then the neighbors came in and took it away. She screamed so loud you see. I won't ever have a chance to kill her now. She died of a fever a month after that happened."

THE THINKER

THE house in which Seth Richmond of Winesburg lived with his mother had been at one time the show place of the town, but when young Seth lived there its glory had become somewhat dimmed. The huge brick house which Banker White had built on Buckeye Street had overshadowed it. The Richmond place was in a little valley far out at the end of Main Street. Farmers coming into town by a dusty road from the south passed by a grove of walnut trees, skirted the Fair Ground with its high board fence covered with advertisements, and trotted their horses down through the valley past the Richmond place into town. As much of the country north and south of Winesburg was devoted to fruit and berry raising, Seth saw wagon-loads of berry pickers—boys, girls, and women—going to the fields in the morning and returning covered with dust in the evening. The chattering crowd, with their rude jokes cried out from wagon to wagon, sometimes irritated him sharply. He regretted that he also could not laugh boisterously, shout meaningless jokes and make of himself a figure in the endless stream of moving, giggling activity that went up and down the road.

The Richmond house was built of limestone, and although it was said in the village to have become run down, had in reality grown more beautiful with every passing year. Already time had begun a little to color the stone, lending a golden richness to its surface and in the evening or on dark days touching the shaded places beneath the eaves with wavering patches of browns and blacks.

The house had been built by Seth's grandfather, a stone quarryman, and it, together with the stone quarries on Lake Erie eighteen miles to the north, had been left to his son, Clarence Richmond, Seth's father. Clarence Richmond, a quiet passionate man extraordinarily admired by his neighbors, had been killed in a street fight with the editor of a newspaper in Toledo, Ohio. The fight concerned the publication of Clarence Richmond's name coupled with that of a woman school teacher, and as the dead man had begun the row by firing upon the editor, the effort to punish the slayer was unsuccessful. After the quarryman's death it was found that much of the money left to him had been squandered in speculation and in insecure investments made through the influence of friends.

Left with but a small income, Virginia Richmond had settled down to a retired life in the village and to the raising of her son. Although she had been deeply moved by the death of the husband and father, she did not at all believe the stories concerning him that ran about after his death. To her mind, the sensitive, boyish man whom all had instinctively loved, was but an unfortunate, a being too fine for everyday life. "You'll be hearing all sorts of stories, but you are not to believe what you hear," she said to her son. "He was a good man, full of tenderness for everyone, and should not have tried to be a man of affairs. No matter how much I were to plan and dream of your future, I could not imagine anything better for you than that you turn out as good a man as your father."

Several years after the death of her husband, Virginia Richmond had become alarmed at the growing demands upon her income and had set herself to the task of increasing it. She had learned stenography and through the influence of her husband's friends got the position of court stenographer at the county seat. There she went by train each morning during the sessions of the court and when no court sat, spent her days working among the rosebushes in her garden. She was a tall, straight figure of a woman with a plain face and a great mass of brown hair.

In the relationship between Seth Richmond and his mother, there was a quality that even at eighteen had begun to color all of his traffic with

men.   An almost unhealthy respect for the youth
kept the mother for the most part silent in his
presence.   When she did speak sharply to him he
had only to look steadily into her eyes to see
dawning there the puzzled look he had already no-
ticed in the eyes of others when he looked at them.

The truth was that the son thought with remarkable clearness and the mother did not.   She
expected from all people certain conventional re-
actions to life.   A boy was your son, you scolded
him and he trembled and looked at the floor.
When you had scolded enough he wept and all was
forgiven.   After the weeping and when he had
gone to bed, you crept into his room and kissed
him.

Virginia Richmond could not understand why
her son did not do these things.   After the se-
verest reprimand, he did not tremble and look at
the floor but instead looked steadily at her, caus-
ing uneasy doubts to invade her mind.   As for
creeping into his room—after Seth had passed his
fifteenth year, she would have been half afraid to
do anything of the kind.

Once when he was a boy of sixteen, Seth in company with two other boys, ran away from home.
The three boys climbed into the open door of an
empty freight car and rode some forty miles to a
town where a fair was being held.   One of the
boys had a bottle filled with a combination of

whiskey and blackberry wine, and the three sat with legs dangling out of the car door drinking from the bottle. Seth's two companions sang and waved their hands to idlers about the stations of the towns through which the train passed. They planned raids upon the baskets of farmers who had come with their families to the fair. "We will live like kings and won't have to spend a penny to see the fair and horse races," they declared boastfully.

After the disappearance of Seth, Virginia Richmond walked up and down the floor of her home filled with vague alarms. Although on the next day she discovered, through an inquiry made by the town marshal, on what adventure the boys had gone, she could not quiet herself. All through the night she lay awake hearing the clock tick and telling herself that Seth, like his father, would come to a sudden and violent end. So determined was she that the boy should this time feel the weight of her wrath that, although she would not allow the marshal to interfere with his adventure, she got out pencil and paper and wrote down a series of sharp, stinging reproofs she intended to pour out upon him. The reproofs she committed to memory, going about the garden and saying them aloud like an actor memorizing his part.

And when, at the end of the week, Seth returned, a little weary and with coal soot in his ears and about his eyes, she again found herself unable to reprove him. Walking into the house he hung his cap on a nail by the kitchen door and stood looking steadily at her. "I wanted to turn back within an hour after we had started," he explained. "I didn't know what to do. I knew you would be bothered, but I knew also that if I didn't go on I would be ashamed of myself. I went through with the thing for my own good. It was uncomfortable, sleeping on wet straw, and two drunken negroes came and slept with us. When I stole a lunch basket out of a farmer's wagon I couldn't help thinking of his children going all day without food. I was sick of the whole affair, but I was determined to stick it out until the other boys were ready to come back."

"I'm glad you did stick it out," replied the mother, half resentfully, and kissing him upon the forehead pretended to busy herself with the work about the house.

On a summer evening Seth Richmond went to the New Willard House to visit his friend, George Willard. It had rained during the afternoon, but as he walked through Main Street, the sky had partially cleared and a golden glow lit up the west. Going around a corner, he turned in at the door of the hotel and began to climb the stairway leading up to his friend's room. In the hotel office the proprietor and two traveling men were engaged in a discussion of politics.

On the stairway Seth stopped and listened to the voices of the men below. They were excited and talked rapidly. Tom Willard was berating the traveling men. "I am a Democrat but your talk makes me sick," he said. "You don't understand McKinley. McKinley and Mark Hanna are friends. It is impossible perhaps for your mind to grasp that. If anyone tells you that a friendship can be deeper and bigger and more worth while than dollars and cents, or even more worth while than state politics, you snicker and laugh."

The landlord was interrupted by one of the guests, a tall grey-mustached man who worked for a wholesale grocery house. "Do you think that I've lived in Cleveland all these years without knowing Mark Hanna?" he demanded. "Your talk is piffle. Hanna is after money and nothing else. This McKinley is his tool. He has McKinley bluffed and don't you forget it."

The young man on the stairs did not linger to hear the rest of the discussion, but went on up the stairway and into a little dark hall. Something in the voices of the men talking in the hotel office started a chain of thoughts in his mind. He was lonely and had begun to think that loneliness was a part of his character, something that would al-

ways stay with him.   Stepping into a side hall he
stood by a window that looked into an alleyway.
At the back of his shop stood Abner Groff, the
town baker.   His tiny bloodshot eyes looked up
and down the alleyway.   In his shop someone
called the baker who pretended not to hear.   The
baker had an empty milk bottle in his hand and an
angry sullen look in his eyes.

In Winesburg, Seth Richmond was called the
"deep one."   "He's like his father," men said
as he went through the streets.   "He'll break out
some of these days.   You wait and see."

The talk of the town and the respect with
which men and boys instinctively greeted him, as
all men greet silent people, had affected Seth
Richmond's outlook on life and on himself.   He,
like most boys, was deeper than boys are given
credit for being, but he was not what the men of
the town, and even his mother, thought him to be.
No great underlying purpose lay back of his ha-
bitual silence, and he had no definite plan for his
life.   When the boys with whom he associated
were noisy and quarrelsome, he stood quietly at
one side.   With calm eyes he watched the gestic-
ulating lively figures of his companions.   He
wasn't particularly interested in what was going
on, and sometimes wondered if he would ever be
particularly interested in anything.   Now, as he
stood in the half-darkness by the window watching

the baker, he wished that he himself might become thoroughly stirred by something, even by the fits of sullen anger for which Baker Groff was noted. "It would be better for me if I could become excited and wrangle about politics like windy old Tom Willard," he thought, as he left the window and went again along the hallway to the room occupied by his friend, George Willard.

George Willard was older than Seth Richmond, but in the rather odd friendship between the two, it was he who was forever courting and the younger boy who was being courted. The paper on which George worked had one policy. It strove to mention by name in each issue, as many as possible of the inhabitants of the village. Like an excited dog, George Willard ran here and there, noting on his pad of paper who had gone on business to the county seat or had returned from a visit to a neighboring village. All day he wrote little facts upon the pad. "A. P. Wringlet has received a shipment of straw hats. Ed Byerbaum and Tom Marshall were in Cleveland Friday. Uncle Tom Sinnings is building a new barn on his place on the Valley Road."

The idea that George Willard would some day become a writer had given him a place of distinction in Winesburg, and to Seth Richmond he talked continually of the matter. "It's the easiest of all lives to live," he declared, becoming excited and boastful. "Here and there you go and there is no one to boss you. Though you are in India or in the South Seas in a boat, you have but to write and there you are. Wait till I get my name up and then see what fun I shall have."

In George Willard's room, which had a window looking down into an alleyway and one that looked across railroad track's to Biff Carter's Lunch Room facing the railroad station, Seth Richmond sat in a chair and looked at the floor. George Willard who had been sitting for an hour idly playing with a lead pencil, greeted him effusively. "I've been trying to write a love story," he explained, laughing nervously. Lighting a pipe he began walking up and down the room. "I know what I'm going to do. I'm going to fall in love. I've been sitting here and thinking it over and I'm going to do it."

As though embarrassed by his declaration, George went to a window and turning his back to his friend leaned out. "I know who I'm going to fall in love with," he said sharply. "It's Helen White. She is the only girl in town with any 'get-up' to her."

Struck with a new idea, young Willard turned and walked towards his visitor. "Look here," he said. "You know Helen White better than I do. I want you to tell her what I said. You just get to talking to her and say that I'm in love with

her. See what she says to that. See how she
takes it, and then you come and tell me."

Seth Richmond arose and went towards the
door. The words of his comrade irritated him
unbearably. "Well, good-bye," he said briefly.

George was amazed. Running forward he
stood in the darkness trying to look into Seth's
face. "What's the matter? What are you going to do? You stay here and let's talk," he
urged.

A wave of resentment directed against his
friend, the men of the town who were, he thought,
perpetually talking of nothing, and most of all,
against his own habit of silence, made Seth half
desperate. "Aw, speak to her yourself," he
burst forth and then going quickly through the
door, slammed it sharply in his friend's face.
"I'm going to find Helen White and talk to her,
but not about him," he muttered.

Seth went down the stairway and out at the
front door of the hotel muttering with wrath.
Crossing a little dusty street and climbing a low
iron railing, he went to sit upon the grass in the
station yard. George Willard he thought a profound fool, and he wished that he had said so
more vigorously. Although his acquaintanceship
with Helen White, the banker's daughter, was
outwardly but casual, she was often the subject
of his thoughts and he felt that she was some-

thing private and personal to himself. "The busy fool with his love stories," he muttered, staring back over his shoulder at George Willard's room, "why does he never tire of his eternal talking."

It was berry harvest time in Winesburg and upon the station platform men and boys loaded the boxes of red, fragrant berries into two express cars that stood upon the siding. A June moon was in the sky, although in the west a storm threatened, and no street lamps were lighted. In the dim light the figures of the men standing upon the express truck and pitching the boxes in at the doors of the cars were but dimly discernible. Upon the iron railing that protected the station lawn sat other men. Pipes were lighted. Village jokes went back and forth. Away in the distance a train whistled and the men loading the boxes into the cars worked with renewed activity.

Seth arose from his place on the grass and went silently past the men perched upon the railing and into Main Street. He had come to a resolution. "I'll get out of here," he told himself. "What good am I here? I'm going to some city and go to work. I'll tell mother about it to-morrow."

Seth Richmond went slowly along Main Street, past Wacker's Cigar Store and the Town Hall, and into Buckeye Street. He was depressed by the thought that he was not a part of the life in his own town, but the depression did not cut deeply as he did not think of himself as at fault. In the heavy shadows of a big tree before Dr. Welling's house, he stopped and stood watching half-witted Turk Smollet, who was pushing a wheelbarrow in the road. The old man with his absurdly boyish mind had a dozen long boards on the wheelbarrow, and as he hurried along the road, balanced the load with extreme nicety. "Easy there, Turk! Steady now, old boy!" the old man shouted to himself, and laughed so that the load of boards rocked dangerously.

Seth knew Turk Smollet, the half dangerous old wood chopper whose peculiarities added so much of color to the life of the village. He knew that when Turk got into Main Street he would become the center of a whirlwind of cries and comments, that in truth the old man was going far out of his way in order to pass through Main Street and exhibit his skill in wheeling the boards. "If George Willard were here, he'd have something to say," thought Seth. "George belongs to this town. He'd shout at Turk and Turk would shout at him. They'd both be secretly pleased by what they had said. It's different with me. I don't belong. I'll not make a fuss about it, but I'm going to get out of here."

Seth stumbled forward through the half darkness, feeling himself an outcast in his own town. He began to pity himself, but a sense of the ab-

surdity of his thoughts made him smile.   In the
end he decided that he was simply old beyond his
years and not at all a subject for self-pity.   "I'm
made to go to work.   I may be able to make a
place for myself by steady working, and I might
as well be at it," he decided.

Seth went to the house of Banker White and
stood in the darkness by the front door.   On the
door hung a heavy brass knocker, an innovation
introduced into the village by Helen White's
mother, who had also organized a woman's club
for the study of poetry.   Seth raised the knocker
and let it fall.   Its heavy clatter sounded like a
report from distant guns.   "How awkward and
foolish I am," he thought.   "If Mrs. White
comes to the door, I won't know what to say."

It was Helen White who came to the door and
found Seth standing at the edge of the porch.
Blushing with pleasure, she stepped forward, closing the door softly.   "I'm going to get out of
town.   I don't know what I'll do, but I'm going to get out of here and go to work.   I think
I'll go to Columbus," he said.   "Perhaps I'll get
into the State University down there.   Anyway,
I'm going.   I'll tell mother to-night."   He hesitated and looked doubtfully about.   "Perhaps you
wouldn't mind coming to walk with me?"

Seth and Helen walked through the streets beneath the trees.   Heavy clouds had drifted across

the face of the moon, and before them in the deep twilight went a man with a short ladder upon his shoulder. Hurrying forward, the man stopped at the street crossing and, putting the ladder against the wooden lamp post, lighted the village lights so that their way was half lighted, half darkened, by the lamps and by the deepening shadows cast by the low-branched trees. In the tops of the trees the wind began to play, disturbing the sleeping birds so that they flew about calling plaintively. In the lighted space before one of the lamps, two bats wheeled and circled, pursuing the gathering swarm of night flies.

Since Seth had been a boy in knee trousers there had been a half expressed intimacy between him and the maiden who now for the first time walked beside him. For a time she had been beset with a madness for writing notes which she addressed to Seth. He had found them concealed in his books at school and one had been given him by a child met in the street, while several had been delivered through the village post office.

The notes had been written in a round, boyish hand and had reflected a mind inflamed by novel reading. Seth had not answered them, although he had been moved and flattered by some of the sentences scrawled in pencil upon the stationery of the banker's wife. Putting them into the pocket of his coat, he went through the street or stood by

the fence in the school yard with something burning at his side.   He thought it fine that he should
be thus selected as the favorite of the richest and
most attractive girl in town.

Helen and Seth stopped by a fence near where
a low dark building faced the street.   The building had once been a factory for the making of
barrel staves but was now vacant.   Across the
street upon the porch of a house a man and
woman talked of their childhood, their voices coming clearly across to the half-embarrassed youth
and maiden.   There was the sound of scraping
chairs and the man and woman came down the
gravel path to a wooden gate.   Standing outside
the gate, the man leaned over and kissed the
woman.   "For old times' sake," he said and,
turning, walked rapidly away along the sidewalk.

"That's Belle Turner," whispered Helen, and
put her hand boldly into Seth's hand.   "I didn't
know she had a fellow.   I thought she was too
old for that."   Seth laughed uneasily.   The hand
of the girl was warm and a strange, dizzy feeling
crept over him.   Into his mind came a desire to
tell her something he had been determined not
to tell.   "George Willard's in love with you,"
he said, and in spite of his agitation his voice was
low and quiet.   "He's writing a story, and he
wants to be in love.   He wants to know how it

feels.   He wanted me to tell you and see what you
said."

Again Helen and Seth walked in silence.   They
came to the garden surrounding the old Richmond
place and going through a gap in the hedge sat on
a wooden bench beneath a bush.

On the street as he walked beside the girl new
and daring thoughts had come into Seth Richmond's mind.   He began to regret his decision to
get out of town.   "It would be something new and
altogether delightful to remain and walk often
through the streets with Helen White," he
thought.   In imagination he saw himself putting
his arm about her waist and feeling her arms
clasped tightly about his neck.   One of those odd
combinations of events and places made him con-
nect the idea of love making with this girl and a
spot he had visited some days before.   He had
gone on an errand to the house of a farmer who
lived on a hillside beyond the Fair Ground and
had returned by a path through a field.   At the
foot of the hill below the farmer's house Seth had
stopped beneath a sycamore tree and looked about
him.   A soft humming noise had greeted his ears.
For a moment he had thought the tree must be the
home of a swarm of bees.

And then, looking down, Seth had seen the bees
everywhere all about him in the long grass.   He
stood in a mass of weeds that grew waist-high in

the field that ran away from the hillside. The weeds were abloom with tiny purple blossoms and gave forth an overpowering fragrance. Upon the weeds the bees were gathered in armies, singing as they worked.

Seth imagined himself lying on a summer evening, buried deep among the weeds beneath the tree. Beside him, in the scene built in his fancy, lay Helen White, her hand lying in his hand. A peculiar reluctance kept him from kissing her lips, but he felt he might have done that if he wished. Instead, he lay perfectly still, looking at her and listening to the army of bees that sang the sustained masterful song of labor above his head.

On the bench in the garden Seth stirred uneasily. Releasing the hand of the girl, he thrust his hands into his trouser pockets. A desire to impress the mind of his companion with the importance of the resolution he had made came over him and he nodded his head toward the house. "Mother'll make a fuss, I suppose," he whispered. "She hasn't thought at all about what I'm going to do in life. She thinks I'm going to stay on here forever just being a boy."

Seth's voice became charged with boyish earnestness. "You see, I've got to strike out. I've got to get to work. It's what I'm good for."

Helen White was impressed. She nodded her head and a feeling of admiration swept over her.

"This is as it should be," she thought. "This boy is not a boy at all, but a strong, purposeful man." Certain vague desires that had been invading her body were swept away and she sat up very straight on the bench. The thunder continued to rumble and flashes of heat lightning lit up the eastern sky. The garden that had been so mysterious and vast, a place that with Seth beside her might have become the background for strange and wonderful adventures, now seemed no more than an ordinary Winesburg back yard, quite definite and limited in its outlines.

"What will you do up there?" she whispered.

Seth turned half around on the bench, striving to see her face in the darkness. He thought her infinitely more sensible and straightforward than George Willard, and was glad he had come away from his friend. A feeling of impatience with the town that had been in his mind returned, and he tried to tell her of it. "Everyone talks and talks," he began. "I'm sick of it. I'll do something, get into some kind of work where talk don't count. Maybe I'll just be a mechanic in a shop. I don't know. I guess I don't care much. I just want to work and keep quiet. That's all I've got in my mind."

Seth arose from the bench and put out his hand. He did not want to bring the meeting to an end but could not think of anything more to say. "It's the last time we'll see each other," he whispered.

A wave of sentiment swept over Helen. Putting her hand upon Seth's shoulder, she started to draw his face down towards her own upturned face. The act was one of pure affection and cutting regret that some vague adventure that had been present in the spirit of the night would now never be realized. "I think I'd better be going along," she said, letting her hand fall heavily to her side. A thought came to her. "Don't you go with me; I want to be alone," she said. "You go and talk with your mother. You'd better do that now."

Seth hesitated and, as he stood waiting, the girl turned and ran away through the hedge. A desire to run after her came to him, but he only stood staring, perplexed and puzzled by her action as he had been perplexed and puzzled by all of the life of the town out of which she had come. Walking slowly toward the house, he stopped in the shadow of a large tree and looked at his mother sitting by a lighted window busily sewing. The feeling of loneliness that had visited him earlier in the evening returned and colored his thoughts of the adventure through which he had just passed. "Huh!" he exclaimed, turning and staring in the direction taken by Helen White. "That's how things'll turn out. She'll be like the rest. I suppose she'll begin now to look at me in

a funny way." He looked at the ground and pon-
dered this thought. "She'll be embarrassed and
feel strange when I'm around," he whispered to
himself. "That's how it'll be. That's how
everything'll turn out. When it comes to loving
some one, it won't never be me. It'll be some
one else—some fool—some one who talks a lot—
some one like that George Willard."

TANDY

UNTIL she was seven years old she lived in an old unpainted house on an unused road that led off Trunion Pike. Her father gave her but little attention and her mother was dead. The father spent his time talking and thinking of religion. He proclaimed himself an agnostic and was so absorbed in destroying the ideas of God that had crept into the minds of his neighbors that he never saw God manifesting himself in the little child that, half forgotten, lived here and there on the bounty of her dead mother's relatives.

A stranger came to Winesburg and saw in the child what the father did not see. He was a tall, red-haired young man who was almost always drunk. Sometimes he sat in a chair before the New Willard House with Tom Hard, the father. As Tom talked, declaring there could be no God, the stranger smiled and winked at the bystanders. He and Tom became friends and were much together.

The stranger was the son of a rich merchant of Cleveland and had come to Winesburg on a mission. He wanted to cure himself of the habit of drink, and thought that by escaping from his city associates and living in a rural community he would have a better chance in the struggle with the appetite that was destroying him.

His sojourn in Winesburg was not a success. The dullness of the passing hours led to his drinking harder than ever. But he did succeed in doing something. He gave a name rich with meaning to Tom Hard's daughter.

One evening when he was recovering from a long debauch the stranger came reeling along the main street of the town. Tom Hard sat in a chair before the New Willard House with his daughter, then a child of five, on his knees. Beside him on the board sidewalk sat young George Willard. The stranger dropped into a chair beside them. His body shook and when he tried to talk his voice trembled.

It was late evening and darkness lay over the town and over the railroad than ran along the foot of a little incline before the hotel. Somewhere in the distance, off to the west, there was a prolonged blast from the whistle of a passenger engine. A dog that had been sleeping in the roadway arose and barked. The stranger began to babble and made a prophecy concerning the child that lay in the arms of the agnostic.

"I came here to quit drinking," he said, and

tears began to run down his cheeks. He did not look at Tom Hard, but leaned forward and stared into the darkness as though seeing a vision. "I ran away to the country to be cured, but I am not cured. There is a reason." He turned to look at the child who sat up very straight on her father's knee and returned the look.

The stranger touched Tom Hard on the arm. "Drink is not the only thing to which I am addicted," he said. "There is something else. I am a lover and have not found my thing to love. That is a big point if you know enough to realize what I mean. It makes my destruction inevitable, you see. There are few who understand that."

The stranger became silent and seemed overcome with sadness, but another blast from the whistle of the passenger engine aroused him. "I have not lost faith. I proclaim that. I have only been brought to the place where I know my faith will not be realized," he declared hoarsely. He looked hard at the child and began to address her, paying no more attention to the father. "There is a woman coming," he said, and his voice was now sharp and earnest. "I have missed her, you see. She did not come in my time. You may be the woman. It would be like fate to let me stand in her presence once, on such an evening as this, when I have destroyed myself with drink and she is as yet only a child."

The shoulders of the stranger shook violently, and when he tried to roll a cigarette the paper fell from his trembling fingers. He grew angry and scolded. "They think it's easy to be a woman, to be loved, but I know better," he declared. Again he turned to the child. "I understand," he cried. "Perhaps of all men I alone understand."

His glance again wandered away to the darkened street. "I know about her, although she has never crossed my path," he said softly. "I know about her struggles and her defeats. It is because of her defeats that she is to me the lovely one. Out of her defeats has been born a new quality in woman. I have a name for it. I call it Tandy. I made up the name when I was a true dreamer and before my body became vile. It is the quality of being strong to be loved. It is something men need from women and that they do not get."

The stranger arose and stood before Tom Hard. His body rocked back and forth and he seemed about to fall, but instead he dropped to his knees on the sidewalk and raised the hands of the little girl to his drunken lips. He kissed them ecstatically. "Be Tandy, little one," he plead. "Dare to be strong and courageous. That is the road. Venture anything. Be brave enough to dare to be loved. Be something more than man or woman. Be Tandy."

The stranger arose and staggered off down the street. A day or two later he got aboard a train and returned to his home in Cleveland. On the summer evening, after the talk before the hotel, Tom Hard took the girl child to the house of a relative where she had been invited to spend the night. As he went along in the darkness under the trees he forgot the babbling voice of the stranger and his mind returned to the making of arguments by which he might destroy men's faith in God. He spoke his daughter's name and she began to weep.

"I don't want to be called that," she declared. "I want to be called Tandy—Tandy Hard." The child wept so bitterly that Tom Hard was touched and tried to comfort her. He stopped beneath a tree and, taking her into his arms, began to caress her. "Be good, now," he said sharply; but she would not be quieted. With childish abandon she gave herself over to grief, her voice breaking the evening stillness of the street. "I want to be Tandy. I want to be Tandy. I want to be Tandy Hard," she cried, shaking her head and sobbing as though her young strength were not enough to bear the vision the words of the drunkard had brought to her.

THE STRENGTH OF GOD

THE Reverend Curtis Hartman was pastor of the Presbyterian Church of Winesburg, and had been in that position ten years. He was forty years old, and by his nature very silent and reticent. To preach, standing in the pulpit before the people, was always a hardship for him and from Wednesday morning until Saturday evening he thought of nothing but the two sermons that must be preached on Sunday. Early on Sunday morning he went into a little room called a study in the bell tower of the church and prayed. In his prayers there was one note that always predominated. "Give me strength and courage for Thy work, O Lord!" he plead, kneeling on the bare floor and bowing his head in the presence of the task that lay before him.

The Reverend Hartman was a tall man with a brown beard. His wife, a stout, nervous woman, was the daughter of a manufacturer of underwear at Cleveland, Ohio. The minister himself was rather a favorite in the town. The elders of the church liked him because he was quiet and unpretentious and Mrs. White, the banker's wife, thought him scholarly and refined.

The Presbyterian Church held itself somewhat aloof from the other churches of Winesburg. It was larger and more imposing and its minister was better paid. He even had a carriage of his own and on summer evenings sometimes drove about town with his wife. Through Main Street and up and down Buckeye Street he went, bowing gravely to the people, while his wife, afire with secret pride, looked at him out of the corners of her eyes and worried lest the horse become frightened and run away.

For a good many years after he came to Winesburg things went well with Curtis Hartman. He was not one to arouse keen enthusiasm among the worshippers in his church but on the other hand he made no enemies. In reality he was much in earnest and sometimes suffered prolonged periods of remorse because he could not go crying the word of God in the highways and byways of the town. He wondered if the flame of the spirit really burned in him and dreamed of a day when a strong sweet new current of power would come like a great wind into his voice and his soul and the people would tremble before the spirit of God made manifest in him. "I am a poor stick and that will never really happen to me," he mused dejectedly and then a patient smile lit up his features. "Oh well, I suppose I'm doing well enough," he added philosophically.

The room in the bell tower of the church, where on Sunday mornings the minister prayed for an increase in him of the power of God, had but one window. It was long and narrow and swung outward on a hinge like a door. On the window, made of little leaded panes, was a design showing the Christ laying his hand upon the head of a child. One Sunday morning in the summer as he sat by his desk in the room with a large Bible opened before him, and the sheets of his sermon scattered about, the minister was shocked to see, in the upper room of the house next door, a woman lying in her bed and smoking a cigarette while she read a book. Curtis Hartman went on tiptoe to the window and closed it softly. He was horror stricken at the thought of a woman smoking and trembled also to think that his eyes, just raised from the pages of the book of God, had looked upon the bare shoulders and white throat of a woman. With his brain in a whirl he went down into the pulpit and preached a long sermon without once thinking of his gestures or his voice. The sermon attracted unusual attention because of its power and clearness. "I wonder if she is listening, if my voice is carrying a message into her soul," he thought and began to hope that on future Sunday mornings he might be able to say words that would touch and awaken the woman apparently far gone in secret sin.

The house next door to the Presbyterian
Church, through the windows of which the minister had seen the sight that had so upset him, was
occupied by two women. Aunt Elizabeth Swift,
a grey competent-looking widow with money in
the Winesburg National Bank, lived there with
her daughter Kate Swift, a school teacher. The
school teacher was thirty years old and had a neat
trim-looking figure. She had few friends and
bore a reputation of having a sharp tongue.
When he began to think about her, Curtis Hartman remembered that she had been to Europe
and had lived for two years in New York City.
"Perhaps after all her smoking means nothing,"
he thought. He began to remember that when he
was a student in college and occasionally read
novels, good, although somewhat worldly women,
had smoked through the pages of a book that had
once fallen into his hands. With a rush of new
determination he worked on his sermons all
through the week and forgot, in his zeal to reach
the ears and the soul of this new listener, both his
embarrassment in the pulpit and the necessity of
prayer in the study on Sunday mornings.

Reverend Hartman's experience with women
had been somewhat limited. He was the son of
a wagon maker from Muncie, Indiana, and had
worked his way through college. The daughter
of the underwear manufacturer had boarded in

a house where he lived during his school days and he had married her after a formal and prolonged courtship, carried on for the most part by the girl herself. On his marriage day the underwear manufacturer had given his daughter five thousand dollars and he promised to leave her at least twice that amount in his will. The minister had thought himself fortunate in marriage and had never permitted himself to think of other women. He did not want to think of other women. What he wanted was to do the work of God quietly and earnestly.

In the soul of the minister a struggle awoke. From wanting to reach the ears of Kate Swift, and through his sermons to delve into her soul, he began to want also to look again at the figure lying white and quiet in the bed. On a Sunday morning when he could not sleep because of his thoughts he arose and went to walk in the streets. When he had gone along Main Street almost to the old Richmond place he stopped and picking up a stone rushed off to the room in the bell tower. With the stone he broke out a corner of the window and then locked the door and sat down at the desk before the open Bible to wait. When the shade of the window to Kate Swift's room was raised he could see, through the hole, directly into her bed, but she was not there. She also had arisen and had gone for a walk and the hand that raised the shade was the hand of Aunt Elizabeth Swift.

The minister almost wept with joy at this deliverence from the carnal desire to "peep" and went back to his own house praising God. In an ill moment he forgot, however, to stop the hole in the window. The piece of glass broken out at the corner of the window just nipped off the bare heel of the boy standing motionless and looking with rapt eyes into the face of the Christ.

Curtis Hartman forgot his sermon on that Sunday morning. He talked to his congregation and in his talk said that it was a mistake for people to think of their minister as a man set aside and intended by nature to lead a blameless life. "Out of my own experience I know that we, who are the ministers of God's word, are beset by the same temptations that assail you," he declared. "I have been tempted and have surrendered to temptation. It is only the hand of God, placed beneath my head, that has raised me up. As he has raised me so also will he raise you. Do not despair. In your hour of sin raise your eyes to the skies and you will be again and again saved."

Resolutely the minister put the thoughts of the woman in the bed out of his mind and began to be something like a lover in the presence of his wife. One evening when they drove out together he turned the horse out of Buckeye Street and in the darkness on Gospel Hill, above Waterworks Pond, put his arm about Sarah Hartman's waist. When he had eaten breakfast in the morning and was ready to retire to his study at the back of his house he went around the table and kissed his wife on the cheek. When thoughts of Kate Swift came into his head, he smiled and raised his eyes to the skies. "Intercede for me, Master," he muttered, "keep me in the narrow path intent on Thy work."

And now began the real struggle in the soul of the brown-bearded minister. By chance he discovered that Kate Swift was in the habit of lying in her bed in the evenings and reading a book. A lamp stood on a table by the side of the bed and the light streamed down upon her white shoulders and bare throat. On the evening when he made the discovery the minister sat at the desk in the study from nine until after eleven and when her light was put out stumbled out of the church to spend two more hours walking and praying in the streets. He did not want to kiss the shoulders and the throat of Kate Swift and had not allowed his mind to dwell on such thoughts. He did not know what he wanted. "I am God's child and he must save me from myself," he cried, in the darkness under the trees as he wandered in the streets. By a tree he stood and looked at the sky that was covered with hurrying clouds. He began to talk to God intimately and closely. "Please, Father, do not forget me. Give me power to go to-morrow and repair the hole in the window. Lift my eyes again to the skies. Stay with me, Thy servant, in his hour of need."

Up and down through the silent streets walked the minister and for days and weeks his soul was troubled. He could not understand the temptation that had come to him nor could he fathom the reason for its coming. In a way he began to blame God, saying to himself that he had tried to keep his feet in the true path and had not run about seeking sin. "Through my days as a young man and all through my life here I have gone quietly about my work," he declared. "Why now should I be tempted? What have I done that this burden should be laid on me?"

Three times during the early fall and winter of that year Curtis Hartman crept out of his house to the room in the bell tower to sit in the darkness looking at the figure of Kate Swift lying in her bed and later went to walk and pray in the streets. He could not understand himself. For weeks he would go along scarcely thinking of the school teacher and telling himself that he had conquered the carnal desire to look at her body. And then something would happen. As he sat in the study of his own house, hard at work on a sermon, he would become nervous and begin to walk up and down the room. "I will go out into the streets," he told himself and even as he let himself in at the church door he persistently denied to himself the cause of his being there. "I will not repair the hole in the window and I will train myself to come here at night and sit in the presence of this woman without raising my eyes. I will not be defeated in this thing. The Lord has devised this temptation as a test of my soul and I will grope my way out of darkness into the light of righteousness."

One night in January when it was bitter cold and snow lay deep on the streets of Winesburg Curtis Hartman paid his last visit to the room in the bell tower of the church. It was past nine o'clock when he left his own house and he set out so hurriedly that he forgot to put on his overshoes. In Main Street no one was abroad but Hop Higgins the night watchman and in the whole town no one was awake but the watchman and young George Willard, who sat in the office of the *Winesburg Eagle* trying to write a story. Along the street to the church went the minister, plowing through the drifts and thinking that this time he would utterly give way to sin. "I want to look at the woman and to think of kissing her shoulders and I am going to let myself think what I choose," he declared bitterly and tears came into his eyes. He began to think that he would get out of the ministry and try some other way of life. "I shall go to some city and get into business," he declared. "If my nature is such that I cannot resist sin, I shall give myself over to sin. At least I shall not be a hypocrite, preaching the word of God with my mind thinking of the shoulders and neck of a woman who does not belong to me."

It was cold in the room of the bell tower of the church on that January night and almost as soon as he came into the room Curtis Hartman knew that if he stayed he would be ill. His feet were wet from tramping in the snow and there was no fire. In the room in the house next door Kate Swift had not yet appeared. With grim determination the man sat down to wait. Sitting in the chair and gripping the edge of the desk on which lay the Bible he stared into the darkness thinking the blackest thoughts of his life. He thought of his wife and for the moment almost hated her. "She has always been ashamed of passion and has cheated me," he thought. "Man has a right to expect living passion and beauty in a woman. He has no right to forget that he is an animal and in me there is something that is Greek. I will throw off the woman of my bosom and seek other women. I will besiege this school teacher. I will fly in the face of all men and if I am a creature of carnal lusts I will live then for my lusts."

The distracted man trembled from head to

foot, partly from cold, partly from the struggle in which he was engaged. Hours passed and a fever assailed his body. His throat began to hurt and his teeth chattered. His feet on the study floor felt like two cakes of ice. Still he would not give up. "I will see this woman and will think the thoughts I have never dared to think," he told himself, gripping the edge of the desk and waiting.

Curtis Hartman came near dying from the effects of that night of waiting in the church, and also he found in the thing that happened what he took to be the way of life for him. On other evenings when he had waited he had not been able to see, through the little hole in the glass, any part of the school teacher's room except that occupied by her bed. In the darkness he had waited until the woman suddenly appeared sitting in the bed in her white night-robe. When the light was turned up she propped herself up among the pillows and read a book. Sometimes she smoked one of the cigarettes. Only her bare shoulders and throat were visible.

On the January night, after he had come near dying with cold and after his mind had two or three times actually slipped away into an odd land of fantasy so that he had by an exercise of will power to force himself back into consciousness, Kate Swift appeared. In the room next door a lamp was lighted and the waiting man stared into an empty bed. Then upon the bed before his eyes a naked woman threw herself. Lying face downward she wept and beat with her fists upon the pillow. With a final outburst of weeping she half arose, and in the presence of the man who had waited to look and to think thoughts the woman of sin began to pray. In the lamplight her figure, slim and strong, looked like the figure of the boy in the presence of the Christ on the leaded window.

Curtis Hartman never remembered how he got out of the church. With a cry he arose, dragging the heavy desk along the floor. The Bible fell, making a great clatter in the silence. When the light in the house next door went out he stumbled down the stairway and into the street. Along the street he went and ran in at the door of the *Winesburg Eagle*. To George Willard, who was tramping up and down in the office undergoing a struggle of his own, he began to talk half incoherently. "The ways of God are beyond human understanding," he cried, running in quickly and closing the door. He began to advance upon the young man, his eyes glowing and his voice ringing with fervor. "I have found the light," he cried. "After ten years in this town, God has manifested himself to me in the body of a woman." His voice dropped and he began to whisper. "I did not understand," he said.   "What I took to be a trial of my soul was only a preparation for a new and more beautiful fervor of the spirit.   God has appeared to me in the person of Kate Swift, the school teacher, kneeling naked on a bed.   Do you know Kate Swift?   Although she may not be aware of it, she is an instrument of God, bearing the message of truth."

Reverend Curtis Hartman turned and ran out of the office.   At the door he stopped, and after looking up and down the deserted street, turned again to George Willard.   "I am delivered. Have no fear."   He held up a bleeding fist for the young man to see.   "I smashed the glass of the window," he cried.   "Now it will have to be wholly replaced.   The strength of God was in me and I broke it with my fist."

THE TEACHER

SNOW lay deep in the streets of Winesburg. It had begun to snow about ten o'clock in the morning and a wind sprang up and blew the snow in clouds along Main Street. The frozen mud roads that led into town were fairly smooth and in places ice covered the mud. "There will be good sleighing," said Will Henderson, standing by the bar in Ed Griffith's saloon. Out of the saloon he went and met Sylvester West the druggist stumbling along in the kind of heavy overshoes called arctics. "Snow will bring the people into town on Saturday," said the druggist. The two men stopped and discussed their affairs. Will Henderson, who had on a light overcoat and no overshoes, kicked the heel of his left foot with the toe of the right. "Snow will be good for the wheat," observed the druggist sagely.

Young George Willard, who had nothing to do, was glad because he did not feel like working that day. The weekly paper had been printed and taken to the post office on Wednesday evening and the snow began to fall on Thursday. At eight o'clock, after the morning train had passed, he put

a pair of skates in his pocket and went up to
Waterworks Pond but did not go skating. Past
the pond and along a path that followed Wine
Creek he went until he came to a grove of beech
trees. There he built a fire against the side of a
log and sat down at the end of the log to think.
When the snow began to fall and the wind to blow
he hurried about getting fuel for the fire.

The young reporter was thinking of Kate Swift
who had once been his school teacher. On the
evening before he had gone to her house to get a
book she wanted him to read and had been alone
with her for an hour. For the fourth or fifth
time the woman had talked to him with great
earnestness and he could not make out what she
meant by her talk. He began to believe she
might be in love with him and the thought was
both pleasing and annoying.

Up from the log he sprang and began to pile
sticks on the fire. Looking about to be sure he
was alone he talked aloud pretending he was in the
presence of the woman. "Oh, you're just letting
on, you know you are," he declared. "I am going
to find out about you. You wait and see."

The young man got up and went back along the
path toward town leaving the fire blazing in the
wood. As he went through the streets the skates
clanked in his pocket. In his own room in the
New Willard House he built a fire in the stove

and lay down on top of the bed.   He began to
have lustful thoughts and pulling down the shade
of the window closed his eyes and turned his face
to the wall.   He took a pillow into his arms and
embraced it thinking first of the school teacher,
who by her words had stirred something within
him and later of Helen White, the slim daughter
of the town banker, with whom he had been for
a long time half in love.

By nine o'clock of that evening snow lay deep
in the streets and the weather had become bitter
cold.   It was difficult to walk about.   The stores
were dark and the people had crawled away to
their houses.   The evening train from Cleveland
was very late but nobody was interested in its ar-
rival.   By ten o'clock all but four of the eighteen
hundred citizens of the town were in bed.

Hop Higgins, the night watchman, was partially awake.   He was lame and carried a heavy
stick.   On dark nights he carried a lantern.   Between nine and ten o'clock he went his rounds.
Up and down Main Street he stumbled through
the drifts trying the doors of the stores.   Then
he went into alleyways and tried the back doors.
Finding all tight he hurried around the corner to
the New Willard House and beat on the door.
Through the rest of the night he intended to stay
by the stove.   "You go to bed.   I'll keep the

stove going," he said to the boy who slept on a cot in the hotel office.

Hop Higgins sat down by the stove and took off his shoes. When the boy had gone to sleep he began to think of his own affairs. He intended to paint his house in the spring and sat by the stove calculating the cost of paint and labor. That led him into other calculations. The night watchman was sixty years old and wanted to retire. He had been a soldier in the Civil War and drew a small pension. He hoped to find some new method of making a living and aspired to become a professional breeder of ferrets. Already he had four of the strangely shaped savage little creatures, that are used by sportsmen in the pursuit of rabbits, in the cellar of his house. "Now I have one male and three females," he mused. "If I am lucky by spring I shall have twelve or fifteen. In another year I shall be able to begin advertising ferrets for sale in the sporting papers."

The night watchman settled into his chair and his mind became a blank. He did not sleep. By years of practice he had trained himself to sit for hours through the long nights neither asleep nor awake. In the morning he was almost as refreshed as though he had slept.

With Hop Higgins safely stowed away in the

chair behind the stove only three people were awake in Winesburg. George Willard was in the office of the *Eagle* pretending to be at work on the writing of a story but in reality continuing the mood of the morning by the fire in the wood. In the bell tower of the Presbyterian Church the Reverend Curtis Hartman was sitting in the darkness preparing himself for a revelation from God, and Kate Swift, the school teacher, was leaving her house for a walk in the storm.

It was past ten o'clock when Kate Swift set out and the walk was unpremeditated. It was as though the man and the boy, by thinking of her, had driven her forth into the wintry streets. Aunt Elizabeth Swift had gone to the county seat concerning some business in connection with mortgages in which she had money invested and would not be back until the next day. By a huge stove, called a base burner, in the living room of the house sat the daughter reading a book. Suddenly she sprang to her feet and, snatching a cloak from a rack by the front door, ran out of the house.

At the age of thirty Kate Swift was not known in Winesburg as a pretty woman. Her complexion was not good and her face was covered with blotches that indicated ill health. Alone in the night in the winter streets she was lovely. Her back was straight, her shoulders square and her features were as the features of a tiny goddess on a pedestal in a garden in the dim light of a summer evening.

During the afternoon the school teacher had been to see Dr. Welling concerning her health. The doctor had scolded her and had declared she was in danger of losing her hearing. It was foolish for Kate Swift to be abroad in the storm, foolish and perhaps dangerous.

The woman in the streets did not remember the words of the doctor and would not have turned back had she remembered. She was very cold but after walking for five minutes no longer minded the cold. First she went to the end of her own street and then across a pair of hay scales set in the ground before a feed barn and into Trunion Pike. Along Trunion Pike she went to Ned Winter's barn and turning east followed a street of low frame houses that led over Gospel Hill and into Sucker Road that ran down a shallow valley past Ike Smead's chicken farm to Waterworks Pond. As she went along, the bold, excited mood that had driven her out of doors passed and then returned again.

There was something biting and forbidding in the character of Kate Swift. Everyone felt it. In the schoolroom she was silent, cold, and stern, and yet in an odd way very close to her pupils. Once in a long while something seemed to have come over her and she was happy. All of the children in the schoolroom felt the effect of her happiness. For a time they did not work but sat back in their chairs and looked at her.

With hands clasped behind her back the school teacher walked up and down in the schoolroom and talked very rapidly. It did not seem to matter what subject came into her mind. Once she talked to the children of Charles Lamb and made up strange intimate little stories concerning the life of the dead writer. The stories were told with the air of one who had lived in a house with Charles Lamb and knew all the secrets of his private life. The children were somewhat confused, thinking Charles Lamb must be someone who had once lived in Winesburg.

On another occasion the teacher talked to the children of Benvenuto Cellini. That time they laughed. What a bragging, blustering, brave, lovable fellow she made of the old artist! Concerning him also she invented anecdotes. There was one of a German music teacher who had a room above Cellini's lodgings in the city of Milan that made the boys guffaw. Sugars McNutts, a fat boy with red cheeks, laughed so hard that he became dizzy and fell off his seat and Kate Swift laughed with him. Then suddenly she became again cold and stern.

On the winter night when she walked through the deserted snow-covered streets, a crisis had come into the life of the school teacher. Although no one in Winesburg would have suspected it, her life had been very adventurous. It was still adventurous. Day by day as she worked in the schoolroom or walked in the streets, grief, hope, and desire fought within her. Behind a cold exterior the most extraordinary events transpired in her mind. The people of the town thought of her as a confirmed old maid and because she spoke sharply and went her own way thought her lacking in all the human feeling that did so much to make and mar their own lives. In reality she was the most eagerly passionate soul among them, and more than once, in the five years since she had come back from her travels to settle in Winesburg and become a school teacher, had been compelled to go out of the house and walk half through the night fighting out some battle raging within. Once on a night when it rained she had stayed out six hours and when she came home had a quarrel with Aunt Elizabeth Swift. "I am glad you're not a man," said the mother sharply. "More than once I've waited for your father to come home, not knowing what new mess he had got into. I've had my share of uncertainty and you cannot blame me if I do not want to see the worst side of him reproduced in you."

.   .   .   .

Kate Swift's mind was ablaze with thoughts of George Willard. In something he had written as a school boy she thought she had recognized the spark of genius and wanted to blow on the spark. One day in the summer she had gone to the *Eagle* office and finding the boy unoccupied had taken him out Main Street to the fair ground, where the two sat on a grassy bank and talked. The school teacher tried to bring home to the mind of the boy some conception of the difficulties he would have to face as a writer. "You will have to know life," she declared, and her voice trembled with earnestness. She took hold of George Willard's shoulders and turned him about so that she could look into his eyes. A passer-by might have thought them about to embrace. "If you are to become a writer you'll have to stop fooling with words," she explained. "It would be better to give up the notion of writing until you are better prepared. Now it's time to be living. I don't want to frighten you, but I would like to make you understand the import of what you think of attempting. You must not become a mere peddler of words. The thing to learn is to know what people are thinking about, not what they say."

On the evening before that stormy Thursday

night, when the Reverend Curtis Hartman sat in
the bell tower of the church waiting to look at her
body, young Willard had gone to visit the teacher
and to borrow a book. It was then the thing
happened that confused and puzzled the boy. He
had the book under his arm and was preparing to
depart. Again Kate Swift talked with great earnestness. Night was coming on and the light in
the room grew dim. As he turned to go she spoke
his name softly and with an impulsive movement
took hold of his hand. Because the reporter was
rapidly becoming a man something of his man's
appeal, combined with the winsomeness of the
boy, stirred the heart of the lonely woman. A
passionate desire to have him understand the import of life, to learn to interpret it truly and hon-
estly, swept over her. Leaning forward, her lips
brushed his cheek. At the same moment he for
the first time became aware of the marked beauty
of her features. They were both embarrassed,
and to relieve her feeling she became harsh and
domineering. "What's the use? It will be ten
years before you begin to understand what I mean
when I talk to you," she cried passionately.

.   .   .   .

On the night of the storm and while the minister sat in the church waiting for her, Kate Swift
went to the office of the *Winesburg Eagle*, in-
tending to have another talk with the boy. After

the long walk in the snow she was cold, lonely, and tired.   As she came through Main Street she saw the light from the print shop window shining on the snow and on an impulse opened the door and went in.   For an hour she sat by the stove in the office talking of life.   She talked with passionate earnestness.   The impulse that had driven her out into the snow poured itself out into talk. She became inspired as she sometimes did in the presence of the children in school.   A great eagerness to open the door of life to the boy, who had been her pupil and whom she thought might possess a talent for the understanding of life, had possession of her.   So strong was her passion that it became something physical.   Again her hands took hold of his shoulders and she turned him about.   In the dim light her eyes blazed.   She arose and laughed, not sharply as was customary with her, but in a queer, hesitating way.   "I must be going," she said.   "In a moment, if I stay, I'll be wanting to kiss you."

In the newspaper office a confusion arose.   Kate Swift turned and walked to the door.   She was a teacher but she was also a woman.   As she looked at George Willard, the passionate desire to be loved by a man, that had a thousand times before swept like a storm over her body, took possession of her.   In the lamplight George Willard looked

no longer a boy, but a man ready to play the part
of a man.

The school teacher let George Willard take her
into his arms. In the warm little office the air
became suddenly heavy and the strength went out
of her body. Leaning against a low counter by
the door she waited. When he came and put a
hand on her shoulder she turned and let her body
fall heavily against him. For George Willard
the confusion was immediately increased. For a
moment he held the body of the woman tightly
against his body and then it stiffened. Two sharp
little fists began to beat on his face. When the
school teacher had run away and left him alone, he
walked up and down in the office swearing furiously.

It was into this confusion that the Reverend
Curtis Hartman protruded himself. When he
came in George Willard thought the town had
gone mad. Shaking a bleeding fist in the air, the
minister proclaimed the woman George had only
a moment before held in his arms an instrument
of God bearing a message of truth.

.   .   .   .

George blew out the lamp by the window and
locking the door of the print shop went home.
Through the hotel office, past Hop Higgins lost in
his dream of the raising of ferrets, he went and up

into his own room.   The fire in the stove had
gone out and he undressed in the cold.   When he
got into bed the sheets were like blankets of dry
snow.

George Willard rolled about in the bed on
which he had lain in the afternoon hugging the
pillow and thinking thoughts of Kate Swift.   The
words of the minister, who he thought had gone
suddenly insane, rang in his ears.   His eyes stared
about the room.   The resentment, natural to the
baffled male, passed and he tried to understand
what had happened.   He could not make it out.
Over and over he turned the matter in his mind.
Hours passed and he began to think it must be
time for another day to come.   At four o'clock he
pulled the covers up about his neck and tried to
sleep.   When he became drowsy and closed his
eyes, he raised a hand and with it groped about in
the darkness.   "I have missed something.   I
have missed something Kate Swift was trying to
tell me," he muttered sleepily.   Then he slept
and in all Winesburg he was the last soul on that
winter night to go to sleep.

LONELINESS

HE was the son of Mrs. Al Robinson who once owned a farm on a side road leading off Trunion Pike, east of Winesburg and two miles beyond the town limits. The farmhouse was painted brown and the blinds to all of the windows facing the road were kept closed. In the road before the house a flock of chickens, accompanied by two guinea hens, lay in the deep dust. Enoch lived in the house with his mother in those days and when he was a young boy went to school at the Winesburg High School. Old citizens remembered him as a quiet, smiling youth inclined to silence. He walked in the middle of the road when he came into town and sometimes read a book. Drivers of teams had to shout and swear to make him realize where he was so that he would turn out of the beaten track and let them pass.

When he was twenty-one years old Enoch went to New York City and was a city man for fifteen years. He studied French and went to an art school, hoping to develop a faculty he had for drawing. In his own mind he planned to go to

Paris and to finish his art education among the masters there, but that never turned out.

Nothing ever turned out for Enoch Robinson. He could draw well enough and he had many odd delicate thoughts hidden away in his brain that might have expressed themselves through the brush of a painter, but he was always a child and that was a handicap to his worldly development. He never grew up and of course he couldn't understand people and he couldn't make people understand him. The child in him kept bumping against things, against actualities like money and sex and opinions. Once he was hit by a street car and thrown against an iron post. That made him lame. It was one of the many things that kept things from turning out for Enoch Robinson.

In New York City, when he first went there to live and before he became confused and disconcerted by the facts of life, Enoch went about a good deal with young men. He got into a group of other young artists, both men and women, and in the evenings they sometimes came to visit him in his room. Once he got drunk and was taken to a police station where a police magistrate frightened him horribly, and once he tried to have an affair with a woman of the town met on the sidewalk before his lodging house. The woman and Enoch walked together three blocks and then the young man grew afraid and ran away. The woman had been drinking and the incident amused her. She leaned against the wall of a building and laughed so heartily that another man stopped and laughed with her. The two went away together, still laughing, and Enoch crept off to his room trembling and vexed.

The room in which young Robinson lived in New York faced Washington Square and was long and narrow like a hallway. It is important to get that fixed in your mind. The story of Enoch is in fact the story of a room almost more than it is the story of a man.

And so into the room in the evening came young Enoch's friends. There was nothing particularly striking about them except that they were artists of the kind that talk. Everyone knows of the talking artists. Throughout all of the known history of the world they have gathered in rooms and talked. They talk of art and are passionately, almost feverishly, in earnest about it. They think it matters much more than it does.

And so these people gathered and smoked cigarettes and talked and Enoch Robinson, the boy from the farm near Winesburg, was there. He stayed in a corner and for the most part said nothing. How his big blue childlike eyes stared about! On the walls were pictures he had made, crude things, half finished. His friends talked of these. Leaning back in their chairs, they talked.

and talked with their heads rocking from side to side. Words were said about line and values and composition, lots of words, such as are always being said.

Enoch wanted to talk too but he didn't know how. He was too excited to talk coherently. When he tried he sputtered and stammered and his voice sounded strange and squeaky to him. That made him stop talking. He knew what he wanted to say, but he knew also that he could never by any possibility say it. When a picture he had painted was under discussion, he wanted to burst out with something like this: "You don't get the point," he wanted to explain: "the picture you see doesn't consist of the things you see and say words about. There is something else, something you don't see at all, something you aren't intended to see. Look at this one over here, by the door here, where the light from the window falls on it. The dark spot by the road that you might not notice at all is, you see, the beginning of everything. There is a clump of elders there such as used to grow beside the road before our house back in Winesburg, Ohio, and in among the elders there is something hidden. It is a woman, that's what it is. She has been thrown from a horse and the horse has run away out of sight. Do you not see how the old man who drives a cart looks anxiously about? That is Thad Gray-back who has a farm up the road. He is taking corn to Winesburg to be ground into meal at Comstock's mill. He knows there is something in the elders, something hidden away, and yet he doesn't quite know.

"It's a woman you see, that's what it is! It's a woman and, oh, she is lovely! She is hurt and is suffering but she makes no sound. Don't you see how it is? She lies quite still, white and still, and the beauty comes out from her and spreads over everything. It is in the sky back there and all around everywhere. I didn't try to paint the woman, of course. She is too beautiful to be painted. How dull to talk of composition and such things! Why do you not look at the sky and then run away as I used to do when I was a boy back there in Winesburg, Ohio?"

That is the kind of thing young Enoch Robinson trembled to say to the guests who came into his room when he was a young fellow in New York City, but he always ended by saying nothing. Then he began to doubt his own mind. He was afraid the things he felt were not getting expressed in the pictures he painted. In a half indignant mood he stopped inviting people into his room and presently got into the habit of locking the door. He began to think that enough people had visited him, that he did not need people any more. With quick imagination he began to invent his own people to whom he could really talk and to whom he explained the things he had been unable to explain to living people.   His room began to be inhabited by the spirits of men and women among whom he went, in his turn saying words.   It was as though every one Enoch Robinson had ever seen had left with him some essence of himself, something he could mould and change to suit his own fancy, something that understood all about such things as the wounded woman behind the elders in the pictures.

The mild, blue-eyed young Ohio boy was a complete egotist, as all children are egotists.   He did not want friends for the quite simple reason that no child wants friends.   He wanted most of all the people of his own mind, people with whom he could really talk, people he could harangue and scold by the hour, servants, you see, to his fancy. Among these people he was always self-confident and bold.   They might talk, to be sure, and even have opinions of their own, but always he talked last and best.   He was like a writer busy among the figures of his brain, a kind of tiny blue-eyed king he was, in a six-dollar room facing Washington Square in the city of New York.

Then Enoch Robinson got married.   He began to get lonely and to want to touch actual flesh and bone people with his hands.   Days passed when his room seemed empty.   Lust visited his body and desire grew in his mind. At night strange fevers, burning within, kept him awake. He married a girl who sat in a chair next to his own in the art school and went to live in an apartment house in Brooklyn. Two children were born to the woman he married, and Enoch got a job in a place where illustrations are made for advertisements.

That began another phase of Enoch's life. He began to play at a new game. For a while he was very proud of himself in the rôle of producing citizen of the world. He dismissed the essence of things and played with realities. In the fall he voted at an election and he had a newspaper thrown on his porch each morning. When in the evening he came home from work he got off a street car and walked sedately along behind some business man, striving to look very substantial and important. As a payer of taxes he thought he should post himself on how things are run. "I'm getting to be of some moment, a real part of things, of the state and the city and all that," he told himself with an amusing miniature air of dignity. Once coming home from Philadelphia, he had a discussion with a man met on a train. Enoch talked about the advisability of the government's owning and operating the railroads and the man gave him a cigar. It was Enoch's notion that such a move on the part of the government would be a good thing, and he grew quite excited as he talked. Later he remembered his own words with pleasure. "I gave him something to think about, that fellow," he muttered to himself as he climbed the stairs to his Brooklyn apartment.

To be sure, Enoch's marriage did not turn out. He himself brought it to an end. He began to feel choked and walled in by the life in the apartment, and to feel toward his wife and even toward his children as he had felt concerning the friends who once came to visit him. He began to tell little lies about business engagements that would give him freedom to walk alone in the street at night and, the chance offering, he secretly re-rented the room facing Washington Square. Then Mrs. Al Robinson died on the farm near Winesburg, and he got eight thousand dollars from the bank that acted as trustee of her estate. That took Enoch out of the world of men altogether. He gave the money to his wife and told her he could not live in the apartment any more. She cried and was angry and threatened, but he only stared at her and went his own way. In reality the wife did not care much. She thought Enoch slightly insane and was a little afraid of him. When it was quite sure that he would never come back, she took the two children and went to a village in Connecticut where she had lived as a girl. In the end she

married a man who bought and sold real estate
and was contented enough.

And so Enoch Robinson stayed in the New
York room among the people of his fancy, playing with them, talking to them, happy as a child is
happy. They were an odd lot, Enoch's people.
They were made, I suppose, out of real people he
had seen and who had for some obscure reason
made an appeal to him. There was a woman
with a sword in her hand, an old man with a long
white beard who went about followed by a dog, a
young girl whose stockings were always coming
down and hanging over her shoe tops. There
must have been two dozen of the shadow people,
invented by the child-mind of Enoch Robinson,
who lived in the room with him.

And Enoch was happy. Into the room he went
and locked the door. With an absurd air of importance he talked aloud, giving instructions, making comments on life. He was happy and satisfied to go on making his living in the advertising
place until something happened. Of course something did happen. That is why he went back to
live in Winesburg and why we know about him.
The thing that happened was a woman. It would
be that way. He was too happy. Something
had to come into his world. Something had to
drive him out of the New York room to live out
his life, an obscure, jerky little figure, bobbing up

and down on the streets of an Ohio town at evening when the sun was going down behind the roof
of Wesley Moyer's livery barn.

About the thing that happened.　Enoch told
George Willard about it one night.　He wanted
to talk to someone, and he chose the young newspaper reporter because the two happened to be
thrown together at a time when the younger man
was in a mood to understand.

Youthful sadness, young man's sadness, the
sadness of a growing boy in a village at the year's
end opened the lips of the old man.　The sadness
was in the heart of George Willard and was without meaning, but it appealed to Enoch Robinson.

It rained on the evening when the two met and
talked, a drizzly wet October rain.　The fruition
of the year had come and the night should have
been fine with a moon in the sky and the crisp
sharp promise of frost in the air, but it wasn't
that way.　It rained and little puddles of water
shone under the street lamps on Main Street.　In
the woods in the darkness beyond the Fair Ground
water dripped from the black trees.　Beneath the
trees wet leaves were pasted against tree roots
that protruded from the ground.　In gardens
back of houses in Winesburg dry shriveled potato
vines lay sprawling on the ground.　Men who had
finished the evening meal and who had planned to
go uptown to talk the evening away with other

men at the back of some store changed their
minds. George Willard tramped about in the
rain and was glad that it rained. He felt that
way. He was like Enoch Robinson on the evenings when the old man came down out of his
room and wandered alone in the streets. He was
like that only that George Willard had become a
tall young man and did not think it manly to weep
and carry on. For a month his mother had been
very ill and that had something to do with his sadness, but not much. He thought about himself
and to the young that always brings sadness.

Enoch Robinson and George Willard met beneath a wooden awning that extended out over the
sidewalk before Voight's wagon shop on Maumee
Street just off the main street of Winesburg.
They went together from there through the rain-
washed streets to the older man's room on the
third floor of the Heffner Block. The young reporter went willingly enough. Enoch Robinson
asked him to go after the two had talked for ten
minutes. The boy was a little afraid but had
never been more curious in his life. A hundred
times he had heard the old man spoken of as a
little off his head and he thought himself rather
brave and manly to go at all. From the very beginning, in the street in the rain, the old man
talked in a queer way, trying to tell the story of
the room in Washington Square and of his life in

the room. "You'll understand if you try hard enough," he said conclusively. "I have looked at you when you went past me on the street and I think you can understand. It isn't hard. All you have to do is to believe what I say, just listen and believe, that's all there is to it."

It was past eleven o'clock that evening when Old Enoch, talking to George Willard in the room in the Heffner Block, came to the vital thing, the story of the woman and of what drove him out of the city to live out his life alone and defeated in Winesburg. He sat on a cot by the window with his head in his hand and George Willard was in a chair by a table. A kerosene lamp sat on the table and the room, although almost bare of furniture, was scrupulously clean. As the man talked George Willard began to feel that he would like to get out of the chair and sit on the cot also. He wanted to put his arms about the little old man. In the half darkness the man talked and the boy listened, filled with sadness.

"She got to coming in there after there hadn't been anyone in the room for years," said Enoch Robinson. "She saw me in the hallway of the house and we got acquainted. I don't know just what she did in her own room. I never went there. I think she was a musician and played a violin. Every now and then she came and knocked at the door and I opened it. In she came and sat down beside me, just sat and looked about and said nothing.   Anyway, she said nothing that mattered."

The old man arose from the cot and moved about the room.   The overcoat he wore was wet from the rain and drops of water kept falling with a soft little thump on the floor.   When he again sat upon the cot George Willard got out of the chair and sat beside him.

"I had a feeling about her.   She sat there in the room with me and she was too big for the room.   I felt that she was driving everything else away.   We just talked of little things, but I couldn't sit still.   I wanted to touch her with my fingers and to kiss her.   Her hands were so strong and her face was so good and she looked at me all the time."

The trembling voice of the old man became silent and his body shook as from a chill.   "I was afraid," he whispered.   "I was terribly afraid. I didn't want to let her come in when she knocked at the door but I couldn't sit still.   'No, no,' I said to myself, but I got up and opened the door just the same.   She was so grown up, you see.   She was a woman.   I thought she would be bigger than I was there in that room."

Enoch Robinson stared at George Willard, his childlike blue eyes shining in the lamplight.   Again he shivered.   "I wanted her and all the time I

didn't want her," he explained. "Then I began
to tell her about my people, about everything that
meant anything to me. I tried to keep quiet, to
keep myself to myself, but I couldn't. I felt just
as I did about opening the door. Sometimes I
ached to have her go away and never come back
any more."

The old man sprang to his feet and his voice
shook with excitement. "One night something
happened. I became mad to make her understand
me and to know what a big thing I was in that
room. I wanted her to see how important I was.
I told her over and over. When she tried to go
away, I ran and locked the door. I followed her
about. I talked and talked and then all of a sudden things went to smash. A look came into her
eyes and I knew she did understand. Maybe she
had understood all the time. I was furious. I
couldn't stand it. I wanted her to understand but,
don't you see, I couldn't let her understand. I
felt that then she would know everything, that
I would be submerged, drowned out, you see.
That's how it is. I don't know why."

The old man dropped into a chair by the lamp
and the boy listened, filled with awe. "Go away,
boy," said the man. "Don't stay here with me
any more.. I thought it might be a good thing to
tell you but it isn't. I don't want to talk any
more. Go away."

George Willard shook his head and a note of command came into his voice. "Don't stop now. Tell me the rest of it," he commanded sharply. "What happened? Tell me the rest of the story."

Enoch Robinson sprang to his feet and ran to the window that looked down into the deserted main street of Winesburg. George Willard followed. By the window the two stood, the tall awkward boy-man and the little wrinkled man-boy. The childish, eager voice carried forward the tale. "I swore at her," he explained. "I said vile words. I ordered her to go away and not to come back. Oh, I said terrible things. At first she pretended not to understand but I kept at it. I screamed and stamped on the floor. I made the house ring with my curses. I didn't want ever to see her again and I knew, after some of the things I said, that I never would see her again."

The old man's voice broke and he shook his head. "Things went to smash," he said quietly and sadly. "Out she went through the door and all the life there had been in the room followed her out. She took all of my people away. They all went out through the door after her. That's the way it was."

George Willard turned and went out of Enoch Robinson's room. In the darkness by the window, as he went through the door, he could hear the thin old voice whimpering and complaining. "I'm alone, all alone here," said the voice. "It was warm and friendly in my room but now I'm all alone."

AN AWAKENING

BELLE CARPENTER had a dark skin, grey eyes and thick lips. She was tall and strong. When black thoughts visited her she grew angry and wished she were a man and could fight someone with her fists. She worked in the millinery shop kept by Mrs. Nate McHugh and during the day sat trimming hats by a window at the rear of the store. She was the daughter of Henry Carpenter, bookkeeper in the First National Bank of Winesburg, and lived with him in a gloomy old house far out at the end of Buckeye Street. The house was surrounded by pine trees and there was no grass beneath the trees. A rusty tin eaves-trough had slipped from its fastenings at the back of the house and when the wind blew it beat against the roof of a small shed, making a dismal drumming noise that sometimes persisted all through the night.

When she was a young girl Henry Carpenter made life almost unbearable for Belle, but as she emerged from girlhood into womanhood he lost his power over her. The bookkeeper's life was made up of innumerable little pettinesses. When he went to the bank in the morning he stepped into a closet and put on a black alpaca coat that had become shabby with age. At night when he returned to his home he donned another black alpaca coat. Every evening he pressed the clothes worn in the streets. He had invented an arrangement of boards for the purpose. The trousers to his street suit were placed between the boards and the boards were clamped together with heavy screws. In the morning he wiped the boards with a damp cloth and stood them upright behind the dining room door. If they were moved during the day he was speechless with anger and did not recover his equilibrium for a week.

The bank cashier was a little bully and was afraid of his daughter. She, he realized, knew the story of his brutal treatment of her mother and hated him for it. One day she went home at noon and carried a handful of soft mud, taken from the road, into the house. With the mud she smeared the face of the boards used for the pressing of trousers and then went back to her work feeling relieved and happy.

Belle Carpenter occasionally walked out in the evening with George Willard. Secretly she loved another man, but her love affair, about which no one knew, caused her much anxiety. She was in love with Ed Handby, bartender in Ed Griffith's Saloon, and went about with the young reporter as a kind of relief to her feelings. She did not think that her station in life would permit her to be seen in the company of the bartender and walked about under the trees with George Willard and let him kiss her to relieve a longing that was very insistent in her nature. She felt that she could keep the younger man within bounds. About Ed Handby she was somewhat uncertain.

Handby, the bartender, was a tall, broad-shouldered man of thirty who lived in a room upstairs above Griffith's saloon. His fists were large and his eyes unusually small, but his voice, as though striving to conceal the power back of his fists, was soft and quiet.

At twenty-five the bartender had inherited a large farm from an uncle in Indiana. When sold, the farm brought in eight thousand dollars which Ed spent in six months. Going to Sandusky, on Lake Erie, he began an orgy of dissipation, the story of which afterward filled his home town with awe. Here and there he went throwing the money about, driving carriages through the streets, giving wine parties to crowds of men and women, playing cards for high stakes and keeping mistresses whose wardrobes cost him hundreds of dollars. One night at a resort called Cedar Point, he got into a fight and ran amuck like a wild thing. With his fist he broke a large mirror in the wash room of a hotel and later went about smashing windows and breaking chairs in dance halls for the joy of hearing the glass rattle on the floor and seeing the terror in the eyes of clerks who had come from Sandusky to spend the evening at the resort with their sweethearts.

The affair between Ed Handby and Belle Carpenter on the surface amounted to nothing. He had succeeded in spending but one evening in her company. On that evening he hired a horse and buggy at Wesley Moyer's livery barn and took her for a drive. The conviction that she was the woman his nature demanded and that he must get her settled upon him and he told her of his desires. The bartender was ready to marry and to begin trying to earn money for the support of his wife, but so simple was his nature that he found it difficult to explain his intentions. His body ached with physical longing and with his body he expressed himself. Taking the milliner into his arms and holding her tightly in spite of her struggles, he kissed her until she became helpless. Then he brought her back to town and let her out of the buggy. "When I get hold of you again I'll not let you go. You can't play with me," he declared as he turned to drive away. Then, jumping out of the buggy, he gripped her shoulders with his strong hands. "I'll keep you for good the next time," he said. "You might as well make up your mind to that. It's you and me for it and I'm going to have you before I get through."

One night in January when there was a new moon George Willard, who was in Ed Handby's mind the only obstacle to his getting Belle Carpenter, went for a walk. Early that evening George went into Ransom Surbeck's pool room with Seth Richmond and Art Wilson, son of the town butcher. Seth Richmond stood with his back against the wall and remained silent, but George Willard talked. The pool room was filled with Winesburg boys and they talked of women. The young reporter got into that vein. He said that women should look out for themselves, that the fellow who went out with a girl was not responsible for what happened. As he talked he looked about, eager for attention. He held the floor for five minutes and then Art Wilson began to talk. Art was learning the barber's trade in Cal Prouse's shop and already began to consider himself an authority in such matters as baseball, horse racing, drinking, and going about with women. He began to tell of a night when he with two men from Winesburg went into a house of prostitution at the county seat. The butcher's son held a cigar in the side of his mouth and as he talked spat on the floor. "The women in the place couldn't embarrass me although they tried hard enough," he boasted. "One of the girls in the house tried to get fresh, but I fooled her.   As soon as she began to talk I went and sat in her lap. Everyone in the room laughed when I kissed her. I taught her to let me alone."

George Willard went out of the pool room and into Main Street.   For days the weather had been bitter cold with a high wind blowing down on the town from Lake Erie, eighteen miles to the north, but on that night the wind had died away and a new moon made the night unusually lovely. Without thinking where he was going or what he wanted to do, George went out of Main Street and began walking in dimly lighted streets filled with frame houses.

Out of doors under the black sky filled with stars he forgot his companions of the pool room. Because it was dark and he was alone he began to talk aloud.   In a spirit of play he reeled along the street imitating a drunken man and then imagined himself a soldier clad in shining boots that reached to the knees and wearing a sword that jingled as he walked.   As a soldier he pictured himself as an inspector, passing before a long line of men who stood at attention.   He began to examine the accoutrements of the men.   Before a tree he stopped and began to scold.   "Your pack is not in order," he said sharply.   "How many times will I have to speak of this matter?   Everything must be in order here.   We have a difficult task before us and no difficult task can be done without order."

Hypnotized by his own words, the young man stumbled along the board sidewalk saying more words. "There is a law for armies and for men too," he muttered, lost in reflection. "The law begins with little things and spreads out until it covers everything. In every little thing there must be order, in the place where men work, in their clothes, in their thoughts. I myself must be orderly. I must learn that law. I must get myself into touch with something orderly and big that swings through the night like a star. In my little way I must begin to learn something, to give and swing and work with life, with the law."

George Willard stopped by a picket fence near a street lamp and his body began to tremble. He had never before thought such thoughts as had just come into his head and he wondered where they had come from. For the moment it seemed to him that some voice outside of himself had been talking as he walked. He was amazed and delighted with his own mind and when he walked on again spoke of the matter with fervor. "To come out of Ransom Surbeck's pool room and think things like that," he whispered. "It is better to be alone. If I talked like Art Wilson the boys would understand me but they wouldn't understand what I've been thinking down here."

In Winesburg, as in all Ohio towns of twenty years ago, there was a section in which lived day laborers. As the time of factories had not yet come, the laborers worked in the fields or were section hands on the railroads. They worked twelve hours a day and received one dollar for the long day of toil. The houses in which they lived were small cheaply constructed wooden affairs with a garden at the back. The more comfortable among them kept cows and perhaps a pig, housed in a little shed at the rear of the garden.

With his head filled with resounding thoughts, George Willard walked into such a street on the clear January night. The street was dimly lighted and in places there was no sidewalk. In the scene that lay about him there was something that excited his already aroused fancy. For a year he had been devoting all of his odd moments to the reading of books and now some tale he had read concerning life in old world towns of the middle ages came sharply back to his mind so that he stumbled forward with the curious feeling of one revisiting a place that had been a part of some former existence. On an impulse he turned out of the street and went into a little dark alleyway behind the sheds in which lived the cows and pigs.

For a half hour he stayed in the alleyway, smelling the strong smell of animals too closely housed and letting his mind play with the strange new thoughts that came to him. The very rankness of the smell of manure in the clear sweet air awoke something heady in his brain. The poor little houses lighted by kerosene lamps, the smoke from the chimneys mounting straight up into the clear air, the grunting of pigs, the women clad in cheap calico dresses and washing dishes in the kitchens, the footsteps of men coming out of the houses and going off to the stores and saloons of Main Street, the dogs barking and the children crying—all of these things made him seem, as he lurked in the darkness, oddly detached and apart from all life.

The excited young man, unable to bear the weight of his own thoughts, began to move cautiously along the alleyway. A dog attacked him and had to be driven away with stones, and a man appeared at the door of one of the houses and swore at the dog. George went into a vacant lot and throwing back his head looked up at the sky. He felt unutterably big and remade by the simple experience through which he had been passing and in a kind of fervor of emotion put up his hands, thrusting them into the darkness above his head and muttering words. The desire to say words overcame him and he said words without meaning, rolling them over on his tongue and saying them because they were brave words, full of meaning.

"Death," he muttered, "night, the sea, fear, love-liness."

George Willard came out of the vacant lot and stood again on the sidewalk facing the houses. He felt that all of the people in the little street must be brothers and sisters to him and he wished he had the courage to call them out of their houses and to shake their hands. "If there were only a woman here I would take hold of her hand and we would run until we were both tired out," he thought. "That would make me feel better." With the thought of a woman in his mind he walked out of the street and went toward the house where Belle Carpenter lived. He thought she would understand his mood and that he could achieve in her presence a position he had long been wanting to achieve. In the past when he had been with her and had kissed her lips he had come away filled with anger at himself. He had felt like one being used for some obscure purpose and had not enjoyed the feeling. Now he thought he had suddenly become too big to be used.

When George got to Belle Carpenter's house there had already been a visitor there before him. Ed Handby had come to the door and calling Belle out of the house had tried to talk to her. He had wanted to ask the woman to come away with him and to be his wife, but when she came and stood by the door he lost his self-assurance and became sullen. "You stay away from that kid," he growled, thinking of George Willard, and then, not knowing what else to say, turned to go away. "If I catch you together I will break your bones and his too," he added. The bartender had come to woo, not to threaten, and was angry with himself because of his failure.

When her lover had departed Belle went indoors and ran hurriedly upstairs. From a window at the upper part of the house she saw Ed Handby cross the street and sit down on a horse block before the house of a neighbor. In the dim light the man sat motionless holding his head in his hands. She was made happy by the sight, and when George Willard came to the door she greeted him effusively and hurriedly put on her hat. She thought that, as she walked through the streets with young Willard, Ed Handby would follow and she wanted to make him suffer.

For an hour Belle Carpenter and the young reporter walked about under the trees in the sweet night air. George Willard was full of big words. The sense of power that had come to him during the hour in the darkness in the alleyway remained with him and he talked boldly, swaggering along and swinging his arms about. He wanted to make Belle Carpenter realize that he was aware of his former weakness and that he had changed. "You'll find me different," he declared, thrusting his hands into his pockets and looking boldly into her eyes. "I don't know why but it is so. You've got to take me for a man or let me alone. That's how it is."

Up and down the quiet streets under the new moon went the woman and the boy. When George had finished talking they turned down a side street and went across a bridge into a path that ran up the side of a hill. The hill began at Waterworks Pond and climbed upwards to the Winesburg Fair Grounds. On the hillside grew dense bushes and small trees and among the bushes were little open spaces carpeted with long grass, now stiff and frozen.

As he walked behind the woman up the hill George Willard's heart began to beat rapidly and his shoulders straightened. Suddenly he decided that Belle Carpenter was about to surrender herself to him. The new force that had manifested itself in him had, he felt, been at work upon her and had led to her conquest. The thought made him half drunk with the sense of masculine power. Although he had been annoyed that as they walked about she had not seemed to be listening to his words, the fact that she had accompanied him to this place took all his doubts away. "It is different. Everything has become different," he thought and taking hold of her shoulder turned

her about and stood looking at her, his eyes shining
with pride.

Belle Carpenter did not resist. When he
kissed her upon the lips she leaned heavily against
him and looked over his shoulder into the darkness. In her whole attitude there was a suggestion of waiting. Again, as in the alleyway,
George Willard's mind ran off into words and,
holding the woman tightly he whispered the words
into the still night. "Lust," he whispered, "lust
and night and women."

George Willard did not understand what happened to him that night on the hillside. Later,
when he got to his own room, he wanted to weep
and then grew half insane with anger and hate.
He hated Belle Carpenter and was sure that all
his life he would continue to hate her. On the
hillside he had led the woman to one of the little
open spaces among the bushes and had dropped to
his knees beside her. As in the vacant lot, by the
laborers' houses, he had put up his hands in grat-
itude for the new power in himself and was waiting for the woman to speak when Ed Handby
appeared.

The bartender did not want to beat the boy,
who he thought had tried to take his woman away.
He knew that beating was unnecessary, that he had
power within himself to accomplish his purpose

without using his fists.   Gripping George by the
shoulder and pulling him to his feet, he held him
with one hand while he looked at Belle Carpenter
seated on the grass.   Then with a quick wide
movement of his arm he sent the younger man
sprawling away into the bushes and began to bully
the woman, who had risen to her feet.   "You're
no good," he said roughly.   "I've half a mind
not to bother with you.   I'd let you alone if I
didn't want you so much."

On his hands and knees in the bushes George
Willard stared at the scene before him and tried
hard to think.   He prepared to spring at the man
who had humiliated him.   To be beaten seemed
to be infinitely better than to be thus hurled igno-
miniously aside.

Three times the young reporter sprang at Ed
Handby and each time the bartender, catching him
by the shoulder, hurled him back into the bushes.
The older man seemed prepared to keep the exercise going indefinitely but George Willard's
head struck the root of a tree and he lay still.
Then Ed Hanby took Belle Carpenter by the arm
and marched her away.

George heard the man and woman making their
way through the bushes.   As he crept down the
hillside his heart was sick within him.   He hated
himself and he hated the fate that had brought
about his humiliation.   When his mind went back

to the hour alone in the alleyway he was puzzled and stopping in the darkness listened, hoping to hear again the voice outside himself that had so short a time before put new courage into his heart. When his way homeward led him again into the street of frame houses he could not bear the sight and began to run, wanting to get quickly out of the neighborhood that now seemed to him utterly squalid and commonplace.

"QUEER"

FROM his seat on a box in the rough board
shed that stuck like a burr on the rear of
Cowley & Son's store in Winesburg, Elmer
Cowley, the junior member of the firm, could
see through a dirty window into the printshop
of the *Winesburg Eagle*. Elmer was putting
new shoelaces in his shoes. They did not go
in readily and he had to take the shoes off.
With the shoes in his hand he sat looking at a
large hole in the heel of one of his stockings.
Then looking quickly up he saw George Willard,
the only newspaper reporter in Winesburg, standing at the back door of the *Eagle* printshop and
staring absent-mindedly about. "Well, well, what
next!" exclaimed the young man with the shoes in
his hand, jumping to his feet and creeping away
from the window.

A flush crept into Elmer Cowley's face and his
hands began to tremble. In Cowley & Son's store
a Jewish traveling salesman stood by the counter
talking to his father. He imagined the reporter
could hear what was being said and the thought
made him furious. With one of the shoes still

held in his hand he stood in a corner of the shed and stamped with a stockinged foot upon the board floor.

Cowley & Son's store did not face the main street of Winesburg. The front was on Maumee Street and beyond it was Voight's wagon shop and a shed for the sheltering of farmers' horses. Beside the store an alleyway ran behind the main street stores and all day drays and delivery wagons, intent on bringing in and taking out goods, passed up and down. The store itself was indescribable. Will Henderson once said of it that it sold everything and nothing. In the window facing Maumee Street stood a chunk of coal as large as an apple barrel, to indicate that orders for coal were taken, and beside the black mass of the coal stood three combs of honey grown brown and dirty in their wooden frames.

The honey had stood in the store window for six months. It was for sale as were also the coat hangers, patent suspender buttons, cans of roof paint, bottles of rheumatism cure and a substitute for coffee that companioned the honey in its patient willingness to serve the public.

Ebenezer Cowley, the man who stood in the store listening to the eager patter of words that fell from the lips of the traveling man, was tall and lean and looked unwashed. On his scrawny neck was a large wen partially covered by a grey beard. He wore a long Prince Albert coat. The coat had been purchased to serve as a wedding garment. Before he became a merchant Ebenezer was a farmer and after his marriage he wore the Prince Albert coat to church on Sundays and on Saturday afternoons when he came into town to trade. When he sold the farm to become a merchant he wore the coat constantly. It had become brown with age and was covered with grease spots, but in it Ebenezer always felt dressed up and ready for the day in town.

As a merchant Ebenezer was not happily placed in life and he had not been happily placed as a farmer. Still he existed. His family, consisting of a daughter named Mabel and the son, lived with him in rooms above the store and it did not cost them much to live. His troubles were not financial. His unhappiness as a merchant lay in the fact that when a traveling man with wares to be sold came in at the front door he was afraid. Behind the counter he stood shaking his head. He was afraid, first that he would stubbornly refuse to buy and thus lose the opportunity to sell again; second that he would not be stubborn enough and would in a moment of weakness buy what could not be sold.

In the store on the morning when Elmer Cowley saw George Willard standing and apparently listening at the back door of the *Eagle* printshop, a situation had arisen that always stirred the son's wrath. The traveling man talked and Ebenezer listened, his whole figure expressing uncertainty. "You see how quickly it is done," said the traveling man who had for sale a small flat metal substitute for collar buttons. With one hand he quickly unfastened a collar from his shirt and then fastened it on again. He assumed a flattering wheedling tone. "I tell you what, men have come to the end of all this fooling with collar buttons and you are the man to make money out of the change that is coming. I am offering you the exclusive agency for this town. Take twenty dozen of these fasteners and I'll not visit any other store. I'll leave the field to you."

The traveling man leaned over the counter and tapped with his finger on Ebenezer's breast. "It's an opportunity and I want you to take it," he urged. "A friend of mine told me about you. 'See that man Cowley,' he said. 'He's a live one.'"

The traveling man paused and waited. Taking a book from his pocket he began writing out the order. Still holding the shoe in his hand Elmer Cowley went through the store, past the two absorbed men, to a glass show case near the front door. He took a cheap revolver from the case and began to wave it about. "You get out of here!" he shrieked. "We don't want any collar fasteners here." An idea came to him. "Mind, I'm not making any threat," he added. "I don't say I'll shoot. Maybe I just took this gun out of the case to look at it. But you better get out. Yes sir, I'll say that. You better grab up your things and get out."

The young storekeeper's voice rose to a scream and going behind the counter he began to advance upon the two men. "We're through being fools here!" he cried. "We ain't going to buy any more stuff until we begin to sell. We ain't going to keep on being queer and have folks staring and listening. You get out of here!"

The traveling man left. Raking the samples of collar fasteners off the counter into a black leather bag, he ran. He was a small man and very bow-legged and he ran awkwardly. The black bag caught against the door and he stumbled and fell. "Crazy, that's what he is—crazy!" he sputtered as he arose from the sidewalk and hurried away.

In the store Elmer Cowley and his father stared at each other. Now that the immediate object of his wrath had fled, the younger man was embarrassed. "Well, I meant it. I think we've been queer long enough," he declared, going to the showcase and replacing the revolver. Sitting on a barrel he pulled on and fastened the shoe he had been holding in his hand. He was waiting for some word of understanding from his father but when Ebenezer spoke his words only served to reawaken the wrath in the son and the young man ran out of the store without replying. Scratching his grey beard with his long dirty fingers, the merchant looked at his son with the same wavering uncertain stare with which he had confronted the traveling man. "I'll be starched," he said softly. "Well, well, I'll be washed and ironed and starched!"

Elmer Cowley went out of Winesburg and along a country road that paralleled the railroad track. He did not know where he was going or what he was going to do. In the shelter of a deep cut where the road, after turning sharply to the right, dipped under the tracks he stopped and the passion that had been the cause of his outburst in the store began to again find expression. "I will not be queer—one to be looked at and listened to," he declared aloud. "I'll be like other people. I'll show that George Willard. He'll find out. I'll show him!"

The distraught young man stood in the middle of the road and glared back at the town. He did not know the reporter George Willard and had no special feeling concerning the tall boy who ran about town gathering the town news. The reporter had merely come, by his presence in the office and in the printshop of the *Winesburg Eagle*, to stand for something in the young merchant's mind. He thought the boy who passed and re-passed Cowley & Son's store and who stopped to talk to people in the street must be thinking of him and perhaps laughing at him. George Willard, he felt, belonged to the town, typified the town, represented in his person the spirit of the town. Elmer Cowley could not have believed that George Willard had also his days of unhappiness, that vague hungers and secret unnamable desires visited also his mind. Did he not represent public opinion and had not the public opinion of Winesburg condemned the Cowleys to queerness? Did he not walk whistling and laughing through Main Street? Might not one by striking his person strike also the greater enemy—the thing that smiled and went its own way—the judgment of Winesburg?

Elmer Cowley was extraordinarily tall and his arms were long and powerful. His hair, his eye-brows, and the downy beard that had begun to grow upon his chin, were pale almost to white-ness. His teeth protruded from between his lips and his eyes were blue with the colorless blueness of the marbles called "aggies" that the boys of Winesburg carried in their pockets. Elmer had lived in Winesburg for a year and had made no friends. He was, he felt, one condemned to go through life without friends and he hated the thought.

Sullenly the tall young man tramped along the road with his hands stuffed into his trouser pockets. The day was cold with a raw wind, but presently the sun began to shine and the road became soft and muddy. The tops of the ridges of frozen mud that formed the road began to melt and the mud clung to Elmer's shoes. His feet became cold. When he had gone several miles he turned off the road, crossed a field and entered a wood. In the wood he gathered sticks to build a fire by which he sat trying to warm himself, miserable in body and in mind.

For two hours he sat on the log by the fire and then, arising and creeping cautiously through a mass of underbrush, he went to a fence and looked across fields to a small farmhouse surrounded by low sheds. A smile came to his lips and he began making motions with his long arms to a man who was husking corn in one of the fields.

In his hour of misery the young merchant had returned to the farm where he had lived through boyhood and where there was another human being to whom he felt he could explain himself. The man on the farm was a half-witted old fellow named Mook. He had once been employed by Ebenezer Cowley and had stayed on the farm when it was sold. The old man lived in one of the unpainted sheds back of the farmhouse and puttered about all day in the fields.

Mook the half-wit lived happily. With child-like faith he believed in the intelligence of the animals that lived in the sheds with him, and when he was lonely held long conversations with the cows, the pigs, and even with the chickens that ran about the barnyard. He it was who had put the expression regarding being "laundered" into the mouth of his former employer. When excited or surprised by anything he smiled vaguely and muttered: "I'll be washed and ironed. Well, well, I'll be washed and ironed and starched."

When the half-witted old man left his husking of corn and came into the wood to meet Elmer Cowley, he was neither surprised nor especially interested in the sudden appearance of the young man. His feet also were cold and he sat on the log by the fire, grateful for the warmth and apparently indifferent to what Elmer had to say.

Elmer talked earnestly and with great freedom, walking up and down and waving his arms about. "You don't understand what's the matter with me so of course you don't care," he declared. "With me it's different. Look how it has always been with me. Father is queer and mother was queer, too. Even the clothes mother used to wear were not like other people's clothes, and look at that coat in which father goes about there in town, thinking he's dressed up, too. Why don't he get a new one? It wouldn't cost much. I'll tell you why. Father doesn't know and when mother was alive she didn't know either. Mabel is different. She knows but she won't say anything. I will, though. I'm not going to be stared at any longer. Why look here, Mook, father doesn't know that his store there in town is just a queer jumble, that he'll never sell the stuff he buys. He knows nothing about it. Sometimes he's a little worried that trade doesn't come and then he goes and buys something else. In the evenings he sits by the fire upstairs and says trade will come after a while. He isn't worried. He's queer. He doesn't know enough to be worried."

The excited young man became more excited. "He don't know but I know," he shouted, stopping to gaze down into the dumb, unresponsive face of the half-wit. "I know too well. I can't stand it. When we lived out here it was different. I worked and at night I went to bed and slept. I wasn't always seeing people and thinking as I am now. In the evening, there in town, I go to the post office or to the depot to see the train come in, and no one says anything to me. Everyone stands around and laughs and they talk but they say nothing to me. Then I feel so queer that I can't talk either. I go away. I don't say any-thing. I can't."

The fury of the young man became uncontrolla-ble. "I won't stand it," he yelled, looking up at the bare branches of the trees. "I'm not made to stand it."

Maddened by the dull face of the man on the log by the fire, Elmer turned and glared at him as he had glared back along the road at the town of Winesburg. "Go on back to work," he screamed. "What good does it do me to talk to you?" A thought came to him and his voice dropped. "I'm a coward too, eh?" he muttered. "Do you know why I came clear out here afoot? I had to tell some one and you were the only one I could tell. I hunted out another queer one, you see. I ran away, that's what I did. I couldn't stand up to some one like that George Willard. I had to come to you. I ought to tell him and I will."

Again his voice arose to a shout and his arms flew about. "I will tell him. I won't be queer. I don't care what they think. I won't stand it."

Elmer Cowley ran out of the woods leaving the half-wit sitting on the log before the fire. Pres-ently the old man arose and climbing over the fence went back to his work in the corn. "I'll be washed and ironed and starched," he declared. "Well, well, I'll be washed and ironed." Mook

was interested. He went along a lane to a field
where two cows stood nibbling at a straw stack.
"Elmer was here," he said to the cows. "Elmer
is crazy. You better get behind the stack where
he don't see you. He'll hurt someone yet, Elmer
will."

At eight o'clock that evening Elmer Cowley
put his head in at the front door of the office of
the *Winesburg Eagle* where George Willard sat
writing. His cap was pulled down over his eyes
and a sullen determined look was on his face.
"You come on outside with me," he said, stepping
in and closing the door. He kept his hand on the
knob as though prepared to resist anyone else
coming in. "You just come along outside. I
want to see you."

George Willard and Elmer Cowley walked
through the main street of Winesburg. The
night was cold and George Willard had on a new
overcoat and looked very spruce and dressed up.
He thrust his hands into the overcoat pockets and
looked inquiringly at his companion. He had
long been wanting to make friends with the young
merchant and find out what was in his mind.
Now he thought he saw a chance and was delighted. "I wonder what he's up to? Perhaps
he thinks he has a piece of news for the paper.
It can't be a fire because I haven't heard the fire
bell and there isn't anyone running," he thought.

In the main street of Winesburg, on the cold
November evening, but few citizens appeared and
these hurried along bent on getting to the stove
at the back of some store. The windows of the
stores were frosted and the wind rattled the tin
sign that hung over the entrance to the stairway
leading to Doctor Welling's office. Before
Hearn's Grocery a basket of apples and a rack
filled with new brooms stood on the sidewalk.
Elmer Cowley stopped and stood facing George
Willard. He tried to talk and his arms began
to pump up and down. His face worked spas-
modically. He seemed about to shout. "Oh,
you go on back," he cried. "Don't stay out here
with me. I ain't got anything to tell you. I
don't want to see you at all."

For three hours the distracted young merchant
wandered through the resident streets of Winesburg blind with anger, brought on by his failure
to declare his determination not to be queer. Bitterly the sense of defeat settled upon him and he
wanted to weep. After the hours of futile sput-
tering at nothingness that had occupied the afternoon and his failure in the presence of the young
reporter, he thought he could see no hope of a
future for himself.

And then a new idea dawned for him. In the
darkness that surrounded him he began to see a
light. Going to the now darkened store, where

Cowley & Son had for over a year waited vainly
for trade to come, he crept stealthily in and felt
about in a barrel that stood by the stove at the
rear. In the barrel beneath shavings lay a tin
box containing Cowley & Son's cash. Every
evening Ebenezer Cowley put the box in the barrel when he closed the store and went upstairs to
bed. "They wouldn't never think of a careless
place like that," he told himself, thinking of rob-
bers.

Elmer took twenty dollars, two ten dollar bills,
from the little roll containing perhaps four hundred dollars, the cash left from the sale of the
farm. Then replacing the box beneath the shavings he went quietly out at the front door and
walked again in the streets.

The idea that he thought might put an end to
all of his unhappiness was very simple. "I will
get out of here, run away from home," he told
himself. He knew that a local freight train passed
through Winesburg at midnight and went on to
Cleveland where it arrived at dawn. He would
steal a ride on the local and when he got to Cleveland would lose himself in the crowds there. He
would get work in some shop and become friends
with the other workmen. Gradually he would become like other men and would be indistinguish-
able. Then he could talk and laugh. He would
no longer be queer and would make friends. Life

would begin to have warmth and meaning for him
as it had for others.

The tall awkward young man, striding through
the streets, laughed at himself because he had been
angry and had been half afraid of George Willard. He decided he would have his talk with
the young reporter before he left town, that he
would tell him about things, perhaps challenge
him, challenge all of Winesburg through him.

Aglow with new confidence Elmer went to the
office of the New Willard House and pounded
on the door. A sleep-eyed boy slept on a cot in
the office. He received no salary but was fed at
the hotel table and bore with pride the title of
"night clerk." Before the boy Elmer was bold,
insistent. "You wake him up," he commanded.
"You tell him to come down by the depot. I got
to see him and I'm going away on the local. Tell
him to dress and come on down. I ain't got
much time."

The midnight local had finished its work in
Winesburg and the trainsmen were coupling cars,
swinging lanterns and preparing to resume their
flight east. George Willard, rubbing his eyes and
again wearing the new overcoat, ran down to the
station platform afire with curiosity. "Well,
here I am. What do you want? You've got
something to tell me, eh?" he said.

Elmer tried to explain. He wet his lips with

his tongue and looked at the train that had begun to groan and get under way. "Well, you see," he began, and then lost control of his tongue. "I'll be washed and ironed. I'll be washed and ironed and starched," he muttered half incoherently.

Elmer Cowley danced with fury beside the groaning train in the darkness on the station platform. Lights leaped into the air and bobbed up and down before his eyes. Taking the two ten dollar bills from his pocket he thrust them into George Willard's hand. "Take them," he cried. "I don't want them. Give them to father. I stole them." With a snarl of rage he turned and his long arms began to flay the air. Like one struggling for release from hands that held him he struck out, hitting George Willard blow after blow on the breast, the neck, the mouth. The young reporter rolled over on the platform half unconscious, stunned by the terrific force of the blows. Springing aboard the passing train and running over the tops of cars, Elmer sprang down to a flat car and lying on his face looked back, trying to see the fallen man in the darkness. Pride surged up in him. "I showed him," he cried. "I guess I showed him. I ain't so queer. I guess I showed him I ain't so queer."

THE UNTOLD LIE

RAY PEARSON and Hal Winters were farm hands employed on a farm three miles north of Winesburg. On Saturday afternoons they came into town and wandered about through the streets with other fellows from the country.

Ray was a quiet, rather nervous man of perhaps fifty with a brown beard and shoulders rounded by too much and too hard labor. In his nature he was as unlike Hal Winters as two men can be unlike.

Ray was an altogether serious man and had a little sharp featured wife who had also a sharp voice. The two, with half a dozen thin legged children, lived in a tumble-down frame house beside a creek at the back end of the Wills farm where Ray was employed.

Hal Winters, his fellow employee, was a young fellow. He was not of the Ned Winters family, who were very respectable people in Winesburg, but was one of the three sons of the old man called Windpeter Winters who had a sawmill near Unionville, six miles away, and who was looked upon by everyone in Winesburg as a confirmed old reprobate.

People from the part of Northern Ohio in which Winesburg lies will remember old Windpeter by his unusual and tragic death. He got drunk one evening in town and started to drive home to Unionville along the railroad tracks. Henry Brattenburg, the butcher, who lived out that way, stopped him at the edge of the town and told him he was sure to meet the down train but Windpeter slashed at him with his whip and drove on. When the train struck and killed him and his two horses a farmer and his wife who were driving home along a nearby road saw the accident. They said that old Windpeter stood up on the seat of his wagon, raving and swearing at the onrushing locomotive, and that he fairly screamed with delight when the team, maddened by his incessant slashing at them, rushed straight ahead to certain death. Boys like young George Willard and Seth Richmond will remember the incident quite vividly because, although everyone in our town said that the old man would go straight to hell and that the community was better off without him, they had a secret conviction that he knew what he was doing and admired his foolish courage. Most boys have seasons of wishing they could die gloriously instead of just being grocery clerks and going on with their humdrum lives.

But this is not the story of Windpeter Winters nor yet of his son Hal who worked on the Wills farm with Ray Pearson. It is Ray's story. It will, however, be necessary to talk a little of young Hal so that you will get into the spirit of it.

Hal was a bad one. Everyone said that. There were three of the Winters boys in that family, John, Hal, and Edward, all broad shouldered big fellows like old Windpeter himself and all fighters and woman-chasers and generally all-around bad ones.

Hal was the worst of the lot and always up to some devilment. He once stole a load of boards from his father's mill and sold them in Winesburg. With the money he bought himself a suit of cheap, flashy clothes. Then he got drunk and when his father came raving into town to find him, they met and fought with their fists on Main Street and were arrested and put into jail together.

Hal went to work on the Wills farm because there was a country school teacher out that way who had taken his fancy. He was only twenty-two then but had already been in two or three of what were spoken of in Winesburg as "women scrapes." Everyone who heard of his infatuation for the school teacher was sure it would turn out badly. "He'll only get her into trouble, you'll see," was the word that went around.

And so these two men, Ray and Hal, were at

work in a field on a day in the late October.
They were husking corn and occasionally something was said and they laughed. Then came silence. Ray, who was the more sensitive and always minded things more, had chapped hands and
they hurt. He put them into his coat pockets and
looked away across the fields. He was in a sad
distracted mood and was affected by the beauty of
the country. If you knew the Winesburg country
in the fall and how the low hills are all splashed
with yellows and reds you would understand his
feeling. He began to think of the time, long ago
when he was a young fellow living with his father,
then a baker in Winesburg, and how on such days
he had wandered away to the woods to gather
nuts, hunt rabbits, or just to loaf about and smoke
his pipe. His marriage had come about through
one of his days of wandering. He had induced a
girl who waited on trade in his father's shop to go
with him and something had happened. He was
thinking of that afternoon and how it had affected
his whole life when a spirit of protest awoke in
him. He had forgotten about Hal and muttered
words. "Tricked by Gad, that's what I was,
tricked by life and made a fool of," he said in a
low voice.

As though understanding his thoughts, Hal
Winters spoke up. "Well, has it been worth
while? What about it, eh? What about mar-

riage and all that?" he asked and then laughed.
Hal tried to keep on laughing but he too was in
an earnest mood. He began to talk earnestly.
"Has a fellow got to do it?" he asked. "Has he
got to be harnessed up and driven through life
like a horse?"

Hal didn't wait for an answer but sprang to his
feet and began to walk back and forth between the
corn shocks. He was getting more and more
excited. Bending down suddenly he picked up an
ear of the yellow corn and threw it at the fence.
"I've got Nell Gunther in trouble," he said. "I'm
telling you, but you keep your mouth shut."

Ray Pearson arose and stood staring. He was
almost a foot shorter than Hal, and when the
younger man came and put his two hands on the
older man's shoulders they made a picture. There
they stood in the big empty field with the quiet
corn shocks standing in rows behind them and the
red and yellow hills in the distance, and from being just two indifferent workmen they had become
all alive to each other. Hal sensed it and because that was his way he laughed. "Well, old
daddy," he said awkwardly, "come on, advise me.
I've got Nell in trouble. Perhaps you've been in
the same fix yourself. I know what every one
would say is the right thing to do, but what do you
say? Shall I marry and settle down? Shall I
put myself into the harness to be worn out like

an old horse? You know me, Ray. There can't
any one break me but I can break myself. Shall
I do it or shall I tell Nell to go to the devil?
Come on, you tell me. Whatever you say, Ray,
I'll do."

Ray couldn't answer. He shook Hal's hands
loose and turning walked straight away toward
the barn. He was a sensitive man and there were
tears in his eyes. He knew there was only one
thing to say to Hal Winters, son of old Windpeter Winters, only one thing that all his own
training and all the beliefs of the people he knew
would approve, but for his life he couldn't say
what he knew he should say.

At half-past four that afternoon Ray was puttering about the barnyard when his wife came up
the lane along the creek and called him. After
the talk with Hal he hadn't returned to the corn
field but worked about the barn. He had already
done the evening chores and had seen Hal, dressed
and ready for a roistering night in town, come out
of the farmhouse and go into the road. Along
the path to his own house he trudged behind his
wife, looking at the ground and thinking. He
couldn't make out what was wrong. Every time
he raised his eyes and saw the beauty of the country in the failing light he wanted to do something
he had never done before, shout or scream or hit
his wife with his fists or something equally unex-

pected and terrifying. Along the path he went scratching his head and trying to make it out. He looked hard at his wife's back but she seemed all right.

She only wanted him to go into town for groceries and as soon as she had told him what she wanted began to scold. "You're always puttering," she said. "Now I want you to hustle. There isn't anything in the house for supper and you-ve got to get to town and back in a hurry."

Ray went into his own house and took an overcoat from a hook back of the door. It was torn about the pockets and the collar was shiny. His wife went into the bedroom and presently came out with a soiled cloth in one hand and three silver dollars in the other. Somewhere in the house a child wept bitterly and a dog that had been sleeping by the stove arose and yawned. Again the wife scolded. "The children will cry and cry. Why are you always puttering?" she asked.

Ray went out of the house and climbed the fence into a field. It was just growing dark and the scene that lay before him was lovely. All the low hills were washed with color and even the little clusters of bushes in the corners by the fences were alive with beauty. The whole world seemed to Ray Pearson to have become alive with something just as he and Hal had suddenly become alive when they stood in the corn field staring into each other's eyes.

The beauty of the country about Winesburg was too much for Ray on that fall evening. That is all there was to it. He could not stand it. Of a sudden he forgot all about being a quiet old farm hand and throwing off the torn overcoat began to run across the field. As he ran he shouted a protest against his life, against all life, against everything that makes life ugly. "There was no promise made," he cried into the empty spaces that lay about him. "I didn't promise my Minnie anything and Hal hasn't made any promise to Nell. I know he hasn't. She went into the woods with him because she wanted to go. What he wanted she wanted. Why should I pay? Why should Hal pay? Why should any one pay? I don't want Hal to become old and worn out. I'll tell him. I won't let it go on. I'll catch Hal before he gets to town and I'll tell him."

Ray ran clumsily and once he stumbled and fell down. "I must catch Hal and tell him," he kept thinking and although his breath came in gasps he kept running harder and harder. As he ran he thought of things that hadn't come into his mind for years—how at the time he married he had planned to go west to his uncle in Portland, Oregon—how he hadn't wanted to be a farm hand, but had thought when he got out west he would

go to sea and be a sailor or get a job on a ranch
and ride a horse into western towns, shouting and
laughing and waking the people in the houses with
his wild cries. Then as he ran he remembered
his children and in fancy felt their hands clutching at him. All of his thoughts of himself were
involved with the thoughts of Hal and he thought
the children were clutching at the younger man
also. "They are the accidents of life, Hal," he
cried. "They are not mine or yours. I had nothing to do with them."

Darkness began to spread over the fields as
Ray Pearson ran on and on. His breath came
in little sobs. When he came to the fence at the
edge of the road and confronted Hal Winters, all
dressed up and smoking a pipe as he walked jaunt-
ily along, he could not have told what he thought
or what he wanted.

Ray Pearson lost his nerve and this is really
the end of the story of what happened to him.
It was almost dark when he got to the fence and
he put his hands on the top bar and stood staring.
Hal Winters jumped a ditch and coming up close
to Ray put his hands into his pockets and laughed.
He seemed to have lost his own sense of what had
happened in the corn field and when he put up a
strong hand and took hold of the lapel of Ray's
coat he shook the old man as he might have shaken
a dog that had misbehaved.

"You came to tell me, eh?" he said. "Well, never mind telling me anything. I'm not a coward and I've already made up my mind." He laughed again and jumped back across the ditch. "Nell ain't no fool," he said. "She didn't ask me to marry her. I want to marry her. I want to settle down and have kids."

Ray Pearson also laughed. He felt like laughing at himself and all the world.

As the form of Hal Winters disappeared in the dusk that lay over the road that led to Winesburg, he turned and walked slowly back across the fields to where he had left his torn overcoat. As he went some memory of pleasant evenings spent with the thin-legged children in the tumble-down house by the creek must have come into his mind, for he muttered words. "It's just as well. Whatever I told him would have been a lie," he said softly, and then his form also disappeared into the darkness of the fields.

DRINK

TOM FOSTER came to Winesburg from Cincinnati when he was still young and could get many new impressions. His grandmother had been raised on a farm near the town and as a young girl had gone to school there when Winesburg was a village of twelve or fifteen houses clustered about a general store on the Trunion Pike.

What a life the old woman had led since she went away from the frontier settlement and what a strong, capable little old thing she was! She had been in Kansas, in Canada, and in New York City, traveling about with her husband, a mechanic, before he died. Later she went to stay with her daughter who had also married a mechanic and lived in Covington, Kentucky, across the river from Cincinnati.

Then began the hard years for Tom Foster's grandmother. First her son-in-law was killed by a policeman during a strike and then Tom's mother became an invalid and died also. The grandmother had saved a little money, but it was swept away by the illness of the daughter and by

254

the cost of the two funerals.   She became a half
worn-out old woman worker and lived with the
grandson above a junk shop on a side street in
Cincinnati.   For five years she scrubbed the floors
in an office building and then got a place as dish
washer in a restaurant.   Her hands were all
twisted out of shape.   When she took hold of a
mop or a broom handle the hands looked like the
dried stems of an old creeping vine clinging to a
tree.

The old woman came back to Winesburg as
soon as she got the chance.   One evening as she
was coming home from work she found a pocketbook containing thirty-seven dollars, and that
opened the way.   The trip was a great adventure
for the boy.   It was past seven o'clock at night
when the grandmother came home with the pocketbook held tightly in her old hands and she was so
excited she could scarcely speak.   She insisted on
leaving Cincinnati that night, saying that if they
stayed until morning the owner of the money
would be sure to find them out and make trouble.
Tom, who was then sixteen years old, had to go
trudging off to the station with the old woman
bearing all of their earthly belongings done up in
a worn-out blanket and slung across his back.   By
his side walked the grandmother urging him forward.   Her toothless old mouth twitched nervously, and when Tom grew weary and wanted to

put the pack down at a street crossing she
snatched it up and if he had not prevented would
have slung it across her own back. When they
got into the train and it had run out of the city
she was as delighted as a girl and talked as the
boy had never heard her talk before.

All through the night as the train rattled along,
the grandmother told Tom tales of Winesburg
and of how he would enjoy his life working in the
fields and shooting wild things in the wood there.
She could not believe that the tiny village of fifty
years before had grown into a thriving town in her
absence, and in the morning when the train came
to Winesburg did not want to get off. "It isn't
what I thought. It may be hard for you here,"
she said, and then the train went on its way and
the two stood confused, not knowing where to
turn, in the presence of Albert Longworth, the
Winesburg baggage master.

But Tom Foster did get along all right. He
was one to get along anywhere. Mrs. White, the
banker's wife, employed his grandmother to work
in the kitchen and he got a place as stable boy in
the banker's new brick barn.

In Winesburg servants were hard to get. The
woman who wanted help in her housework employed a "hired girl" who insisted on sitting at
the table with the family. Mrs. White was sick
of hired girls and snatched at the chance to get

hold of the old city woman. She furnished a room for the boy Tom upstairs in the barn. "He can mow the lawn and run errands when the horses do not need attention," she explained to her husband.

Tom Foster was rather small for his age and had a large head covered with stiff black hair that stood straight up. The hair emphasized the bigness of his head. His voice was the softest thing imaginable, and he was himself so gentle and quiet that he slipped into the life of the town without attracting the least bit of attention.

One could not help wondering where Tom Foster got his gentleness. In Cincinnati he had lived in a neighborhood where gangs of tough boys prowled through the streets, and all through his early formative years he ran about with tough boys. For a while he was messenger for a telegraph company and delivered messages in a neighborhood sprinkled with houses of prostitution. The women in the houses knew and loved Tom Foster and the tough boys in the gangs loved him also.

He never asserted himself. That was one thing that helped him escape. In an odd way he stood in the shadow of the wall of life, was meant to stand in the shadow. He saw the men and women in the houses of lust, sensed their casual and horrible love affairs, saw boys fighting and listened to their tales of thieving and drunkenness unmoved and strangely unaffected.

Once Tom did steal. That was while he still lived in the city. The grandmother was ill at the time and he himself was out of work. There was nothing to eat in the house, and so he went into a harness shop on a side street and stole a dollar and seventy-five cents out of the cash drawer.

The harness shop was run by an old man with a long mustache. He saw the boy lurking about and thought nothing of it. When he went out into the street to talk to a teamster Tom opened the cash drawer and taking the money walked away. Later he was caught and his grandmother settled the matter by offering to come twice a week for a month and scrub the shop. The boy was ashamed, but he was rather glad, too. "It is all right to be ashamed and makes me understand new things," he said to the grandmother, who didn't know what the boy was talking about but loved him so much that it didn't matter whether she understood or not.

For a year Tom Foster lived in the banker's stable and then lost his place there. He didn't take very good care of the horses and he was a constant source of irritation to the banker's wife. She told him to mow the lawn and he forgot. Then she sent him to the store or to the post office and he did not come back but joined a group

of men and boys and spent the whole afternoon
with them, standing about, listening and occasionally, when addressed, saying a few words. As in
the city in the houses of prostitution and with the
rowdy boys running through the streets at night,
so in Winesburg among its citizens he had always
the power to be a part of and yet distinctly apart
from the life about him.

After Tom lost his place at Banker White's he
did not live with his grandmother, although often
in the evening she came to visit him. He rented
a room at the rear of a little frame building be-
longing to old Rufus Whiting. The building
was on Duane Street, just off Main Street, and
had been used for years as a law office by the old
man who had become too feeble and forgetful for
the practice of his profession but did not realize
his inefficiency. He liked Tom and let him have
the room for a dollar a month. In the late afternoon when the lawyer had gone home the boy had
the place to himself and spent hours lying on the
floor by the stove and thinking of things. In the
evening the grandmother came and sat in the lawyer's chair to smoke a pipe while Tom remained
silent, as he always did in the presence of every
one.

Often the old woman talked with great vigor.
Sometimes she was angry about some happening
at the banker's house and scolded away for hours.

Out of her own earnings she bought a mop and regularly scrubbed the lawyer's office. Then when the place was spotlessly clean and smelled clean she lighted her clay pipe and she and Tom had a smoke together. "When you get ready to die then I will die also," she said to the boy lying on the floor beside her chair.

Tom Foster enjoyed life in Winesburg. He did odd jobs, such as cutting wood for kitchen stoves and mowing the grass before houses. In late May and early June he picked strawberries in the fields. He had time to loaf and he enjoyed loafing. Banker White had given him a cast-off coat which was too large for him, but his grandmother cut it down, and he had also an overcoat, got at the same place, that was lined with fur. The fur was worn away in spots, but the coat was warm and in the winter Tom slept in it. He thought his method of getting along good enough and was happy and satisfied with the way life in Winesburg had turned out for him.

The most absurd little things made Tom Foster happy. That, I suppose, was why people loved him. In Hern's grocery they would be roasting coffee on Friday afternoon, preparatory to the Saturday rush of trade, and the rich odor invaded lower Main Street. Tom Foster appeared and sat on a box at the rear of the store. For an hour he did not move but sat perfectly still, filling his being with the spicy odor that made him half drunk with happiness. "I like it," he said gently. "It makes me think of things far away, places and things like that."

One night Tom Foster got drunk. That came about in a curious way. He never had been drunk before, and indeed in all his life had never taken a drink of anything intoxicating, but he felt he needed to be drunk that one time and so went and did it.

In Cincinnati, when he lived there, Tom had found out many things, things about ugliness and crime and lust. Indeed, he knew more of these things than any one else in Winesburg. The matter of sex in particular had presented itself to him in a quite horrible way and had made a deep impression on his mind. He thought, after what he had seen of the women standing before the squalid houses on cold nights and the look he had seen in the eyes of the men who stopped to talk to them, that he would put sex altogether out of his own life. One of the women of the neighborhood tempted him once and he went into a room with her. He never forgot the smell of the room nor the greedy look that came into the eyes of the woman. It sickened him and in a very terrible way left a scar on his soul. He had always before thought of women as quite innocent things, much like his grandmother, but after that one experience in the room he dismissed women from his mind.   So gentle was his nature that he could not hate anything and not being able to understand he decided to forget.

And Tom did forget until he came to Winesburg.   After he had lived there for two years something began to stir in him.   On all sides he saw youth making love and he was himself a youth. Before he knew what had happened he was in love also.   He fell in love with Helen White, daughter of the man for whom he had worked, and found himself thinking of her at night.

That was a problem for Tom and he settled it in his own way.   He let himself think of Helen White whenever her figure came into his mind and only concerned himself with the manner of his thoughts.   He had a fight, a quiet determined little fight of his own, to keep his desires in the channel where he thought they belonged, but on the whole he was victorious.

And then came the spring night when he got drunk.   Tom was wild on that night.   He was like an innocent young buck of the forest that has eaten of some maddening weed.   The thing began, ran its course, and was ended in one night, and you may be sure that no one in Winesburg was any the worse for Tom's outbreak.

In the first place, the night was one to make a sensitive nature drunk.   The trees along the residence streets of the town were all newly clothed in soft green leaves, in the gardens behind the houses men were puttering about in vegetable gardens, and in the air there was a hush, a waiting kind of silence very stirring to the blood.

Tom left his room on Duane Street just as the young night began to make itself felt. First he walked through the streets, going softly and quietly along, thinking thoughts that he tried to put into words. He said that Helen White was a flame dancing in the air and that he was a little tree without leaves standing out sharply against the sky. Then he said that she was a wind, a strong terrible wind, coming out of the darkness of a stormy sea and that he was a boat left on the shore of the sea by a fisherman.

That idea pleased the boy and he sauntered along playing with it. He went into Main Street and sat on the curbing before Wracker's tobacco store. For an hour he lingered about listening to the talk of men, but it did not interest him much and he slipped away. Then he decided to get drunk and went into Willy's saloon and bought a bottle of whiskey. Putting the bottle into his pocket, he walked out of town, wanting to be alone to think more thoughts and to drink the whiskey.

Tom got drunk sitting on a bank of new grass beside the road about a mile north of town. Before him was a white road and at his back an apple orchard in full bloom. He took a drink out of the bottle and then lay down on the grass. He thought of mornings in Winesburg and of how the stones in the graveled driveway by Banker White's house were wet with dew and glistened in the morning light. He thought of the nights in the barn when it rained and he lay awake hearing the drumming of the rain drops and smelling the warm smell of horses and of hay. Then he thought of a storm that had gone roaring through Winesburg several days before and, his mind going back, he relived the night he had spent on the train with his grandmother when the two were coming from Cincinnati. Sharply he remembered how strange it had seemed to sit quietly in the coach and to feel the power of the engine hurling the train along through the night.

Tom got drunk in a very short time. He kept taking drinks from the bottle as the thoughts visited him and when his head began to reel got up and walked along the road going away from Winesburg. There was a bridge on the road that ran out of Winesburg north to Lake Erie and the drunken boy made his way along the road to the bridge. There he sat down. He tried to drink again, but when he had taken the cork out of the bottle he became ill and put it quickly back. His head was rocking back and forth and so he sat on

the stone approach to the bridge and sighed.   His
head seemed to be flying about like a pin wheel and
then projecting itself off into space and his arms
and legs flopped helplessly about.

At eleven o'clock Tom got back into town.
George Willard found him wandering about and
took him into the *Eagle* printshop.   Then he became afraid that the drunken boy would make a
mess on the floor and helped him into the alleyway.

The reporter was confused by Tom Foster.
The drunken boy talked of Helen White and said
he had been with her on the shore of a sea and
had made love to her.   George had seen Helen
White walking in the street with her father during
the evening and decided that Tom was out of his
head.   A sentiment concerning Helen White that
lurked in his own heart flamed up and he became
angry.   "Now you quit that," he said.   "I won't
let Helen White's name be dragged into this.   I
won't let that happen."   He began shaking Tom's
shoulder, trying to make him understand.   "You
quit it," he said again.

For three hours the two young men, thus
strangely thrown together, stayed in the printshop.   When he had a little recovered George
took Tom for a walk.   They went into the country and sat on a log near the edge of a wood.
Something in the still night drew them together

and when the drunken boy's head began to clear they talked.

"It was good to be drunk," Tom Foster said. "It taught me something. I won't have to do it again. I will think more clearly after this. You see how it is."

George Willard did not see, but his anger concerning Helen White passed and he felt drawn towards the pale, shaken boy as he had never before been drawn towards any one. With motherly solicitude, he insisted that Tom get to his feet and walk about. Again they went back to the printshop and sat in silence in the darkness.

The reporter could not get the purpose of Tom Foster's action straightened out in his mind. When Tom spoke again of Helen White he again grew angry and began to scold. "You quit that," he said sharply. "You haven't been with her. What makes you say you have? What makes you keep saying such things? Now you quit it, do you hear?"

Tom was hurt. He couldn't quarrel with George Willard because he was incapable of quarreling, so he got up to go away. When George Willard was insistent he put out his hand, laying it on the older boy's arm, and tried to explain.

"Well," he said softly, "I don't know how it was. I was happy. You see how that was. Helen White made me happy and the night did too. I wanted to suffer, to be hurt somehow. I thought that was what I should do. I wanted to suffer, you see, because every one suffers and does wrong. I thought of a lot of things to do, but they wouldn't work. They all hurt some one else."

Tom Foster's voice arose, and for once in his life he became almost excited. "It was like making love, that's what I mean," he explained. "Don't you see how it is? It hurt me to do what I did and made everything strange. That's why I did it. I'm glad, too. It taught me something, that's it, that's what I wanted. Don't you understand? I wanted to learn things, you see. That's why I did it."

DEATH

THE stairway leading up to Dr. Reefy's office, in the Heffner Block above the Paris Dry Goods Store, was but dimly lighted. At the head of the stairway hung a lamp with a dirty chimney that was fastened by a bracket to the wall. The lamp had a tin reflector, brown with rust and covered with dust. The people who went up the stairway followed with their feet the feet of many who had gone before. The soft boards of the stairs had yielded under the pressure of feet and deep hollows marked the way.

At the top of the stairway a turn to the right brought you to the doctor's door. To the left was a dark hallway filled with rubbish. Old chairs, carpenter's horses, step ladders and empty boxes lay in the darkness waiting for shins to be barked. The pile of rubbish belonged to the Paris Dry Goods Co. When a counter or a row of shelves in the store became useless, clerks carried it up the stairway and threw it on the pile.

Doctor Reefy's office was as large as a barn. A stove with a round paunch sat in the middle of the room. Around its base was piled sawdust, held in place by heavy planks nailed to the floor. By the door stood a huge table that had once been a part of the furniture of Herrick's Clothing Store and that had been used for displaying custom-made clothes. It was covered with books, bottles and surgical instruments. Near the edge of the table lay three or four apples left by John Spaniard, a tree nurseryman who was Doctor Reefy's friend, and who had slipped the apples out of his pocket as he came in at the door.

At middle age Doctor Reefy was tall and awkward. The grey beard he later wore had not yet appeared, but on the upper lip grew a brown mustache. He was not a graceful man, as when he grew older, and was much occupied with the problem of disposing of his hands and feet.

On summer afternoons, when she had been married many years and when her son George was a boy of twelve or fourteen, Elizabeth Willard sometimes went up the worn steps to Doctor Reefy's office. Already the woman's naturally tall figure had begun to droop and to drag itself listlessly about. Ostensibly she went to see the doctor because of her health, but on the half dozen occasions when she had been to see him the outcome of the visits did not primarily concern her health. She and the doctor talked of that but they talked most of her life, of their two lives and

of the ideas that had come to them as they lived
their lives in Winesburg.

In the big empty office the man and the woman
sat looking at each other and they were a good
deal alike.   Their bodies were different as were
also the color of their eyes, the length of their
noses and the circumstances of their existence,
but something inside them meant the same thing,
wanted the same release, would have left the same
impression on the memory of an onlooker.   Later,
and when he grew older and married a young wife,
the doctor often talked to her of the hours spent
with the sick woman and expressed a good many
things he had been unable to express to Elizabeth.
He was almost a poet in his old age and his notion of what happened took a poetic turn.   "I
had come to the time in my life when prayer became necessary and so I invented gods and prayed
to them," he said.   "I did not say my prayers in
words nor did I kneel down but sat perfectly still
in my chair.   In the late afternoon when it was
hot and quiet on Main Street or in the winter when
the days were gloomy, the gods came into the office
and I thought no one knew about them.   Then I
found that this woman Elizabeth knew, that she
worshipped also the same gods.   I have a notion
that she came to the office because she thought the
gods would be there but she was happy to find herself not alone just the same.   It was an experi₂

ence that cannot be explained, although I suppose
it is always happening to men and women in all
sorts of places."

.   .   .   .

On the summer afternoons when Elizabeth and
the doctor sat in the office and talked of their two
lives they talked of other lives also. Sometimes
the doctor made philosophic epigrams. Then he
chuckled with amusement. Now and then after a
period of silence, a word was said or a hint given
that strangely illuminated the life of the speaker,
a wish became a desire, or a dream, half dead,
flared suddenly into life. For the most part the
words came from the woman and she said them
without looking at the man.

Each time she came to see the doctor the hotel
keeper's wife talked a little more freely and after
an hour or two in his presence went down
the stairway into Main Street feeling renewed and
strengthened against the dullness of her days.
With something approaching a girlhood swing to
her body she walked along, but when she had got
back to her chair by the window of her room and
when darkness had come on and a girl from the
hotel dining room brought her dinner on a tray,
she let it grow cold. Her thoughts ran away to
her girlhood with its passionate longing for adventure and she remembered the arms of men that
had held her when adventure was a possible thing

for her. Particularly she remembered one who
had for a time been her lover and who in the moment of his passion had cried out to her more than
a hundred times, saying the same words madly
over and over: "You dear! You dear! You
lovely dear!" The words she thought expressed
something she would have liked to have achieved
in life.

In her room in the shabby old hotel the sick
wife of the hotel keeper began to weep and putting her hands to her face rocked back and forth.
The words of her one friend, Doctor Reefy, rang
in her ears. "Love is like a wind stirring the
grass beneath trees on a black night," he had said.
"You must not try to make love definite. It is
the divine accident of life. If you try to be definite and sure about it and to live beneath the trees,
where soft night winds blow, the long hot day of
disappointment comes swiftly and the gritty dust
from passing wagons gathers upon lips inflamed
and made tender by kisses."

Elizabeth Willard could not remember her
mother who had died when she was but five years
old. Her girlhood had been lived in the most
haphazard manner imaginable. Her father was
a man who had wanted to be let alone and the
affairs of the hotel would not let him alone. He
also had lived and died a sick man. Every

day he arose with a cheerful face, but by ten o'clock in the morning all the joy had gone out of his heart. When a guest complained of the fare in the hotel dining room or one of the girls who made up the beds got married and went away, he stamped on the floor and swore. At night when he went to bed he thought of his daughter growing up among the stream of people that drifted in and out of the hotel and was overcome with sadness. As the girl grew older and began to walk out in the evening with men he wanted to talk to her, but when he tried was not successful. He always forgot what he wanted to say and spent the time complaining of his own affairs.

In her girlhood and young womanhood Elizabeth had tried to be a real adventurer in life. At eighteen life had so gripped her that she was no longer a virgin but, although she had a half dozen lovers before she married Tom Willard, she had never entered upon an adventure prompted by desire alone. Like all the women in the world, she wanted a real lover. Always there was something she sought blindly, passionately, some hidden wonder in life. The tall beautiful girl with the swinging stride who had walked under the trees with men was forever putting out her hand into the darkness and trying to get hold of some other hand. In all the babble of words that fell from

the lips of the men with whom she adventured she
was trying to find what would be for her the true
word.

Elizabeth had married Tom Willard, a clerk in
her father's hotel, because he was at hand and
wanted to marry at the time when the determination to marry came to her.   For a while, like most
young girls, she thought marriage would change
the face of life.   If there was in her mind a doubt
of the outcome of the marriage with Tom she
brushed it aside.   Her father was ill and near
death at the time and she was perplexed because
of the meaningless outcome of an affair in which
she had just been involved.   Other girls of her
age in Winesburg were marrying men she had always known, grocery clerks or young farmers.   In
the evening they walked in Main Street with their
husbands and when she passed they smiled happily.   She began to think that the fact of marriage
might be full of some hidden significance.   Young
wives with whom she talked spoke softly and
shyly.   "It changes things to have a man of your
own," they said.

On the evening before her marriage the perplexed girl had a talk with her father.   Later she
wondered if the hours alone with the sick man
had not led to her decision to marry.   The father
talked of his life and advised the daughter to
avoid being led into another such muddle.   He

abused Tom Willard, and that led Elizabeth to
come to the clerk's defense. The sick man became excited and tried to get out of bed. When
she would not let him walk about he began to
complain. "I've never been let alone," he said.
"Although I've worked hard I've not made the
hotel pay. Even now I owe money at the bank.
You'll find that out when I'm gone."

The voice of the sick man became tense with
earnestness. Being unable to arise, he put out
his hand and pulled the girl's head down beside
his own. "There's a way out," he whispered.
"Don't marry Tom Willard or any one else here
in Winesburg. There is eight hundred dollars in
a tin box in my trunk. Take it and go away."

Again the sick man's voice became querulous.
"You've got to promise," he declared. "If you
won't promise not to marry, give me your word
that you'll never tell Tom about the money. It
is mine and if I give it to you I've the right to
make that demand. Hide it away. It is to make
up to you for my failure as a father. Some time
it may prove to be a door, a great open door to
you. Come now, I tell you I'm about to die, give
me your promise."

.   .   .   .

In Doctor Reefy's office, Elizabeth, a tired
gaunt old woman at forty-one, sat in a chair near
the stove and looked at the floor. By a small

desk near the window sat the doctor.   His hands
played with a lead pencil that lay on the desk.
Elizabeth talked of her life as a married woman.
She became impersonal and forgot her husband,
only using him as a lay figure to give point to her
tale.   "And then I was married and it did not
turn out at all," she said bitterly.   "As soon as I
had gone into it I began to be afraid.   Perhaps
I knew too much before and then perhaps I found
out too much during my first night with him.   I
don't remember.

"What a fool I was.   When father gave me the
money and tried to talk me out of the thought of
marriage, I would not listen.   I thought of what
the girls who were married had said of it and I
wanted marriage also.   It wasn't Tom I wanted,
it was marriage.   When father went to sleep I
leaned out of the window and thought of the life
I had led.   I didn't want to be a bad woman.
The town was full of stories about me.   I even
began to be afraid Tom would change his mind."

The woman's voice began to quiver with excitement.   To Doctor Reefy, who without realizing
what was happening had begun to love her, there
came an odd illusion.   He thought that as she
talked the woman's body was changing, that
she was becoming younger, straighter, stronger.
When he could not shake off the illusion his mind
gave it a professional twist.   "It is good for both

her body and her mind, this talking," he muttered.

The woman began telling of an incident that had happened one afternoon a few months after her marriage. Her voice became steadier. "In the late afternoon I went for a drive alone," she said. "I had a buggy and a little grey pony I kept in Moyer's Livery. Tom was painting and repapering rooms in the hotel. He wanted money and I was trying to make up my mind to tell him about the eight hundred dollars father had given to me. I couldn't decide to do it. I didn't like him well enough. There was always paint on his hands and face during those days and he smelled of paint. He was trying to fix up the old hotel, make it new and smart."

The excited woman sat up very straight in her chair and made a quick girlish movement with her hand as she told of the drive alone on the spring afternoon. "It was cloudy and a storm threatened," she said. "Black clouds made the green of the trees and the grass stand out so that the colors hurt my eyes. I went out Trunion Pike a mile or more and then turned into a side road. The little horse went quickly along up hill and down. I was impatient. Thoughts came and I wanted to get away from my thoughts. I began to beat the horse. The black clouds settled down and it began to rain. I wanted to go at a terri-

ble speed, to drive on and on forever. I wanted
to get out of town, out of my clothes, out of my
marriage, out of my body, out of everything. I
almost killed the horse, making him run, and when
he could not run any more I got out of the buggy
and ran afoot into the darkness until I fell and
hurt my side. I wanted to run away from everything but I wanted to run towards something too.
Don't you see, dear, how it was?"

Elizabeth sprang out of the chair and began to
walk about in the office. She walked as Doctor
Reefy thought he had never seen any one walk before. To her whole body there was a swing, a
rhythm that intoxicated him. When she came
and knelt on the floor beside his chair he took her
into his arms and began to kiss her passionately.
"I cried all the way home," she said, as she tried
to continue the story of her wild ride, but he did
not listen. "You dear! You lovely dear! Oh
you lovely dear!" he muttered and thought he held
in his arms, not the tired out woman of forty-one
but a lovely and innocent girl who had been able
by some miracle to project herself out of the husk
of the body of the tired-out woman.

Doctor Reefy did not see the woman he had
held in his arms again until after her death. On
the summer afternoon in the office when he was
on the point of becoming her lover a half grotesque little incident brought his love-making

quickly to an end.   As the man and woman held
each other tightly heavy feet came tramping up
the office stairs.   The two sprang to their feet
and stood listening and trembling.   The noise on
the stairs was made by a clerk from the Paris
Dry Goods Store Co.   With a loud bang he threw
an empty box on the pile of rubbish in the hallway
and then went heavily down the stairs.   Elizabeth followed him almost immediately.   The
thing that had come to life in her as she talked to
her one friend died suddenly.   She was hysterical,
as was also Doctor Reefy, and did not want to
continue the talk.   Along the street she went with
the blood still singing in her body, but when she
turned out of Main Street and saw ahead the
lights of the New Willard House, she began to
tremble and her knees shook so that for a
moment she thought she would fall in the
street.

The sick woman spent the last few months of
her life hungering for death.   Along the road of
death she went, seeking, hungering.   She personified the figure of death and made him, now a
strong black-haired youth running over hills,
now a stern quiet man marked and scarred by
the business of living.   In the darkness of her
room she put out her hand, thrusting it from under
the covers of her bed, and she thought that death
like a living thing put out his hand to her.   "Be

patient, lover," she whispered. "Keep yourself young and beautiful and be patient."

On the evening when disease laid its heavy hand upon her and defeated her plans for telling her son George of the eight hundred dollars hidden away, she got out of bed and crept half across the room pleading with death for another hour of life. "Wait, dear! The boy! The boy! The boy!" she pleaded as she tried with all of her strength to fight off the arms of the lover she had wanted so earnestly.

.   .   .   .   .   .

Elizabeth died one day in March in the year when her son George became eighteen, and the young man had but little sense of the meaning of her death. Only time could give him that. For a month he had seen her lying white and still and speechless in her bed, and then one afternoon the doctor stopped him in the hallway and said a few words.

The young man went into his own room and closed the door. He had a queer empty feeling in the region of his stomach. For a moment he sat staring at the floor and then jumping up went for a walk. Along the station platform he went, and around through residence streets past the high school building, thinking almost entirely of his own affairs. The notion of death could not get hold of him and he was in fact a little annoyed that his mother had died on that day. He had just received a note from Helen White, the daughter of the town banker, in answer to one from him. "Tonight I could have gone to see her and now it will have to be put off," he thought half angrily.

Elizabeth died on a Friday afternoon at three o'clock. It had been cold and rainy in the morning but in the afternoon the sun came out. Before she died she lay paralyzed for six days unable to speak or move and with only her mind and her eyes alive. For three of the six days she struggled, thinking of her boy, trying to say some few words in regard to his future, and in her eyes there was an appeal so touching that all who saw it kept the memory of the dying woman in their minds for years. Even Tom Willard who had always half resented his wife forgot his resentment and the tears ran out of his eyes and lodged in his mustache. The mustache had begun to turn grey and Tom colored it with dye. There was oil in the preparation he used for the purpose and the tears, catching in the mustache and being brushed away by his hand, formed a fine mist-like vapor. In his grief Tom Willard's face looked like the face of a little dog that has been out a long time in bitter weather.

George came home along Main Street at dark on the day of his mother's death and, after going to his own room to brush his hair and clothes, went along the hallway and into the room where the body lay. There was a candle on the dressing table by the door and Doctor Reefy sat in a chair by the bed. The doctor arose and started to go out. He put out his hand as though to greet the younger man and then awkwardly drew it back again. The air of the room was heavy with the presence of the two self-conscious human beings, and the man hurried away.

The dead woman's son sat down in a chair and looked at the floor. He again thought of his own affairs and definitely decided he would make a change in his life, that he would leave Winesburg. "I will go to some city. Perhaps I can get a job on some newspaper," he thought and then his mind turned to the girl with whom he was to have spent this evening and again he was half angry at the turn of events that had prevented his going to her.

In the dimly lighted room with the dead woman the young man began to have thoughts. His mind played with thoughts of life as his mother's mind had played with the thought of death. He closed his eyes and imagined that the red young lips of Helen White touched his own lips. His body trembled and his hands shook. And then something happened. The boy sprang to his feet and stood stiffly. He looked at the figure of the dead woman under the sheets and shame for his thoughts swept over him so that he began to weep. A new notion came into his mind and he turned and looked guiltily about as though afraid he would be observed.

George Willard became possessed of a madness to lift the sheet from the body of his mother and look at her face. The thought that had come into his mind gripped him terribly. He became convinced that not his mother but some one else lay in the bed before him. The conviction was so real that it was almost unbearable. The body under the sheets was long and in death looked young and graceful. To the boy, held by some strange fancy, it was unspeakably lovely. The feeling that the body before him was alive, that in another moment a lovely woman would spring out of the bed and confront him became so overpowering that he could not bear the suspense. Again and again he put out his hand. Once he touched and half lifted the white sheet that covered her, but his courage failed and he, like Doctor Reefy, turned and went out of the room. In the hallway outside the door he stopped and trembled so that he had to put a hand against the wall to support himself. "That's not my mother. That's not my mother in there," he whispered to himself and again his body shook with fright and uncertainty. When Aunt Elizabeth Swift, who had come to watch over the body, came out of an adjoining room he put his hand into hers and began to sob, shaking his head from side to side, half blind with grief. "My mother is dead," he said, and then forgetting the woman he turned and stared at the door through which he had just come. "The dear, the dear, oh the lovely dear," the boy, urged by some impulse outside himself, muttered aloud.

. . . .

As for the eight hundred dollars, the dead woman had kept hidden so long and that was to give George Willard his start in the city, it lay in the tin box behind the plaster by the foot of his mother's bed. Elizabeth had put it there a week after her marriage, breaking the plaster away with a stick. Then she got one of the workmen her husband was at that time employing about the hotel to mend the wall. "I jammed the corner of the bed against it," she had explained to her husband, unable at the moment to give up her dream of release, the release that after all came to her but twice in her life, in the moments when her lovers Death and Doctor Reefy held her in their arms.

SOPHISTICATION

IT was early evening of a day in the late fall and the Winesburg County Fair had brought crowds of country people into town. The day had been clear and the night came on warm and pleasant. On the Trunion Pike, where the road after it left town stretched away between berry fields now covered with dry brown leaves, the dust from passing wagons arose in clouds. Children, curled into little balls, slept on the straw scattered on wagon beds. Their hair was full of dust and their fingers black and sticky. The dust rolled away over the fields and the departing sun set it ablaze with colors.

In the main street of Winesburg crowds filled the stores and the sidewalks. Night came on, horses whinnied, the clerks in the stores ran madly about, children became lost and cried lustily, an American town worked terribly at the task of amusing itself.

Pushing his way through the crowds in Main Street, young George Willard concealed himself in the stairway leading to Doctor Reefy's office and looked at the people. With feverish eyes he

watched the faces drifting past under the store
lights. Thoughts kept coming into his head and
he did not want to think. He stamped impa-
tiently on the wooden steps and looked sharply
about. "Well, is she going to stay with him all
day? Have I done all this waiting for nothing?"
he muttered.

George Willard, the Ohio village boy, was fast
growing into manhood and new thoughts had been
coming into his mind. All that day, amid the
jam of people at the Fair, he had gone about feeling lonely. He was about to leave Winesburg
to go away to some city where he hoped to get
work on a city newspaper and he felt grown up.
The mood that had taken possession of him was
a thing known to men and unknown to boys. He
felt old and a little tired. Memories awoke in
him. To his mind his new sense of maturity
set him apart, made of him a half-tragic figure.
He wanted someone to understand the feeling
that had taken possession of him after his mother's
death.

There is a time in the life of every boy when he
for the first time takes the backward view of life.
Perhaps that is the moment when he crosses the
line into manhood. The boy is walking through
the street of his town. He is thinking of the
future and of the figure he will cut in the world.
Ambitions and regrets awake within him. Sud-

denly something happens; he stops under a tree
and waits as for a voice calling his name.   Ghosts
of old things creep into his consciousness; the
voices outside of himself whisper a message concerning the limitations of life.   From being quite
sure of himself and his future he becomes not at
all sure.   If he be an imaginative boy a door is
torn open and for the first time he looks out upon
the world, seeing, as though they marched in procession before him, the countless figures of men
who before his time have come out of nothingness
into the world, lived their lives and again disappeared into nothingness.   The sadness of sophistication has come to the boy.   With a little gasp
he sees himself as merely a leaf blown by the wind
through the streets of his village.   He knows that
in spite of all the stout talk of his fellows he must
live and die in uncertainty, a thing blown by the
winds, a thing destined like corn to wilt in the sun.
He shivers and looks eagerly about.   The eighteen
years he has lived seem but a moment, a breath-
ing space in the long march of humanity.   Already
he hears death calling.   With all his heart he
wants to come close to some other human, touch
someone with his hands, be touched by the hand
of another.   If he prefers that the other be a
woman, that is because he believes that a woman
will be gentle, that she will understand.   He
wants, most of all, understanding.

When the moment of sophistication came to
George Willard his mind turned to Helen White,
the Winesburg banker's daughter.   Always he
had been conscious of the girl growing into womanhood as he grew into manhood.   Once on a summer night when he was eighteen, he had walked
with her on a country road and in her presence
had given way to an impulse to boast, to make
himself appear big and significant in her eyes.
Now he wanted to see her for another purpose.
He wanted to tell her of the new impulses that
had come to him.   He had tried to make her think
of him as a man when he knew nothing of manhood and now he wanted to be with her and to
try to make her feel the change he believed had
taken place in his nature.

As for Helen White, she also had come to a
period of change.   What George felt, she in her
young woman's way felt also.   She was no longer
a girl and hungered to reach into the grace and
beauty of womanhood.   She had come home from
Cleveland, where she was attending college, to
spend a day at the Fair.   She also had begun to
have memories.   During the day she sat in the
grandstand with a young man, one of the instruc-
tors from the college, who was a guest of her
mother's.   The young man was of a pedantic turn
of mind and she felt at once he would not do for
her purpose.   At the Fair she was glad to be seen

in his company as he was well dressed and a stran. ger. She knew that the fact of his presence would create an impression. During the day she was happy, but when night came on she began to grow restless. She wanted to drive the instructor away, to get out of his presence. While they sat together in the grand-stand and while the eyes of former schoolmates were upon them, she paid so much attention to her escort that he grew interested. "A scholar needs money. I should marry a woman with money," he mused.

Helen White was thinking of George Willard even as he wandered gloomily through the crowds thinking of her. She remembered the summer evening when they had walked together and wanted to walk with him again. She thought that the months she had spent in the city, the going to theatres and the seeing of great crowds wandering in lighted thoroughfares, had changed her profoundly. She wanted him to feel and be conscious of the change in her nature.

The summer evening together that had left its mark on the memory of both the young man and woman had, when looked at quite sensibly, been rather stupidly spent. They had walked out of town along a country road. Then they had stopped by a fence near a field of young corn and George had taken off his coat and let it hang on his arm. "Well, I've stayed here in Winesburg

—yes—I've not yet gone away but I'm growing up," he had said. "I've been reading books and I've been thinking. I'm going to try to amount to something in life.

"Well," he explained, "that isn't the point. Perhaps I'd better quit talking."

The confused boy put his hand on the girl's arm. His voice trembled. The two started to walk back along the road toward town. In his desperation George boasted, "I'm going to be a big man, the biggest that ever lived here in Winesburg," he declared. "I want you to do something, I don't know what. Perhaps it is none of my business. I want you to try to be different from other women. You see the point. It's none of my business I tell you. I want you to be a beautiful woman. You see what I want."

The boy's voice failed and in silence the two came back into town and went along the street to Helen White's house. At the gate he tried to say something impressive. Speeches he had thought out came into his head, but they seemed utterly pointless. "I thought—I used to think— I had it in my mind you would marry Seth Richmond. Now I know you won't," was all he could find to say as she went through the gate and toward the door of her house.

On the warm fall evening as he stood in the stairway and looked at the crowd drifting through

Main Street, George thought of the talk beside
the field of young corn and was ashamed of the
figure he had made of himself. In the street the
people surged up and down like cattle confined in
a pen. Buggies and wagons almost filled the narrow thoroughfare. A band played and small
boys raced along the sidewalk, diving between
the legs of men. Young men with shining red
faces walked awkwardly about with girls on their
arms. In a room above one of the stores, where
a dance was to be held, the fiddlers tuned their
instruments. The broken sounds floated down
through an open window and out across the mur-
mer of voices and the loud blare of the horns of
the band. The medley of sounds got on young
Willard's nerves. Everywhere, on all sides, the
sense of crowding, moving life closed in about
him. He wanted to run away by himself and
think. "If she wants to stay with that fellow she
may. Why should I care? What difference
does it make to me?" he growled and went along
Main Street and through Hern's grocery into a
side street.

George felt so utterly lonely and dejected that
he wanted to weep but pride made him walk rapidly along, swinging his arms. He came to Westley Moyer's livery barn and stopped in the shadows to listen to a group of men who talked of a
race Westley's stallion, Tony Tip, had won at the

down," he declared as he came up to her. He stopped and stared stupidly. "Come on," he said and took hold of her hand. With hanging heads they walked away along the street under the trees. Dry leaves rustled under foot. Now that he had found her George wondered what he had better do and say.

. . . . . .

At the upper end of the fair ground, in Winesburg, there is a half decayed old grand-stand. It has never been painted and the boards are all warped out of shape. The fair ground stands on top of a low hill rising out of the valley of Wine Creek and from the grand-stand one can see at night, over a cornfield, the lights of the town reflected against the sky.

George and Helen climbed the hill to the fair ground, coming by the path past Waterworks Pond. The feeling of loneliness and isolation that had come to the young man in the crowded streets of his town was both broken and intensified by the presence of Helen. What he felt was reflected in her.

In youth there are always two forces fighting in people. The warm unthinking little animal struggles against the thing that reflects and remembers, and the older, the more sophisticated thing had possession of George Willard. Sensing his mood, Helen walked beside him filled with respect.

When they got to the grand-stand they climbed up under the roof and sat down on one of the long bench-like seats.

There is something memorable in the experience to be had by going into a fair ground that stands at the edge of a Middle Western town on a night after the annual fair has been held. The sensation is one never to be forgotten. On all sides are ghosts, not of the dead, but of living people. Here, during the day just passed, have come the people pouring in from the town and the country around. Farmers with their wives and children and all the people from the hundreds of little frame houses have gathered within these board walls. Young girls have laughed and men with beards have talked of the affairs of their lives. The place has been filled to overflowing with life. It has itched and squirmed with life and now it is night and the life has all gone away. The silence is almost terrifying. One conceals oneself standing silently beside the trunk of a tree and what there is of a reflective tendency in his nature is intensified. One shudders at the thought of the meaninglessness of life while at the same instant, and if the people of the town are his people, one loves life so intensely that tears come into the eyes.

In the darkness under the roof of the grand-stand, George Willard sat beside Helen White both embarrassed and to relieve their embarrassment dropped into the animalism of youth. They laughed and began to pull and haul at each other. In some way chastened and purified by the mood they had been in they became, not man and woman, not boy and girl, but excited little animals.

It was so they went down the hill. In the darkness they played like two splendid young things in a young world. Once, running swiftly forward, Helen tripped George and he fell. He squirmed and shouted. Shaking with laughter, he rolled down the hill. Helen ran after him. For just a moment she stopped in the darkness. There is no way of knowing what woman's thoughts went through her mind but, when the bottom of the hill was reached and she came up to the boy, she took his arm and walked beside him in dignified silence. For some reason they could not have explained they had both got from their silent evening together the thing needed. Man or boy, woman or girl, they had for a moment taken hold of the thing that makes the mature life of men and women in the modern world possible.

DEPARTURE

YOUNG George Willard got out of bed at four in the morning. It was April and the young tree leaves were just coming out of their buds. The trees along the residence streets in Winesburg are maple and the seeds are winged. When the wind blows they whirl crazily about, filling the air and making a carpet underfoot.

George came down stairs into the hotel office carrying a brown leather bag. His trunk was packed for departure. Since two o'clock he had been awake thinking of the journey he was about to take and wondering what he would find at the end of his journey. The boy who slept in the hotel office lay on a cot by the door. His mouth was open and he snored lustily. George crept past the cot and went out into the silent deserted main street. The east was pink with the dawn and long streaks of light climbed into the sky where a few stars still shone.

Beyond the last house on Trunion Pike in Winesburg there is a great stretch of open fields. The fields are owned by farmers who live in town

and drive homeward at evening along Trunion
Pike in light creaking wagons. In the fields are
planted berries and small fruits. In the late afternoon in the hot summers when the road and the
fields are covered with dust, a smoky haze lies over
the great flat basin of land. To look across it is
like looking out across the sea. In the spring
when the land is green the effect is somewhat different. The land becomes a wide green billiard
table on which tiny human insects toil up and
down.

All through his boyhood and young manhood
George Willard had been in the habit of walking
on Trunion Pike. He had been in the midst of
the great open place on winter nights when it
was covered with snow and only the moon looked
down at him; he had been there in the fall when
bleak winds blew and on summer evenings when
the air vibrated with the song of insects. On the
April morning he wanted to go there again, to
walk again in the silence. He did walk to where
the road dipped down by a little stream two miles
from town and then turned and walked silently
back again. When he got to Main Street clerks
were sweeping the sidewalks before the stores.
"Hey, you George. How does it feel to be going
away?" they asked.

The west bound train leaves Winesburg at seven
forty-five in the morning. Tom Little is conduc-

tor. His train runs from Cleveland to where
it connects with a great trunk line railroad with
terminals in Chicago and New York. Tom has
what in railroad circles is called an "easy run."
Every evening he returned to his family. In the
fall and spring he spends his Sundays fishing in
Lake Erie. He has a round red face and small
blue eyes. He knows the people in the towns
along his railroad better than a city man knows
the people who live in his apartment building.

George came down the little incline from the
New Willard House at seven o'clock. Tom Willard carried his bag. The son had become taller
than the father.

On the station platform everyone shook the
young man's hand. More than a dozen people
waited about. Then they talked of their own affairs. Even Will Henderson, who was lazy and
often slept until nine, had got out of bed. George
was embarrassed. Gertrude Wilmot, a tall thin
woman of fifty who worked in the Winesburg post
office, came along the station platform. She had
never before paid any attention to George. Now
she stopped and put out her hand. In two words
she voiced what everyone felt. "Good luck," she
said sharply and then turning went on her way.

When the train came into the station George
felt relieved. He scampered hurriedly aboard.
Helen White came running along Main Street

hoping to have a parting word with him, but he had found a seat and did not see her. When the train started Tom Little punched his ticket, grinned and, although he knew George well and knew on what adventure he was just setting out, made no comment. Tom had seen a thousand George Willards go out of their towns to the city. It was a commonplace enough incident with him. In the smoking car there was a man who had just invited Tom to go on a fishing trip to Sandusky Bay. He wanted to accept the invitation and talk over details.

George glanced up and down the car to be sure no one was looking then took out his pocketbook and counted his money. His mind was occupied with a desire not to appear green. Almost the last words his father had said to him concerned the matter of his behavior when he got to the city. "Be a sharp one," Tom Willard had said. "Keep your eyes on your money. Be awake. That's the ticket. Don't let any one think you're a greenhorn."

After George counted his money he looked out of window and was surprised to see that the train was still in Winesburg.

The young man, going out of his town to meet the adventure of life, began to think but he did not think of anything very big or dramatic. Things like his mother's death, his departure from

Winesburg, the uncertainty of his future life in the city, the serious and larger aspects of his life did not come into his mind.

He thought of little things—Turk Smallet wheeling boards through the main street of his town in the morning, a tall woman, beautifully gowned, who had once stayed over night at his father's hotel, Butch Wheeler the lamp lighter of Winesburg hurrying through the streets on a summer evening and holding a torch in his hand, Helen White standing by a window in the Winesburg post office and putting a stamp on an envelope.

The young man's mind was carried away by his growing passion for dreams. One looking at him would not have thought him particularly sharp. With the recollection of little things occupying his mind he closed his eyes and leaned back in the car seat. He stayed that way for a long time and when he aroused himself and again looked out of the car window the town of Winesburg had disappeared and his life there had become but a background on which to paint the dreams of his manhood.

THE END

The Best of the World's Best Books
COMPLETE LIST OF TITLES IN
THE MODERN LIBRARY

For convenience in ordering use number at right of title

ADAMS, HENRY	The Education of Henry Adams 76
AESCHYLUS	The Complete Greek Tragedies, Vol. I 310
AIKEN, CONRAD (Editor)	A Comprehensive Anthology of American Poetry 101
AIKEN, CONRAD (Editor)	20th-Century American Poetry 127
ALEICHEM, SHOLOM	Selected Stories of 145
ANDERSON, SHERWOOD	Winesburg, Ohio 104
AQUINAS, ST. THOMAS	Introduction to St. Thomas Aquinas 259
ARISTOTLE	Introduction to Aristotle 248
ARISTOTLE	Politics 228
ARISTOTLE	Rhetoric and Poetics 246
AUDEN, W. H.	Selected Poetry of 160
AUGUSTINE, ST.	The Confessions of 263
AUSTEN, JANE	Pride and Prejudice and Sense and Sensibility 264
BACON, FRANCIS	Selected Writings of 256
BALZAC	Cousin Bette 299
BALZAC	Droll Stories 193
BALZAC	Père Goriot and Eugénie Grandet 245
BEERBOHM, MAX	Zuleika Dobson 116
BELLAMY, EDWARD	Looking Backward 22
BENNETT, ARNOLD	The Old Wives' Tale 184
BERGSON, HENRI	Creative Evolution 231
BLAKE, WILLIAM	Selected Poetry & Prose of 285
BOCCACCIO	The Decameron 71
BOSWELL, JAMES	The Life of Samuel Johnson 282
BRONTË, CHARLOTTE	Jane Eyre 64
BRONTË, EMILY	Wuthering Heights 106
BROWNING, ROBERT	Selected Poetry of 198
BUCK, PEARL	The Good Earth 15
BURCKHARDT, JACOB	The Civilization of the Renaissance in Italy 32
BURK, JOHN N.	The Life and Works of Beethoven 241
BURKE, EDMUND	Selected Writings of 289
BUTLER, SAMUEL	Erewhon and Erewhon Revisited 136
BUTLER, SAMUEL	The Way of All Flesh 13
BYRON, LORD	The Selected Poetry of 195
BYRON, LORD	Don Juan 24
CAESAR, JULIUS	The Gallic War and Other Writings of 295
CALDWELL, ERSKINE	God's Little Acre 51
CALDWELL, ERSKINE	Tobacco Road 249
CAMUS, ALBERT	The Plague 109
CARROLL, LEWIS	Alice in Wonderland, etc. 79
CASANOVA, JACQUES	Memoirs of Casanova 165
CELLINI, BENVENUTO	Autobiography of Cellini 150
CERVANTES	Don Quixote 174
CHAUCER	The Canterbury Tales 161

CHEKHOV, ANTON	Best Plays by 171
CHEKHOV, ANTON	The Short Stories of 50
CICERO	The Basic Works of 272
COLERIDGE	Selected Poetry and Prose of 279
COLETTE	Six Novels by 251
COMMAGER, HENRY STEELE & NEVINS, ALLAN	A Short History of the United States 235
CONFUCIUS	The Wisdom of Confucius 306
CONRAD, JOSEPH	Lord Jim 186
CONRAD, JOSEPH	Nostromo 275
CONRAD, JOSEPH	Victory 34
COOPER, JAMES FENIMORE	The Pathfinder 105
CORNEILLE & RACINE	Six Plays of Corneille and Racine 194
CRANE, STEPHEN	The Red Badge of Courage 130
CUMMINGS, E. E.	The Enormous Room 214
DANA, RICHARD HENRY	Two Years Before the Mast 236
DANTE	The Divine Comedy 208
DA VINCI, LEONARDO	The Notebooks of 156
DEFOE, DANIEL	Moll Flanders 122
DEFOE, DANIEL	Robinson Crusoe and A Journal of the Plague Year 92
DESCARTES, RENE	Philosophical Writings 43
DEWEY, JOHN	Human Nature and Conduct 173
DICKENS, CHARLES	David Copperfield 110
DICKENS, CHARLES	Pickwick Papers 204
DICKENS, CHARLES	Our Mutual Friend 308
DICKENS, CHARLES	A Tale of Two Cities 189
DICKINSON, EMILY	Selected Poems of 25
DINESEN, ISAK	Out of Africa 23
DINESEN, ISAK	Seven Gothic Tales 54
DONNE, JOHN	Complete Poetry and Selected Prose of 12
DOS PASSOS, JOHN	Three Soldiers 205
DOSTOYEVSKY, FYODOR	The Best Short Stories of 293
DOSTOYEVSKY, FYODOR	The Brothers Karamazov 151
DOSTOYEVSKY, FYODOR	Crime and Punishment 199
DOSTOYEVSKY, FYODOR	The Possessed 55
DOUGLAS, NORMAN	South Wind 5
DOYLE, SIR ARTHUR CONAN	The Adventures and Memoirs of Sherlock Holmes 206
DREISER, THEODORE	Sister Carrie 8
DUMAS, ALEXANDRE	Camille 69
DUMAS, ALEXANDRE	The Three Musketeers 143
DU MAURIER, DAPHNE	Rebecca 227
EMERSON, RALPH WALDO	The Journals of 192
EMERSON, RALPH WALDO	Essays and Other Writings 91
EURIPIDES	The Complete Greek Tragedies, Vol. V 314
FAULKNER, WILLIAM	Absalom, Absalom! 271
FAULKNER, WILLIAM	Go Down, Moses 175
FAULKNER, WILLIAM	Light in August 88
FAULKNER, WILLIAM	Sanctuary 61
FAULKNER, WILLIAM	The Sound and the Fury and As I Lay Dying 187
FIELDING, HENRY	Joseph Andrews 117
FIELDING, HENRY	Tom Jones 185
FLAUBERT, GUSTAVE	Madame Bovary 28
FORESTER, C. S.	The African Queen 102
FRANCE, ANATOLE	Penguin Island 210

FRANK, ANNE	Diary of a Young Girl 298
FRANKLIN, BENJAMIN	Autobiography, etc. 39
FREUD, SIGMUND	The Interpretation of Dreams 96
FROST, ROBERT	The Poems of 242
GALSWORTHY, JOHN	The Apple Tree (in Great Modern Short Stories 168)
GEORGE, HENRY	Progress and Poverty 36
GOETHE	Faust 177
GOGOL, NIKOLAI	Dead Souls 40
GOLDSMITH, OLIVER	The Vicar of Wakefield and other Writings 291
GRAVES, ROBERT	I, Claudius 20
GUNTHER, JOHN	Death Be Not Proud 286
HACKETT, FRANCIS	The Personal History of Henry the Eighth 265
HAGGARD, H. RIDER	She and King Solomon's Mines 163
HARDY, THOMAS	Jude the Obscure 135
HARDY, THOMAS	The Mayor of Casterbridge 17
HARDY, THOMAS	The Return of the Native 121
HARDY, THOMAS	Tess of the D'Urbervilles 72
HART & KAUFMAN	Six Plays by 233
HARTE, BRET	The Best Stories of 250
HAWTHORNE, NATHANIEL	The Scarlet Letter 93
HEGEL	The Philosophy of 239
HELLMAN, LILLIAN	Six Plays by 223
HENRY, O.	Best Short Stories of 26
HERODOTUS	The Persian Wars 255
HOMER	The Iliad 166
HOMER	The Odyssey 167
HORACE	The Complete Works of 141
HOWARD, JOHN TASKER	World's Great Operas 302
HOWELLS, WILLIAM DEAN	The Rise of Silas Lapham 277
HUDSON, W. H.	Green Mansions 89
HUGO, VICTOR	The Hunchback of Notre Dame 35
HUXLEY, ALDOUS	Antic Hay 209
HUXLEY, ALDOUS	Brave New World 48
HUXLEY, ALDOUS	Point Counter Point 180
IBSEN, HENRIK	Six Plays by 305
IBSEN, HENRIK	The Wild Duck and Other Plays 307
IRVING, WASHINGTON	Selected Writings of 240
JAMES, HENRY	The Bostonians 16
JAMES, HENRY	The Portrait of a Lady 107
JAMES, HENRY	The Turn of the Screw 169
JAMES, HENRY	Washington Square 269
JAMES, HENRY	The Wings of the Dove 244
JAMES, WILLIAM	The Philosophy of William James 114
JAMES, WILLIAM	The Varieties of Religious Experience 70
JEFFERSON, THOMAS	The Life and Selected Writings of 234
JOYCE, JAMES	Dubliners 124
JUNG, C. G.	Basic Writings of 300
KAFKA, FRANZ	The Trial 318
KAFKA, FRANZ	Selected Stories of 283
KANT	Critique of Pure Reason 297
KANT	The Philosophy of 266
KAUFMAN & HART	Six Plays by 233
KEATS	The Complete Poetry and Selected Prose of 273
KIPLING, RUDYARD	Kim 99

KOESTLER, ARTHUR	Darkness at Noon 74
LAOTSE	The Wisdom of 262
LAWRENCE, D. H.	Lady Chatterley's Lover 148
LAWRENCE, D. H.	The Rainbow 128
LAWRENCE, D. H.	Sons and Lovers 109
LAWRENCE, D. H.	Women in Love 68
LEWIS, SINCLAIR	Dodsworth 252
LEWIS, SINCLAIR	Cass Timberlane 221
LONGFELLOW, HENRY W.	Poems 56
LOUYS, PIERRE	Aphrodite 77
LUDWIG, EMIL	Napoleon 95
MACHIAVELLI	The Prince and The Discourses 65
MALRAUX, ANDRE	Man's Fate 33
MALTHUS, THOMAS ROBERT	On Population 309
MANN, THOMAS	Death in Venice (in Great German Short Novels and Stories 108)
MARQUAND, JOHN P.	The Late George Apley 182
MARX, KARL	Capital and Other Writings 202
MAUGHAM, W. SOMERSET	The Best Short Stories of 14
MAUGHAM, W. SOMERSET	Cakes and Ale 270
MAUGHAM, W. SOMERSET	The Moon and Sixpence 27
MAUGHAM, W. SOMERSET	Of Human Bondage 176
MAUPASSANT, GUY DE	Best Short Stories 98
MAUROIS, ANDRÉ	Disraeli 46
McCORD, DAVID (Editor)	What Cheer: An Anthology of Humorous and Witty Verse 190
MELVILLE, HERMAN	Moby Dick 119
MEREDITH, GEORGE	The Egoist 253
MEREDITH, GEORGE	The Ordeal of Richard Feverel 134
MEREJKOWSKI, DMITRI	The Romance of Leonardo da Vinci 138
MICHENER, JAMES A.	Selected Writings of 296
MILTON, JOHN	The Complete Poetry and Selected Prose of John Milton 132
MOLIÈRE	Eight Plays by 78
MONTAIGNE	Selected Essays of 218
NASH, OGDEN	The Selected Verse of Ogden Nash 191
NEVINS, ALLAN & COMMAGER, HENRY STEELE	A Short History of the United States 235
NEWMAN, CARDINAL JOHN H.	Apologia Pro Vita Sua 113
NIETZSCHE, FRIEDRICH	Thus Spake Zarathustra 9
NOSTRADAMUS	Oracles of 81
ODETS, CLIFFORD	Six Plays of 67
O'HARA, JOHN	Appointment in Samarra 42
O'HARA, JOHN	Selected Short Stories of 211
O'NEILL, EUGENE	The Emperor Jones, Anna Christie and The Hairy Ape 146
O'NEILL, EUGENE	The Long Voyage Home: Seven Plays of the Sea 111
PALGRAVE, FRANCIS (Editor)	The Golden Treasury 232
PARKER, DOROTHY	The Collected Short Stories of 123
PARKER, DOROTHY	The Collected Poetry of 237
PARKMAN, FRANCIS	The Oregon Trail 267
PASCAL, BLAISE	Pensées and The Provincial Letters 164
PATER, WALTER	The Renaissance 86
PEPYS, SAMUEL	Passages from the Diary of 103
PERELMAN, S. J.	The Best of 247
PLATO	The Republic 153

PLATO	The Works of Plato 181
POE, EDGAR ALLAN	Selected Poetry and Prose 82
POLO, MARCO	The Travels of Marco Polo 196
POPE, ALEXANDER	Selected Works of 257
PORTER, KATHERINE ANNE	Flowering Judas 284
PORTER, KATHERINE ANNE	Pale Horse, Pale Rider 45
PROUST, MARCEL	The Captive 120
PROUST, MARCEL	Cities of the Plain 220
PROUST, MARCEL	The Guermantes Way 213
PROUST, MARCEL	The Past Recaptured 278
PROUST, MARCEL	Swann's Way 59
PROUST, MARCEL	The Sweet Cheat Gone 260
PROUST, MARCEL	Within a Budding Grove 172
RACINE & CORNEILLE	Six Plays by 194
READE, CHARLES	The Cloister and the Hearth 62
REED, JOHN	Ten Days that Shook the World 215
RENAN, ERNEST	The Life of Jesus 140
RICHARDSON, SAMUEL	Clarissa 10
RODGERS AND HAMMERSTEIN	Six Plays by 200
ROSTAND, EDMOND	CYRANO de Bergerac 154
ROUSSEAU, JEAN JACQUES	The Confessions of 243
RUNYON, DAMON	Famous Stories 53
RUSSELL, BERTRAND	Selected Papers of Bertrand Russell 137
SAKI	The Short Stories of 280
SALINGER, J. D.	Nine Stories 301
SALINGER, J. D.	The Catcher in the Rye 90
SANTAYANA, GEORGE	The Sense of Beauty 292
SCHOPENHAUER	The Philosophy of Schopenhauer 52
SCHULBERG, BUDD	What Makes Sammy Run? 281
SHAKESPEARE, WILLIAM	Tragedies, 2, 3—complete, 2 vols.
SHAKESPEARE, WILLIAM	Comedies, 4, 5—complete, 2 vols.
SHAKESPEARE, WILLIAM	Histories, 6 } complete, 2 vols. Histories, Poems, 7
SHAW, BERNARD	Four Plays by 19
SHAW, BERNARD	Saint Joan, Major Barbara, and Androcles and the Lion 294
SHAW, IRWIN	The Young Lions 112
SHELLEY	The Selected Poetry & Prose of 274
SMOLLETT, TOBIAS	Humphry Clinker 159
SOPHOCLES	The Complete Greek Tragedies, Vol. III 312
SPINOZA	The Philosophy of Spinoza 60
STEINBECK, JOHN	In Dubious Battle 115
STEINBECK, JOHN	Of Mice and Men 29
STEINBECK, JOHN	Tortilla Flat 216
STENDHAL	The Red and the Black 157
STERNE, LAURENCE	Tristram Shandy 147
STEWART, GEORGE R.	Storm 254
STOKER, BRAM	Dracula 31
STONE, IRVING	Lust for Life 11
STOWE, HARRIET BEECHER	Uncle Tom's Cabin 261
STRACHEY, LYTTON	Eminent Victorians 212
SUETONIUS	Lives of the Twelve Caesars 188
SWIFT, JONATHAN	Gulliver's Travels and Other Writings 100
SYMONDS, JOHN A.	The Life of Michelangelo 49
TACITUS	The Complete Works of 222
TENNYSON	Selected Poetry of 230

THACKERAY, WILLIAM   Henry Esmond 80
THACKERAY, WILLIAM   Vanity Fair 131
THOMPSON, FRANCIS   Complete Poems 38
THOREAU, HENRY DAVID   Walden and Other Writings 155
THUCYDIDES   The Complete Writings of 58
THURBER, JAMES   The Thurber Carnival 85
TOLSTOY, LEO   Anna Karenina 37
TROLLOPE, ANTHONY   Barchester Towers and The Warden 41
TURGENEV, IVAN   Fathers and Sons 21
TWAIN, MARK   A Connecticut Yankee in King Arthur's
                              Court 162
VASARI, GIORGIO   Lives of the Most Eminent Painters,
                              Sculptors and Architects 190
VEBLEN, THORSTEIN   The Theory of the Leisure Class 63
VIRGIL   The Aeneid, Eclogues & Georgics 75
VOLTAIRE   Candide and Other Writings 47
WALPOLE, HUGH   Fortitude 178
WARREN, ROBERT PENN   All The King's Men 170
WEBB, MARY   Precious Bane 219
WEIDMAN, JEROME   I Can Get It For You Wholesale 225
WELLS, H. G.   Tono Bungay 197
WELTY, EUDORA   Selected Stories of 290
WHARTON, EDITH   The Age of Innocence 229
WHITMAN, WALT   Leaves of Grass 97
WILDE, OSCAR   Dorian Gray, De Profundis 125
WILDE, OSCAR   The Plays of Oscar Wilde 83
WILDE, OSCAR   Poems and Fairy Tales 84
WODEHOUSE, P. J.   Selected Stories 126
WORDSWORTH   Selected Poetry of 268
YEATS, W. B. (Editor)   Irish Fairy and Folk Tales 44
YOUNG, G. F.   The Medici 179
ZIMMERN, ALFRED   The Greek Commonwealth 207
ZOLA, EMILE   Nana 142

MISCELLANEOUS

An Anthology of Irish Literature 288
The Arabian Nights' Entertain-
  ments 201
Best Amer. Humorous Short Stories 87
Best Russian Short Stories 18
Best Spanish Stories 129
The Complete Greek Tragedies Vol. I
  310
The Complete Greek Tragedies Vol. III
  312
A Comprehensive Anthology of Ameri-
  can Poetry 101
The Consolation of Philosophy 226
Eight Famous Elizabethan Plays 94
Eighteenth-Century Plays 224
Famous Ghost Stories 73
The Federalist 139
Five Great Modern Irish Plays 30
Fourteen Great Detective Stories 144
Great German Short Novels and Stories
  108
Great Modern Short Stories 168
Great Tales of the American West 238
The Greek Poets 203
Stories of Modern Italy 118
A Kierkegaard Anthology 303
The Latin Poets 217
The Making of Man: An Outline of
  Anthology 149
Making of Society 183
Medieval Romances 133
The Modern Library Dictionary 1
New Voices in the American Theatre
  258
Outline of Abnormal Psychology 152
Outline of Psychoanalysis 66
Restoration Plays 287
Seven Famous Greek Plays 158
The Short Bible 57
Six Modern American Plays 276
Six American Plays For Today 38
Twentieth-Century Amer. Poetry 127